I0603436

BEYOND HOPE'S RIDGE

SILVER MCKENZIE

HOPE'S RIDGE BOOK #2

CONTENTS

Once you choose hope, anything is possible.

CHRISTOPHER REEVE

1

A scream caught in Steph's throat, her eyes flew open, and she sat up, adrenaline pumping through her body.

She took a deep breath and reached for the glass of water on the bedside table as her alarm clock display cast a green glow in the dark room. It was only three.

She threw off the bed covers and made her way to the kitchen, her heart still racing. Would the nightmares ever stop? More than a year had passed since the accident, and if anything, they seemed to be getting worse. She sighed. She was doing everything she could to try to move on. She practiced yoga most days, ate a clean diet, and was seeing Dan, the local psychologist, once a month, yet almost nightly, she was plagued with dreams of a little girl desperate for Steph to help her.

She put a pot of water on the stove to boil and reached into the cupboard for her favorite chamomile tea. She automatically took two mugs from the shelf before giving a small shake of her head and returning one. The likelihood of Zane being home was slim. She was so glad things had worked out for her roommate and her sister. It was still early days in their relationship, only a month had passed since Zane quit his job and proved his love for Asha, but it was obvious to see they were meant to be together.

"Yes, please."

Steph startled and spun around at the sound of Zane's voice in the kitchen doorway. She brought her hand to her chest. "You gave me a heart attack! I thought you were with Ash tonight?"

Zane grinned and stepped into the kitchen. "Nope. I'm here. I miss our middle of the night chats, so I need to make sure I'm home some nights."

Steph smiled as she took the second mug back down from the shelf and added some tea leaves to the infuser. "Why don't you go out and light the heat lamp, and I'll bring these out in a minute. It's cold, but the sky's clear, so it's probably beautiful out there."

"I'll grab a couple of blankets and see you out there soon," Zane said.

Steph organized a small tray for the mugs and teapot, and a few minutes later, she was sitting across from Zane, the night lit only by the heat lamp. She wrapped the blanket he held out to her around her legs.

"More dreams about Holly?"

Steph flinched. She rarely referred by name to the little girl who'd lost her life. It made it all too real. "They're getting more vivid every night and she looks more and more desperate in each dream." She shuddered picturing the little girl. "Her face is at the car window, her eyes wide with fear, and I'm paralyzed, unable to do anything to help. Can't move, can't scream, can't do anything."

Zane's eyes filled with sympathy. "I thought you said stress brought on the dreams. Has something happened?"

Steph sighed. "Not really. I guess Buster's played on my

mind a little since the anniversary of the accident. I wanted to speak to him, explain how sorry I was that I'd been unable to save his little girl, but I've been too gutless to seek him out. Actually, I did see him in town a few weeks ago, and instead of seizing the opportunity, I turned and practically ran in the other direction. I guess that's left me feeling another layer of guilt."

Zane's smile was gentle. "There's an easy solution to that. Buster doesn't blame you. His ex-wife was driving, Steph. She'd been drinking and should never have been behind the wheel. I know Buster's grateful you weren't hurt and that your car didn't follow hers into the lake. You need to speak to him, so you hear it for yourself."

Steph fell silent, her gaze fixing on a constellation high above the ridge in the distance.

"Really, Steph. You should speak to him."

Steph brought her gaze back to meet Zane's. "I don't want him to feel like he needs to tell me it wasn't my fault. I know I wasn't to blame for the accident, but I contributed to it, and I was unable to save his daughter. Nothing will ever change those two things."

Zane opened his mouth to object, but Steph bought up a hand to silence him. "Let's just enjoy the stars. Right now, I'm looking to escape the nightmares, not discuss them." As a heaviness settled on her shoulders, Steph wondered, for the umpteenth time, whether she would ever escape these feelings.

───────

Buster wiped his eyes and pushed himself up off the rock he'd been sitting on. It had been a mistake to come here. Surely he knew that by now. Lake Hopeful. What a joke. There was nothing hopeful about this lake. It had crushed his dreams and ruined his life. He made his way back across the lakefront to where he'd parked.

It seemed like only moments, not thirty minutes later, that he was climbing out of his pickup in his driveway. The drive back to Drayson's Landing had disappeared in a blur of memories.

"Morning, Henry."

Buster forced a smile and waved to Mrs. Anderson, his elderly neighbor, as he shut the door of his truck.

"Been anywhere nice this morning?"

Buster hesitated, wondering for just a moment what she would say if he told her the truth; that he'd driven thirty minutes to the neighboring town of Hope's Ridge to sit by the lake that had swallowed his daughter, hoping to feel close to her.

She'd probably become teary and say what a lovely thing it was to do.

Until he explained that the trip hadn't done that. Instead it had brought back the memories of Holly's death and, once again, left him wracked with guilt.

"No, Mrs. Anderson. Just out for a little drive. And call me Buster. Everyone else does."

Mrs. Anderson tut-tutted. "I don't care what anyone else calls you, I will call you by your christened name. My Henry would be turning in his grave to think you turned your back on such a strong identity. It means hero, you know."

"And your Henry was a true hero, Mrs. Anderson."

The older lady wrung her hands together. "And a gentleman too. Now I'll let you go. Enjoy your day, Henry."

Buster couldn't help but smile as he unlocked his front door and went inside. He would always be Henry to his neighbor.

He kicked off his shoes, padded through to the kitchen, and placed a mug of water in the microwave. After the morning he'd had, he felt like a beer. But as it wasn't even lunchtime, he would settle for instant coffee.

He picked up a photo frame that sat on the kitchen counter—him and Holly on her fifth, and last, birthday. One of the moms who'd attended the small party he'd thrown for her had snapped the shot of the two of them laughing as they blew bubbles into the air. They were happy and carefree. Tears filled his eyes as he wished, for the millionth time, he could turn back the clock. Go back to that birthday, knowing what he did now, and have the ability to change what happened.

He put the photo down as the microwave beeped, a lump expanding in his throat. Everywhere he looked in the house, there were memories of Holly. Her bedroom was still exactly as it had been the day she died, and while he rarely opened the bedroom door, there were reminders throughout the rest of the house too. There were reminders throughout their town, Drayson's Landing, and the neighboring town of Hope's Ridge, where Holly had died.

He made his coffee and took it through the French doors that opened out onto a small back garden. He sat down at the table and did his best to ignore the playhouse and sandpit. It was impossible, though. He half expected Holly to push open the door of the playhouse and jump out to surprise him. What he wouldn't give for that to happen. Or to beg him to let her bury him in the sandpit, just like they'd done so many times at the beach.

Buster closed his eyes and sipped his coffee. He'd hoped that by now, he'd be coping better, but if anything, it was getting harder.

He was beginning to think his mom might be right. That the only way he'd be able to move on was by having a fresh start. By moving away from Drayson's Landing, Hope's Ridge, and all of the places that were a constant reminder of his former life. She'd begged him after the accident to move back to the town of Tall Oaks, where his parents now lived, but his business was in Drayson's Landing, and so, he'd thought, was his life. He'd hate to let down Travis, his business partner, but he couldn't go on like this.

He opened his eyes, relieved to have clarity about his decision. His mother was right, he needed a fresh start, and it was time to do something about it.

Steph wiped her face with a towel, the usual contentment she felt after teaching the early morning yoga class absent. She plastered on a smile as the class participants filed out of the room, many thanking her on the way. Usually, the energy of the class brought a genuine smile to her lips, and after her interrupted night, she'd been looking forward to the escape she knew the sunrise class would bring. Teaching and practicing yoga usually gave her a reprieve from the nightmares and feelings that plagued her. But not today.

She waited until the last person left the room before collecting her own water bottle and mat and walking through to the reception area. Bodhi was chatting with one of the class participants, his face pale and lacking its usual enthusiasm. She'd never seen him look like this, and he'd certainly never walked out of one of her classes partway through like he had that morning. He hadn't given her any suggestion that anything was wrong, but clearly, something was.

"Want to talk about it?" she asked when he'd finished his conversation and they were the only two left in the studio.

Bodhi looked briefly in her direction before returning his focus to the computer screen he'd been studying. "Sorry, I shouldn't have walked out of class like that. It doesn't send the best message to our clients."

Steph waited. What about the message it gave her? She couldn't think of anything she could have done to upset her boss, but he'd never acted like this around her before.

"Bodhi, you need to let me know if I've done something to upset you."

This time he met her gaze, his eyes filled with concern. "You've done nothing wrong at all, Steph. Which is what makes this hard."

Nausea swirled in the pit of Steph's stomach. "You're firing me?"

Bodhi's eyes widened. "What would make you think that?"

"You're acting strangely, that's why."

Bodhi sighed. "Let me make us some tea, and I'll explain what's going on. Then you'll see why this is so difficult."

Five minutes later, Steph sat opposite Bodhi in the small lounge area they'd created for their clients. Bodhi's hand trembled as he brought his drink to his lips. Whatever was going on was affecting him. She nestled her mug against her chest, waiting for him to speak.

"I don't know how to tell you this, but I've decided to leave Hope's Ridge."

Steph almost dropped her tea. Nothing had prepared her for this announcement. She sat forward in her chair. "What? Why?"

"I need to be closer to my mom and dad. Dad's dementia has gone downhill, and we're going to have to move him into care. Some days, he doesn't recognize Mom and starts screaming at her to get out of his house. As you can imagine, it's upsetting her, and they can't go on like that."

Steph reached across and squeezed Bodhi's hand. "Of course, they can't."

7

"I'm going to move in with Mom and help her out. She doesn't drive, so she'll need my help to visit Dad. I also think she'll just need me around. Becca's going to move back too. My sister's lucky that she can transfer to the planning office in Tall Oaks. She's started seeing someone there, so it's working out quite well."

A lump rose in Steph's throat. "But what about you? You've spent so long building up this place." She gestured around the studio.

"There are a few studios in Tall Oaks, so I expect I'll be able to do some teaching. Depending on what happens with Dad, I might consider opening my own business again."

Steph nodded. "And what about Heat Wave?"

"I need to sell it, Steph. I wanted to talk to you and offer you the first option, of course. I've been dreading telling you because I know how much you love working here, and I'm assuming purchasing it might be out of your reach."

Steph swallowed. He was right, she hardly had any savings, and her income barely covered her living expenses. She wasn't in a position to buy a business. "I could run the business for you," Steph said. "That way, you'd still have an income from it and the possibility to return to it down the road."

Bodhi shook his head. "I'm going to need the money from the sale of the business. Putting Dad into care isn't going to be cheap. To be honest, if it isn't you buying Heat Wave, then I would imagine someone will buy it for the land and buildings. The yoga business itself isn't worth a lot. It's the land I'm sitting on that could make a huge difference to my parents."

Steph blinked back tears. She loved working with Bodhi, and she loved Heat Wave. It was hard to imagine it being closed down.

8

"You could still run classes," Bodhi said. "Rent some space in town. It's not the end of yoga for you."

"I know, but you've created an oasis here. A room in town won't be the same."

"*We* created an oasis. In fact, you did most of it. You'll do the same elsewhere. Your own home is a testament to that."

"Do you have anyone else in mind to buy it?"

"I was hoping it would be you," Bodhi said. "But I'll have to chat with Andy. See if he's got anyone on his realtor books that might be interested."

"Matt Law might be," Steph said.

Bodhi raised an eyebrow. "He's the last person I thought you'd suggest after what he did to Asha. Buying the Sandstone Cafe and preventing her from taking on the lease she'd been promised was bad enough. But then having her evicted from her trading location and trying to close her business down took his vindictive streak to another level. I'm surprised you'd consider recommending him for anything."

Steph shrugged. "In amongst his awful behavior he's done some good things for the town. He's talked about a wellness center for a long time, although I don't think it's in his immediate plans." She thought back to a conversation she'd had with Zane when rumors had circulated that Matt was going to build a yoga and wellness center as part of his Lake Drive development. "I think it's a few years off for him, but it might be worth talking to him at least."

Bodhi nodded. "Thanks, Steph. I told Mom I'd move back at the end of the month. It gives me a few weeks to get things rolling at least for a sale. I realize it might take longer than that, and you're welcome to keep running the studio after I've gone until a sale happens. Of course, if you set yourself up somewhere else, I'm happy for you to take our clients with you."

Steph nodded. She wasn't sure what to say. It wasn't a conversation or situation she'd anticipated.

"I am sorry, Steph. I know I've let you down."

Steph's heart contracted at the pain on Bodhi's face. She retook his hand and squeezed it. "You haven't let me down. Leaving to help your parents reconfirms what a selfless and amazing person you are. I just hope you'll find happiness for yourself in Tall Oaks." She smiled. "Remember, I'm a true believer that life unfolds as it's meant to. We can't plan everything or know what's around the corner. We just need to roll with it." Steph was glad to see the tension drain from Bodhi's face. However, the irony of her advice didn't go unnoticed. If only she applied it to each part of her own life, she might enjoy a full night's sleep.

Buster collected the drawings he'd done for his newest client, glad that he'd spent the previous afternoon working and exercising rather than drinking, which after that morning by the lake had been a real possibility. He'd slept surprisingly well and was ready for the week ahead. A lightness had settled over him after making his decision the previous day. He did need a fresh start, and it was time to do something about it.

He put the drawings, his computer, and work bag into his pickup and walked back inside the house. The only downside to his thoughts of a fresh start was leaving this home behind him, Holly's home. He and his ex-wife, Eve, had bought the property the year after they'd married. The deterioration of their marriage after Holly's birth meant the home was now filled with a combination of happy memories and sadness. It would be difficult to turn his back on those happy memories, but not on the sadness.

He was drawn to his daughter's room but stopped at the closed door. What would he do if he did sell the house and move? He'd have to pack up her room. Right now, he stood frozen outside it. If he opened the door, he'd have to deal with the overwhelming rush of emotions that would hit him. He didn't have time for that before his meetings today. But thinking about moving made him realize he couldn't imagine giving away his daughter's clothes or toys. He needed to remind himself that Holly was in his heart and his thoughts, not in material possessions. Regardless, he knew it was still going to be hard.

He glanced at his watch. He needed to get moving if he'd be on time for his nine o'clock meeting. He had contemplated ducking into the office to speak to Travis about this decision first but realized it was too early in the day. Travis would also be out for most of the afternoon, so the discussion about Buster leaving would need to wait until Tuesday. He wouldn't leave him in the lurch, of course, some projects needed to be completed, but just knowing he'd made the decision and would be leaving the area provided him with relief and lightness he hadn't felt for a long time.

Steph pulled her jacket tight around her as an icy wind cut across the lake. The last of the fall leaves crunched underfoot as she made her way along the lake trail toward Irresistables, the food truck her sister ran her business from. She still couldn't believe the conversation she'd just had with Bodhi. It was entirely out of left field for her. She felt incredibly sorry for him and his family. It was an awful situation that no family wanted to be presented with. It didn't surprise her that Bodhi was putting his parents' needs before his own. If it were her parents, she'd be doing the same. However, she wasn't sure what this meant for her. Deep down, Steph did believe everything happened for a reason. She was just going to need to remind herself of this.

Steph did her best to push her morning out of her thoughts and quickened her pace as Asha waved to her from the food truck's service window. It was almost nine, but knowing her sister, she'd probably been up baking muffins since five.

"Hey, hon," Asha called as Steph reached the food truck. "Coffee?"

Steph hesitated for a split second, causing Asha to raise an eyebrow.

"Finally remembering your body is your temple and all that?"

Steph smiled. "Something like that, and I've already taught a class, so I'm wide awake." That and Bodhi's news was enough to keep her wide awake too. "I'll have green tea, thanks."

"Does that mean you've given coffee up again? That you're sleeping better?"

Steph's smile slipped. "Sleeping's still hit and miss, as I'm sure Zane's mentioned to you."

Asha nodded. "Sounds like he hasn't been much better, considering he's up chatting with you at three in the morning."

"We're well suited as far as roommates go." Steph hesitated. She'd planned to talk to Asha about Bodhi and Heat Wave but realized Asha would be full of questions and advice Steph wasn't sure she was ready to hear just yet. She needed to get her head around the situation first. Instead, she decided to focus on her sister. "How was the weekend? I thought you'd be too hungover to function today. Jenna's visits usually leave you in a coma."

"Not this one. We behaved." Asha sighed. "I'll be glad

when this engagement party is over. She was talking about ice sculptures on Saturday night! Who on earth does that for an engagement party?"

"It still seems very sudden," Steph said. "I know Jenna can be impulsive, but she hardly knows him."

Asha handed Steph her tea. "You should have heard Zane yesterday. Jenna almost lost it with him. It's given Zane something to bond with his dad over. I think it's the first time they've ever agreed on anything. Not that that's much help to Jenna."

"What does her mom think?"

"Same as the rest of us. Too soon. But she's also excited. She knows Jenna better than anyone, and once Jenna makes up her mind, there's no changing it. It's easier to just go along with the plans. It's only the engagement party. There will be at least another six months until the wedding. That's more time to get to know each other, at least."

Steph sipped her tea. "I guess we need to be less skeptical and more embracing of love at first sight."

"It was love at first sight for my beloved Ying Yue and me."

Steph turned at the sound of Charlie Li's voice. The older man bowed slightly in greeting, a broad smile on his face.

"How are you, Charlie?"

"Very well, thank you, Steph."

"Here to collect your rent?" Asha called from the food truck. Only a month earlier, when Asha and her business were forcibly removed from the township-owned area on the lake's shoreline, Charlie had offered her a prime lakefront position on land he owned. The rent he'd requested was in the form of bottomless tea and coffee, and muffins on occasion for himself and his three neighbors. It was the only payment he would accept.

"A coffee, perhaps. But it's not the reason for my visit. There's something I wanted to talk to you about."

Asha raised an eyebrow. "Is everything okay?"

Steph saw the concern on her sister's face. After the dramas initiated by property developer Matt Law concerning Charlie, Steph wasn't surprised Asha was concerned.

Charlie's smile widened. "Yes, yes. Better than okay. I have an idea that I hope you will like."

Asha looked to Steph, a sparkle in her eye. "We're all ears, Charlie."

He laughed and checked his watch. "Not yet. My surprise will arrive in a few minutes."

"In that case, I'll make your coffee while we wait."

Steph smiled at the joy in Asha's voice. Asha had had a rough time when Matt had decided to firstly prevent her business expansion plans, and secondly, make life as difficult as possible for her. Still, with that behind her and now in a new relationship with Zane, she couldn't be happier.

"You're not going to give us a hint about the surprise?" Steph asked as Charlie rubbed his hands together, his beaming smile still fixed in place.

Charlie's eyes traveled past Steph to Lake Drive as a silver pickup stopped in the small area designated as parking for the food truck's customers. "No need, here he is."

Steph didn't recognize the pickup. She watched with interest as the back of a tall, broad-shouldered man appeared. He leaned down and scooped up a computer bag and a long tube before turning and facing them. His short blonde hair and tanned complexion made him instantly recognizable.

Steph's hand froze midair as she brought her drink to her

mouth. Her heart raced when she realized it was Buster. She closed her eyes momentarily, reminding herself to breathe.

"Steph?"

Concern laced Asha's tone.

Steph opened her eyes, her heart continuing to hammer.

"Everything okay?" Charlie glanced from Steph to Asha and back again.

Steph nodded. "I have...I have to go." She placed her tea on the food truck's counter, stuffed her hands deep in her jacket pocket and, with her head down, hurried in the opposite direction of Buster to the lake trail.

Buster watched as Steph practically ran from the food truck. She was definitely in a hurry. The meeting this morning was supposed to be between himself, Asha, and Charlie, so he hadn't expected to see her. Had his appearance caused her to leave so suddenly? He remembered Zane's words a couple of months ago. *Did you know Steph Jones relives the accident every day too? Blames herself.* He'd convinced himself that Zane had it wrong. Steph had done everything she could to save Holly. Sure, she would have been affected by what happened, but she was hardly to blame. He probably should have spoken to her about it, but until today, he hadn't seen her. And he certainly hadn't set out looking for her. If he was honest, he knew it was guilt that stopped him. Steph had walked away from the accident with minor injuries, but they could have been so much worse. If only he hadn't... He pushed the thought from his mind as he neared the food truck. This was a client meeting, and he needed to be professional.

"Henry!" Charlie clapped him on the back. "Thank you for coming this morning."

Buster smiled. "You're very welcome. And call me Buster, everyone else does." He turned to Asha. "Hey Ash, how are you?"

"Confused. Charlie said he had a surprise for me this morning, and now you've turned up. I'm scrambling to think of why you're here and how it might affect me."

Buster raised an eyebrow and turned to Charlie. "You haven't told her?"

Charlie shook his head, his smile widening with each shake.

Buster laughed. "Wow, okay. This *is* going to be a surprise then."

"Come and sit down," Charlie insisted. "And then you can tell Asha what's going on."

Buster followed the older man's instructions and sat down at one of the large tables beside the food truck.

"Can I get you some coffee?" Asha asked.

"No, I'm good, thanks. I might get one to go when we're finished. I do think you might want to be sitting when I explain what Charlie's asked me to do."

Asha sat down opposite him, and Buster took a deep breath, turning to Charlie for final confirmation that he wanted Buster to be the one to tell Asha. The older man gave a small nod.

"Charlie came and saw me a few weeks ago and asked me to draw up some preliminary plans."

"For what?"

Buster took the lid from the long tube and slid out the rolled-up plans. "For a pavilion." He couldn't help but smile when Asha's mouth dropped open. Charlie clapped his hands together like a delighted child.

"Surprise!"

Asha turned to Charlie. "What do you mean? You can't do this."

"Why not? I have the money and, more importantly," he spread his arms wide, indicating the area around them, "I have the location. We will build a beautiful pavilion complete with flooring so your customers can sit and enjoy the view. We can add some of those patio heaters so that they can sit year-round in comfort. Rain or shine, you'll have plenty of customers."

"But..." Asha's voice trailed off. She appeared lost for words.

Buster spread the plans out in front of them. "These are very early plans, but Charlie wanted me to provide some suggestions for different approaches we could take. We'll also need to work out exactly where to locate it to ensure the best views, but so it's also easily accessible from the food truck."

Charlie clapped his hands together again. "A covered boardwalk from the service window to the seating area. We must add that. That way, if it's raining, no one gets wet."

Asha was shaking her head. "No, Charlie, this is too much. It's one thing to let me run my business on your land; it's another to do this."

Charlie frowned. "Your dream is to have a cafe one day. Correct?"

Asha nodded.

"This will give you more of a cafe feel. You could consider expanding your menu, even upgrading the food truck if you need something bigger. I would be happy to help you do that too. I was thinking about building a proper cafe, but I think the food truck concept and open-air seating area brings something unique to the lake."

"All of this will cost a lot, Charlie. The materials, let alone the construction."

"That part is not your concern. What *is* your concern is giving us your input about the layout of the seating area and exactly how you would like it set up. Now, let's get back to business. Henry...I mean, Buster has other ideas to show us, and I'm very excited to see them."

Buster grinned. He wished he'd thought to take some video of Charlie and Asha's discussion. Of Asha's shock and Charlie's delight. He opened his computer bag and took out his laptop. "Based on some of Charlie's suggestions and my thoughts as to what I believe will fit in with the look and feel of the area, I've come up with a few initial design ideas." He turned the computer so Asha and Charlie could see the first design on the screen. "Of course, these are just suggestions to give us a starting point. There are a few restrictions based on the town plan that we do have to take into consideration, mainly height and what the structure might block as far as views from the houses on Lake Drive, but overall we have a lot of flexibility."

Charlie gave a low whistle as he looked at the design. "This is perfect. When can you start building?"

Buster laughed. "I'm sure there will be a lot to discuss before we get anywhere near the point of submitting plans. But I'm glad you like these initial concepts. How about you, Ash?"

Asha looked from Charlie to Buster, her eyes brimming with tears. "It's amazing. To be honest, there's so much to think about I don't even know where to start."

Buster nodded. "How about I send you both copies of these initial ideas for you to start thinking about. Once you get your head around the concept, Ash, I think you'll have a lot of ideas you'll want to incorporate. I've got a little more research to do into the zoning laws and restrictions, so if you want to meet again in a few days, I'll make sure I have all of that information confirmed."

Asha nodded, her lips turning up in a small grin. "Matt Law's not going to be happy about this."

"A dream come true," Charlie said.

They all laughed.

"But really," Asha said. "Won't this cause problems for you since you're already working with him? It makes the food truck a more permanent business, which he definitely won't like. I'm sure he's trying to find a loophole to get me removed from this location or secure the land for himself."

"Matt's a client, and we're doing our best to keep him happy. You and Charlie are also clients. While neither of you might be happy with what the other is doing, that's not our concern. As long as all of our projects are completed within the law, then we're happy to work with anyone."

Asha nodded. "I wouldn't want to be around him when he finds out, that's all I'll say."

"That boy deserves every bad thing that comes his way," Charlie said, shaking his head. "He is a bad seed, from which nothing good grows."

Buster looked from Charlie to Asha, who was nodding. He understood that they both had intense feelings about Matt, but he was Buster's client, and he felt he should say something. "You know, Matt's only looking to improve the town."

"That I have no problem with," Charlie said. "The way he goes about it, however, I do. Karma will come back to haunt that boy, and I, for one, will be pleased when it happens."

Even from Charlie, the words sounded harsh. But then again, Buster had heard rumors of Matt trying to get Charlie declared unfit to take care of himself and put in LakeView, Hope's Ridge's long-term care facility.

"What problems are we likely to come up against with this development?" Charlie asked.

"Possible objections from the town," Buster said. "You're

planning to build on an area that is currently available for recreation."

"But it is my land."

"It is, and you're within your rights to build. It's just that some of the town might not be too thrilled. It will change the lakefront from what they're used to. Some people hate change regardless of whether it will improve things."

"Perhaps we should give it more thought, Charlie," Asha said. "I don't want to upset anyone. My food truck is one thing, but a permanent structure is another altogether."

Charlie shook his head. "No, we move ahead. This is my land, and I'm entitled to do whatever I like. I'm also popular with the town, so I will ensure everyone is behind the project." He winked. "It is amazing what the promise of free coffee and cake can do. Okay?"

Asha nodded, and Buster gathered his belongings. "Let's meet again later in the week," he suggested. "It gives Asha a chance to get her head around the idea and her thoughts for how she'd like it positioned and laid out. Call me with any questions, of course."

Charlie stood. "Very good. Now you'll need to excuse me. I have someone I need to speak to." His eyes twinkled, and he rubbed his hands together. "A very important conversation that I've been looking forward to."

Buster looked from Charlie to Asha, who shrugged. He smiled at the older man. "Okay, well, enjoy your conversation, and I'll contact you to schedule a time for our next meeting."

He watched as the older man practically skipped along the path in the direction of Main Street.

2

_A_fter dashing from the food truck that morning, Steph had spent most of the day in the garden, pulling weeds and chastising herself over her extreme reaction to Buster. Zane was right, she did need to talk to him, but she just couldn't bring herself to do it. The sick feeling that plagued her anytime she saw him had worsened as time moved on. If she'd spoken to him straight after the accident, maybe she could have avoided this situation altogether. Her thoughts had flickered between Buster and Heat Wave, where she'd returned in the afternoon to take the four o'clock class.

Now, her conversation with Bodhi replayed in her mind as she chopped vegetables for the stir fry she was making. It would be exciting to see Heat Wave expand, but she wasn't sure if involving Matt Law would be to anyone's benefit, except possibly Matt's.

"You look deep in thought." Zane entered the kitchen and opened the fridge. "Everything okay?" He took out a bottle of water.

Steph nodded. "Just a few things happening at work.

How about you, are you here for dinner? There's plenty if you are."

"Knock, knock." Asha's voice floated down the hallway from the front door before Zane had a chance to answer. He grinned and went to meet her.

Steph smiled at the muffled voices as she picked up a zucchini and began to chop it. She looked up as Zane returned to the kitchen, hand-in-hand with her sister. "Hey, what's happening?"

Asha dropped Zane's hand and took a seat on one of the stools at the kitchen counter. "Came to see if you were okay. You left in a bit of a hurry this morning."

Steph shrugged. "I'm fine. I just had a lot to do."

"Steph?"

Steph continued chopping, unable to look at Asha.

"Have I missed something?" Zane asked.

"Buster arrived at the food truck this morning, and Steph took off like a frightened rabbit."

Steph stopped chopping and held up her knife. "I just didn't want to talk to him, okay? I know I need to, but I want to plan what I'm going to say, not be put on the spot. I wasn't expecting to see him in Hope's Ridge."

"He's likely to be in the Ridge a lot more over the coming months," Asha said. "You might want to think about talking to him, so you're not running away every time you see him."

Steph's breathing quickened. "Why is he going to be here more?"

Asha's lips turned up at the edges. She was trying to suppress a smile.

"Ash, what's going on?"

Steph listened as Asha explained Charlie's plan to build the pavilion on the lakefront and Buster's involvement as far as preparing the architectural and engineering plans.

"That's amazing." Zane put an arm around Asha and pulled her to him. "What an opportunity!"

Steph forced a smile. She was happy for Asha, but dread settled in the pit of her stomach. Even if she did talk to Buster, how would she cope with seeing him regularly? She knew running from him was ridiculous, but the moment she saw him, it was as if instinct took over, and she had to flee. She'd watched his little girl drown and had been utterly useless in doing anything to stop it happening. It was bad enough getting through each day with that playing on her mind, but seeing Buster increased the weight she carried around tenfold. This man woke up every day missing his daughter, and she was partially responsible. How could he ever forgive her when she would never be able to forgive herself?

"I don't think Matt's going to be too happy," Asha said, breaking into Steph's thoughts.

She glanced at her sister. "Do you think he'll try to ruin the opportunity for you?"

"I'm sure he'll do his best. He's got his development happening along Lake Drive, but we know he wanted that to be bigger and wants Charlie's lakefront land."

"Hopefully, he'll have another project on the go and be too busy to stir up trouble for you," Zane said.

Asha rolled her eyes. "That, I doubt. I think one of his life ambitions is to stir up trouble for me. And anyway, what other developments does he even have?"

Steph smiled. "Funny you should ask that." She told them of Bodhi's news and that Matt could be a possible target for the sale of the land, properties, and business.

Asha's face clouded over immediately. "Oh, Steph. I'm so sorry. Matt's the last person you'd want to be involved in Heat Wave."

Steph shrugged. "Bodhi needs a sale, and he's an

obvious buyer as he's expressed interest in doing a wellness center or retreat. There's nothing to say I have to stay on. It might be time for me to open something of my own. I guess for now I'll just wait and see what happens. It's unlikely anything will happen quickly, so I'm assuming I'll have a couple of months to make my plans." That was one good thing about living in a small town. Finding a buyer, even if Matt was interested, was unlikely to be a quick process.

Nerves spiraled in the pit of Buster's stomach as he pushed open the door of the construction office the next morning. Jodi, the office manager, and Travis' wife greeted him.

"Hey, Buster, coffee?"

Buster smiled, Jodi's standard morning greeting quashing his nerves. He'd never felt nervous entering the office before, but today, the day he needed to tell Travis his plans, had left him feeling uncomfortable. He hated letting people down, although according to his ex-wife, he was a master at doing that. He stopped. Where had that thought come from? He did his best not to think of Eve and certainly not to invest any energy in raking over the accusations she'd spat at him.

"Buster? Coffee?" Jodi repeated the question.

He pulled a small tray from behind his back, holding three takeout coffees.

Jodi's eyes widened. "You didn't have to do that."

Buster handed Jodi her coffee. "Why not? It's not part of your job description to make me coffee every morning. I wanted you to know I appreciate that you do. You're an amazing team player."

Jodi blushed, unused to praise from Buster. He probably

should have acknowledged her more often, he realized, also realizing it was a bit late to start now. "Travis in?"

Jodi nodded toward her husband's office as she took a sip from her cup.

Buster smiled and strode into his partner's office. Travis looked up from his computer and pushed his dark hair out of his eyes. Buster held out a coffee to him, which he accepted gratefully.

"You need a haircut."

Travis laughed. "And you need a facelift, but I don't hassle you about it."

Buster sat down across from his business partner, realizing he would miss their good-natured ribbing.

Travis glanced at his watch. "I just had a call from Matt Law. He's dropping in soon. I'd like you in on the meeting as he sounded pretty upset about the shoreline development."

Buster put his coffee down on Travis' desk. "Word spreads quickly. I only met with Asha and Charlie yesterday. How did he find out about it?"

Travis' eyes twinkled. "I gather Charlie decided to fill him in. Went out of his way, according to Matt, to rile him up."

Buster laughed. That must have been who Charlie had hurried off to see following their meeting. "Good old Charlie. Matt probably deserves it after the way he treated him. Trying to get an old man declared unfit to look after himself was pretty harsh."

"Well, keep that opinion to yourself, okay? We need to remember that Matt's our client and whether we approve of the way he chooses to operate or not, right now we can't afford to lose his business. Other than the regular council jobs, there's not a lot happening here in the Landing or Hope's Ridge. If we lose Matt, we'll need to tender for jobs in Tall Oaks, and I don't relish the drive."

Buster cleared his throat. He needed to tell Travis of his decision.

Travis raised an eyebrow. "Everything okay?"

"No, not really." Buster went on to tell Travis how difficult he was finding the constant reminders of Holly in Drayson's Landing and Hope's Ridge.

Travis nodded, in the compassionate and considerate way he always did, as Buster told him of his need for a fresh start.

"I hate to think that me leaving might cause problems for the business, and you and Jodi," Buster said. "But I also know that there's nothing for me here now. My marriage exploded, my daughter died, and while I have loved working with you both, it isn't enough to keep me here."

Travis leaned back in his chair. "Jodi was right. She's been saying for ages that she's surprised you've been able to keep going as well as you have. Would you consider opening a branch of the company somewhere else?"

Buster nodded slowly. "Maybe. I think I need a complete break to start with. A few months to maybe travel, or head to the beach and surf. Ski even. Something different to give me a chance to reset."

"Have you thought about whether you want to stay an owner in the business?"

Buster hesitated. "To be honest, I haven't decided on that one. I guess if we considered opening another branch, then it would make sense to remain an owner. I just wasn't sure whether you'd want me to do that. I thought it might suit you to have someone else buy in and have a partnership like we have."

"I'll need to give it more thought," Travis said. "When did you want to finish up?"

"I'll see my current projects through," Buster said.

Travis raised an eyebrow. "Through the construction phase as well?"

"No, I was thinking up to the stage of plan approval. I can draw up the project plans for construction and go over them with you. But with Matt's Lake Drive development, I'd be here for months if I agreed to see that project through. You usually take over at the construction part anyway, so the timing makes sense."

An instant message pinged on Travis' computer. He glanced at it and typed something before returning his focus to Buster. "Jodi says Matt's here."

Both men stood. "Let's both think about your situation and discuss it again further. I'll be sad to see you go, but I do understand."

Buster swallowed the lump that formed in his throat as Matt's wide frame filled the doorway.

His cheeks were flushed, and he looked agitated as he stepped inside Travis' office.

"Matt, grab a seat." Travis pointed to the empty chair next to Buster. "Coffee?"

Matt shook his head. "No thanks. Jodi already offered. I just wanted to speak to you both, see what we can do to stop Charlie Li's development from going ahead."

Travis shot a glance at Buster, one telling Buster to be careful with what he said.

"I'm not sure there is anything," Travis said. "It's his land, and the zoning of the area does allow for development."

"You'd be the first to develop the site if it was yours," Buster added.

Matt's cheek twitched as he looked at Buster. "And that's the whole point. It's not my site, so what can we do about it? Surely there must be a way to get it caught up in red tape if nothing else. I will be lodging objections, but I thought you two would have a few ideas on how to slow it right down or stop it."

Buster bit the inside of his cheek, trying to work out the best way to approach this discussion. "Matt, are you aware that Charlie's given us the contract to design the pavilion?"

Travis dropped his head and muttered something under his breath.

Matt nodded. "I am, which is another reason I'm here. Surely you realize it's a conflict of interest? We're competition, and you're working with both of us."

"I don't think Charlie would consider you competition, Matt. He's doing something nice for Asha, nothing more. He has money to invest, and I think it's giving him great pleasure to do it."

Matt managed a wry smile. "It certainly gave him great pleasure to come and tell me all about it yesterday. He suggested Asha might invest in a larger food truck and expand her menu. Make it more of a cafe and create more competition for the Sandstone Cafe."

"I'm not sure that's in Asha's plans," Buster said. "She only learned of the development plans yesterday, so I doubt she's had the time to decide. She might, of course, but right now, I imagine Charlie's going to enjoy winding you up."

Matt sighed. "And I imagine there's a good argument that I deserve anything he dishes out."

Buster chose not to respond to that comment. "I can reassure you that the development won't affect the view from the Sandstone Cafe," he said.

"But it will affect the views from the apartments. The food truck already does. What if I make you choose? You either work with me or you work with them."

"That would be disappointing," Travis said before Buster had a chance to answer. "There are benefits for both parties involved—and the town—of us working on both projects. It means all development will be done to a similar standard and in keeping with the look and feel the town wants to maintain. If Charlie was to use someone else, we can't guarantee what the result would be. We'll be advising wherever possible that the design be developed to enhance what you're doing and also to make sure neither project impacts the other negatively."

Matt nodded slowly. "Good answer." He sighed again. "Fine, well, keep working for both of us, but if they do anything foolish, I want to be the first to hear. Now, where are we at with the rooftop bar for the cafe? It looks like I might have a tenant ready to go in, and I want to update them on what to expect as far as interruptions."

"That's great news," Buster said. "Anyone we know?"

"Do you remember Ryan Williams? Artist guy who grew up in Hope's Ridge? He was a bit older than me."

Buster nodded. "I met him a few times. He was a good guy. And an amazing talent. The last I heard, he was working as a gallery director in some fancy New York gallery. I think he even had exhibitions of his work."

"That was a few years ago," Matt said. "He's had a bit of a change of pace since then. Anyway, he and his sister, Margie, are moving back to Hope's Ridge to run the cafe. They arrive tomorrow and will be opening the cafe at the end of next week."

"That's great, Matt."

Matt stood. "It is. You should both come out with us on Saturday. Ryan's an adventure junkie. We're meeting up at the Bluff around eleven to do some free solo climbing. We'll take some equipment too in case free soloing is too scary for anyone planning to join us. You up for it?"

A shot of adrenaline rushed through Buster at the thought. He hadn't done any climbing for years. He used to love it and the thrill the danger element of free soloing provided. He'd had a couple of slips but no major accidents. It was an activity that made you live in the moment. There was no time to think of anything other than precisely what it was you were supposed to be doing. An image of Holly appeared in his mind as he had this thought. He pushed it away, aware that Matt was waiting for his answer. He spent most Saturdays avoiding his thoughts, particularly thoughts about Holly. Climbing sounded like the perfect way to escape.

"Love to."

"Me too," Travis added.

Matt grinned. "Good, I'll meet you both out there. I'll find out the time from Ryan and let you know. And in the meantime, if you do have any golden ideas of how to get rid of Charlie Li's development, feel free to act on them. There'd be a hefty bonus from me if you made that happen."

Steph waited for the red Range Rover Sport to pass before crossing Main Street. She was surprised any tourist would visit Hope's Ridge at this time of the year, but the kayak on top the vehicle suggested someone was mad enough to. She shivered at the thought of paddling out across the icy lake. She stepped inside the bakery to pick up a sourdough loaf to accompany the pumpkin soup Zane had promised to make for dinner.

As she stepped back onto the sidewalk, a loaf of bread in hand, she stopped, a wide smile forming on her lips. "Ryan Williams!"

The tall, slim, dark-haired man in front of her mirrored her smile, opening his arms and leaning forward to hug Steph around the bread awkwardly. "Steph! It's so good to see you. It's been years."

Steph pulled back, laughing. "It has. How are you? Or can I answer that for you, Mr. Famous?"

The dimples in Ryan's cheeks deepened as his cheeks flushed red. "Not sure about that."

"Really? An exhibition at The Met makes you famous."

Ryan raised an eyebrow. "You've been keeping tabs on me?"

"Of course I have! I've loved your artwork since I first saw it displayed at school. I knew you'd be famous one day. I make a point of checking the arts sections of the papers every week in case you're mentioned. I would have loved to have come to New York for your exhibition. It must have been so exciting."

Ryan smiled. "It was. Exciting and stressful."

"Are you working in a gallery too?"

"Not anymore. Time for a change. Do you remember Margie, my sister?"

"Of course. Didn't she go on to become a pastry chef? She went to France to do some courses or something."

"Wow, you do keep informed. I don't think Margie's success has been in the local papers." His eyes twinkled. "Are you a Facebook stalker by any chance?"

Steph laughed. "I choose not to own a cell phone, let alone a computer. You won't find me on Facebook. You should remember that I live in a small town. The same one your mom lives in. She takes quite a few yoga classes at Heat Wave, where I work, and I live on Emerald Bay Drive, so we're neighbors."

Ryan slapped his forehead. "Of course. I'd forgotten how much Mom loves to gossip and brag. Sorry if she's bored you."

"Of course she hasn't. I've been so happy to hear about your success. Anyway, you asked if I remembered Margie. Is everything okay?"

"Kind of. She needs a change of scenery. Her marriage recently ended, and she's had a few other things going on. She was talking to me about slowing down, possibly coming back to the Ridge. At the same time, I had a phone call out of the blue from Matt Law. You know him?"

Steph raised an eyebrow. "Everyone knows Matt Law. He's ruffling feathers all over the place at the moment."

Ryan frowned. "Really? Hopefully, that won't cause problems for us. He's asked Margie and me to run the old Sandstone Cafe. We take over on Monday and hope to be reopened by Friday."

Steph stared at him.

"Everything okay?"

"Did he mention what's been going on between him and Asha?"

Ryan shook his head. "No, he just made us an offer to run the cafe with free rein to do whatever we want. He's going to be doing some renovations, but they won't affect us too much. He didn't mention Asha. What do I need to know?"

"Asha was about to sign a five-year lease on the cafe when Matt came in under her and purchased it. He and Asha then fell out over it, and he managed to get her business shut down. She has the food truck by the lake, which she sells coffee and muffins from."

"But I've just come from there," Ryan said. "Her coffee is fantastic as was the muffin I indulged in. She wasn't closed down."

"It was only temporary. Matt forced the council to have her removed from their land, and where she's operating now is privately owned, so he can't touch her."

"Okay, problem sorted."

"It is, but I just thought I'd give you a heads-up. Things have worked out for Asha, but no thanks to Matt. The

Sandstone Cafe was her dream, and he completely crushed it in a pretty horrible way. You might want to be a little sensitive around her."

Ryan nodded. "Thanks for the heads-up. I'll pop back to see Asha now and let her know what's going on. Try to get off on the right foot. I'd much prefer we are friendly competition rather than anything else. Margie and I are moving back to de-stress and live a more relaxed life. We don't want any animosity surrounding us."

"What about your painting? Are you going to still be doing that?"

Ryan nodded. "I'm hoping to find a house with a separate building I can turn into a studio, or I might build one. I'm also planning to run some classes from the cafe once we're up and running. I love teaching, so I thought it might be a nice thing to do to get involved with the community again."

"Sounds great." Steph smiled.

"I hope so. The change of pace will be nice. I'm also planning to get up to the Bluff to do some climbing and hopefully get out mountain biking again. Do you hike or climb at all?"

"I love to hike. I haven't been doing enough of it, though. I've done a little bit of climbing but not for a few years. I don't own the equipment and wouldn't risk free solo climbing."

"Come up to the Bluff with me on Saturday," Ryan said. "I'm hoping to get Margie and maybe a couple of others up for some climbing. I've got all the equipment so you'd only need to bring yourself. We might do some free soloing too, but there's no pressure to do that. We can have a picnic and make a day of it. Give us a chance to get to know each other again."

Steph hesitated. She didn't have a reason to say no, and it

would be nice to get out of town, but getting to the Bluff meant driving the road out of Hope's Ridge. *The road.* She thought back to her last session with Dan. *You need to step outside your comfort zone, Steph. Avoiding car travel, for instance, isn't viable long term. Short trips will get you back in the rhythm, and hopefully, with each one, it will make it easier.* He was right. She took a deep breath. "What time are you going? I'm teaching an early morning class on Saturday. I'll be free by nine."

"I can work around you," Ryan said. "Why don't we say ten o'clock?"

Steph hesitated only for a second before nodding. "I'd love to come if you don't mind me traveling with you? I don't have a car right now. I'm at 4 Emerald Bay Drive."

"Three doors down from Mom and Dad. I can probably remember that." He grinned. "I've been back in town less than an hour, and things are already looking up."

Steph found herself smiling as she walked home carrying the bread. As much as she loved the routine of her life, since the accident, she'd become more and more of a homebody. Not wanting to drive limited what she could do, of course, but she'd also found herself shying away from invites to join friends at the local bar, Traders, for drinks on a weekend or a meal. Initially, it had been to avoid conversations about the accident and to limit the likelihood of bumping into Buster. But now, over a year later, it was time to move on. As Dan said, she needed to step outside her comfort zone and get back into the land of the living. An outing with a different group of friends on Saturday might be the new start she needed. Regardless, for the first time in a long time, she found herself looking forward to something.

A lightness settled over Buster as the automatic doors on his garage opened, and he maneuvered the pickup inside. He climbed out, aware that he was having a good day. A *really* good day. He could honestly say he hadn't had a good day in a very long time, or more to the point he hadn't allowed himself to. Travis' reaction to his announcement was better than he could have hoped for. He truly was a good friend. The suggestion that Buster set up an office elsewhere wasn't one that he was going to dismiss. He wasn't sure if it was what he wanted to do, but having it as a possibility made the thought of selling his house and moving away less daunting.

The decision had left him feeling like something in him had shifted. When Matt suggested he go rock climbing on the weekend, rather than immediately make an excuse and decline the offer, which he'd done with most social invitations since Holly's death, he'd felt a surge of excitement. Was he going to allow himself to get out and start living again?

His mother's words played over in his head as he put his computer and work bag in his small home office before moving through to the kitchen and taking a beer from the fridge. *You have to allow yourself to live, Henry. We're all devastated to lose Holly, but we can't lose you too. You're only thirty-two, you have a long life ahead, and you deserve to enjoy it.* It was the word *deserve* that had thrown him. He wasn't sure he *deserved* any happiness after what had happened, but maybe he had to give himself a break from time to time. He swigged his beer, a wry smile forming on his lips. It was probably more the idea of free soloing that had caused the shift in him. It was dangerous, and if the universe thought he should be punished, it was the perfect opportunity.

His phone rang as he had this thought. The caller display confirmed his mother's ESP must be finely tuned today. She'd often call when he was thinking of her. He put the phone to his ear, deciding that he wouldn't tell her about his idea for a fresh start just yet.

"Hey, Ma."

"Henry, how are you, love?"

"Good, how are you?"

His mother hesitated for a split second.

"Ma?"

She cleared her throat. "I had a call from Cora, Eve's mother."

Buster put his beer down on the counter, his chest instantly tightening. "Why's she calling you?"

"Eve's asked to see you. She wants to talk to you."

"I have nothing to say to her."

"That's what I told Cora you'd say, but she asked me to contact you regardless. Eve's been working with a psychologist, and part of her therapy involves talking to people whose lives her behavior has affected."

"Ruined, you mean." Buster practically spat the words.

"I know, love. Forgiving Eve, or even talking to her, will be tough."

"I will never forgive her." *Or myself.*

"Perhaps you need to tell her that."

Buster sighed. "What good would that do? I'm sure that's not what she's hoping would come out of talking to me. She's probably going to cry and ask me to forgive her. That's what she did for most of our marriage." *Including having affairs, flaunting them in my face, and then expecting me to forgive her.* Buster didn't add that in. His mother didn't need all of the details.

"It might be good for you, Henry. You're carrying around so much hatred toward Eve. It might do you good to release some of it."

Buster gave a small laugh. "I can't believe you're

encouraging me to rip through Eve, that's not really like you, Ma."

"I'm not. I just think talking to her could benefit you, that's all. Help you move on a little."

They were silent for a moment.

"What should I tell Cora?"

"Let me think about it, okay? I've got Cora's number. I'll call her over the weekend."

"Okay, love. Now, when are we going to see you? It's been weeks since you visited."

Buster chatted with his mother for a few more minutes, promising to make the drive out to visit his parents in Tall Oaks in the coming weeks, before ending the call.

He picked up his beer and took a large swig. So much for his good day. The first day in over a year when he felt a little positive, and it was ruined—ruined by the person who'd also destroyed his life. Anger surged within him. Maybe his mother was right. Perhaps he did need to talk to her. Make her realize what she'd done to him. But as quickly as he had the thought, it was replaced with another. *And what he'd done to her.*

3

*S*teph sank into the leather seats of the Range Rover, looking forward to the day ahead.

"Margie's hoping to meet us there later," Ryan said, as he headed up the winding road that led out of Hope's Ridge toward the Bluff.

Steph automatically tensed as they passed *the corner*, which didn't go unnoticed by Ryan.

"Everything okay?"

Steph nodded. It was unlikely Ryan knew about the accident, which was good. She wanted to enjoy the day, treat it like a fresh start.

"You sure? You're kind of pale." Ryan's brow creased in concern.

Steph forced a smile. "I'm good. Can't wait. It's been ages since I climbed. I hope my upper body strength is good enough."

Ryan's eyes traveled over her upper body before returning his focus to the road. "I think your yoga has prepared you for this."

Steph couldn't remember the last time a man had looked at her with the appreciation she saw in Ryan's eyes. Or maybe she couldn't remember the last time she'd noticed. It gave her a confidence boost but nothing more. Asha had teased her the previous night about today being a *date*, but it wasn't. She and Ryan had been friends years ago when they were in high school; she'd reminded Asha. That's all they'd been then and all they'd be now. He was like a worn, comfy pair of jeans you could slip back on at any time and feel comfortable in. Reliable and dependable.

"I should warn you, Matt's coming out today with a couple of the guys he works with," Ryan said. "Hope that's okay? I know you said there were some issues with him."

"Nothing that affected me directly," Steph said. "The issues were more with Asha than with me." She chose her words carefully. "I wouldn't mind spending some time with him." She went on to tell him Bodhi's plans for selling Heat Wave. "Matt's expressed interest in setting up a wellness center for some time. The timing might not be right for him, but it would be interesting to see what he thinks." She laughed. "I might not have him hold my ropes. I'm not sure I trust him that much."

"No problem. I think he's planning some free soloing anyway, so we might split into a couple of different groups." He glanced over at Steph, his lips curling into a wicked grin. "You can always give him a little nudge off the cliff face if you think he's up to no good."

Steph laughed. "Don't tempt me."

An hour later, as she breathed in a lungful of the fresh mountain air, Steph couldn't help but laugh at Matt's jokes as he and Ryan prepared the harnesses and climbing equipment. He'd arrived with a helmet under his arm, gloves, and expensive La Sportiva climbing shoes on his feet. He was serious about the climbing, but not so serious when relaying stories of a climb he'd done a few months earlier.

"I finally got to the ledge we'd been aiming for and

nearly had a heart attack," he said. "A massive mountain goat was sitting down on all fours watching me. I pulled myself up over the ledge and was about to climb up for a rest when I saw it. It just stared at me." He laughed. "I nearly wet my pants. To be honest, I was lucky to be harnessed, or I probably would have fallen straight off the rock face and plummeted to my death. This was about a month before the debacle with Asha and the cafe, so she'd probably be wishing we were free soloing that day."

"How did the goat get down?" Steph asked, causing Matt to laugh harder.

"That's your question? Not how did I survive, and were we all okay? You want to know about the goat?"

Steph shrugged. "Just wondering how he got there and if he was able to get down."

"There was a small track leading off the back of the ledge. He must have got there that way, so I assume left that way too."

"Who do you normally climb with? The climbing club?"

Matt shook his head. "No, occasionally with Travis Moore." A black pickup drove up next to them as Matt spoke. He gave a little wave. "Here he is now. Hopefully, we won't encounter any goats today."

Steph smiled. As funny as the story was, she wasn't keen on a goat encounter either. Or a mountain lion, black bear or any other dangerous creature. She didn't know Travis very well, but it was nice to be doing something with different people, even if Matt technically was the enemy. In Asha's eyes, anyway.

The doors to the pickup opened, and Travis climbed out from the driver's seat, dressed similarly to Matt. The passenger door opened, and as Buster stepped out, Steph's heart sank.

A twinge of nerves fluttered through Buster's stomach the moment he saw Steph's smile disappear and her face pale. Her eyes flitted to the ground. She wasn't happy to see him. The exchange didn't go unnoticed by Ryan either, who looked from Steph to Buster, the question in his eyes.

Buster gave his head a gentle shake. He needed to speak to Steph without anyone else around. He held out his hand to Ryan. "Good to see you, bro. It's been years."

Ryan shook it, his smile broadening. "You too, Buster. I'm so glad Matt got you and Travis to come along. I've only been back a few days, and from the moment I arrived," he glanced over at Steph and continued, "I knew it was the right decision to come home. Everyone's been so welcoming."

Buster couldn't help but swallow the lump that had formed in his throat. It was a shame Steph wasn't so welcoming of him.

"Let's get moving," Matt said, rubbing his hands together. "I'm looking to free solo, who's with me?"

"Definitely," Travis said.

Buster looked over to Steph. "How about you, Steph? Game?"

She shook her head but didn't meet his eyes. "No, the harnesses are for me." She turned to Ryan. "I think I might head off and do a bit of a hike, let you guys do some free soloing first. I can climb after lunch if there's time."

"Don't be silly," Ryan said. "We just got the harness ready for you. Why don't you climb Bear's Drop first and then we can work out the rest of the day? Matt can take the boys off and do a bit of a warm-up climb."

Steph stood, and Buster could see her leg trembling. She wasn't in the right frame of mind to climb. She shook her head. "No, I think I'll go for a walk. I'll meet you back here later." She didn't wait for Ryan to respond. Instead, she picked up her pack and headed toward one of the trailheads.

Ryan turned to the small group. "What just happened?"

Buster sighed. "Me. I didn't know Steph was going to be here, and I assume she had no idea I would be, or I'm guessing she wouldn't have come."

Ryan raised an eyebrow. "You guys date or something?"

"No, but I need to talk to her." He clenched his teeth. Today was about putting everything out of his mind and enjoying the freedom the climb was supposed to bring. He turned to Travis. "Fill Ryan in. He probably isn't aware of what happened. But," he addressed all of them, "today was supposed to be a fresh start for me, doing something new. After I speak to Steph, I'd appreciate it if we move on with the day. I don't want to discuss the past. At all."

Both Travis and Matt nodded while Ryan's eyes flicked between them. The concern on his face confirmed he knew nothing of the accident. Buster grabbed a bottle of water from Ryan's stash and headed for the trailhead. The speed with which Steph had departed had him question whether he'd even be able to catch her.

"Steph, wait up."

Steph quickened her pace to match her heart rate as she heard Buster call out. She told herself she was being ridiculous, but it didn't help. Her legs continued to pound along the track, her body operating entirely independently of her mind. She pushed along, conscious the track had begun a steep climb upward, and her legs burned as she continued on. Why hadn't she thought to ask Ryan who was coming? Today was the first day in ages she'd looked forward to getting away from everything and just enjoying the different company and something new. The universe did like to punish her.

"Steph!"

Steph's legs froze with the second call of her name, and she felt Buster put a hand on her shoulder. Her breath caught in her throat, even as she tried to breathe normally. Turning to face him, she saw that his cheeks were red, and he was breathing hard. He pointed to some flat rocks just off the side of the track.

"Sit down for a minute. We need to talk."

Steph obeyed his instructions, her body tense. She couldn't imagine being able to string a sentence together. Her tongue was frozen, or at least it felt like it was.

Buster ran a hand through his blonde hair, sweat beading on his forehead. He gave a wry smile. "Your idea of a hike is kind of like a mountain sprint. Ever thought of trail running?"

Steph stared at him. Words flitted through her brain but refused to come out of her mouth. He'd think she was mad.

"Look. I wanted to say sorry."

A gurgling noise escaped Steph's lips. She closed her eyes. Why was he sorry? She was the one who needed forgiveness, not that she ever expected to receive it.

"Zane mentioned to me a while back that you were having a hard time over the accident and…," he cleared his throat, "…that you blamed yourself."

Steph managed a nod.

"Steph." Buster's voice was gentle, laced with concern. "It wasn't your fault. There was nothing you could have done to save Holly. Once the car went into the lake, no one could have helped her. It was a miracle Eve got out alive. There's only one person to blame, and that's my ex-wife. And even she didn't mean for this to happen. As much as I hate her at times, deep down, I know she's just as devastated as I am, except she has a real reason to blame herself. You don't."

Steph forced her eyes open, tears slipping down her cheeks. "I see her every day. Your beautiful little girl's eyes, her face. They're always there. Always asking for my help. If I hadn't been on the road that day, the accident would never have happened."

"But Steph, you were just driving home. You weren't doing anything wrong. Eve had been drinking, and she was angry. Angry with me. If I hadn't threatened her, she would have stayed in Hope's Ridge with Holly for longer. She wouldn't have had any reason to speed up the winding road and veer across the road and hit you."

Steph stared at him. Did he blame himself? "It wasn't your fault."

Buster pushed a hand through his hair again. "I'd just won full custody of Holly. I didn't trust Eve because of her drinking. She was angry and upset. She picked up Holly from school early, even though the school had it on record that she wasn't allowed to. Then she brought her to Hope's Ridge for a special treat, a picnic in a canoe on the lake. She called me so I wouldn't worry and wouldn't go to get Holly from school. Instead of saying okay and letting her have this treat, I went ballistic. I told her it was against court orders, and I'd be reporting her. Then I threatened that I was coming to pick up Holly." Tears filled his eyes, causing Steph's heart to ache. "If I'd handled it differently, she'd still be alive."

Steph put her hand on Buster's arm. "If the school had handled it differently. If Eve hadn't taken her to start with. If I'd been able to get her out of the car. There are so many ifs, but unfortunately, none of us had the opportunity to create a different outcome."

Buster gave her a sad smile. "No, we didn't. Steph, I can't

control how you think or feel about what happened, but the one thing I can tell you is I don't blame you. I never have. I've only ever been eternally grateful that you tried to help Holly. And I'm sorry."

"Sorry?"

"I should have sought you out the moment Zane mentioned to me that you were struggling. I honestly thought he might have it wrong about you blaming yourself. I should have come and talked to you then and made sure you knew how grateful I am for what you tried to do."

A weight lifted from Steph's shoulders as Buster's words sank in. She'd avoided him for over twelve months, absolutely crippled with guilt, unable to look him in the eye, yet in his own words, he was grateful to her. Tears rolled down her cheeks, and she was dismayed to see Buster's eyes well up too.

She wiped her tears. "I'm sorry, I think they're partially from relief, but now I've upset you."

Buster pushed his sleeve roughly across his eyes. "I just didn't expect someone else to care so much."

Steph moved toward Buster and took him in her arms. She could feel him trying to calm his breathing and wondered how he'd coped since his daughter's death. Did he have someone to hold him, to comfort him? She'd been so caught up in avoiding him, she hadn't allowed herself to think beyond that. She stroked his back, feeling him relax against her. Eventually, he pulled back, his cheeks tear-stained, but his eyes reflected his smile.

"I thought I was getting away from everything Holly-related today," he said. "I didn't expect this. I'm glad we had a chance to talk, Steph."

Steph smiled. "Me too. I promise I won't run the other way when I see you next time."

Buster laughed and stood. He held out a hand to Steph

and helped her up. "How about we go back and join the others? I can be the anchor for your harness if you're still in the mood to climb."

Steph nodded. "I'd like that."

Buster watched as Steph found a handhold and pulled herself up the rock face. She was nearly at the top. They'd chosen one of the easier climbs. There were a few places at the Bluff that had pre-installed bolts and anchors, making it relatively easy to progress. It also meant that as soon as Steph reached the top, Buster could join her. He could have done this as a free solo climb, but today he would use the equipment instead. His discussion with Steph had him distracted, and knowing the focus required for free soloing, he decided it was best to play it safe. He watched as her lean body moved farther up the rock face. She was so athletic. He imagined it was the yoga that attributed to that, and her healthy glow. Her eyes were bright, and her skin flawless. Eve had caked-on makeup and still had the unhealthy look of someone who overindulged. He didn't think Steph wore any makeup. He smiled to himself. She didn't need to; she was gorgeous.

He froze. Where had that come from? Women were entirely out of bounds, no matter how gorgeous they might appear. After Eve he would never go there again.

"Great job," he called as Steph pulled herself over the top ledge and stood up waving to him. He bet her muscles were screaming after that. She made it look easy, but it wasn't. There had been no sign of the others when they'd returned to the parking area, but the climbing equipment had been carefully placed in the back of Ryan's pickup, so they'd finished adjusting it and started the climb.

"Your turn," Steph called down from above.

Buster grinned, adjusted his harness, and reached for the first handhold.

His muscles ached, and he was breathing hard by the time he traversed the final section of the climb and pulled himself onto the rock ledge where Steph was waiting. "How did you make that look so easy?" he panted, lying on the ground next to where she sat.

Steph laughed. "If it's any consolation, I don't think I can move. I definitely can't do another climb. My arms are shot."

"We can walk back down," Buster said. "The walking track winds down behind us. It's a pretty quick walk. Not that I think I could do it right away. I'm exhausted."

"Just relax and enjoy the view," Steph said, looking out across the valley. "It's beautiful up here."

Buster pulled himself up to sitting and drank in the view. He could see across the valley to the edge of Lake Hopeful. "You're right; it's an incredible view." He scanned the scenery around them and nudged Steph. "And look over there." He pointed to a rock face in the distance where Matt's bright red shirt pinpointed where he was. He could just make out Ryan and Travis on a crevice above Matt.

Steph shuddered. "That scares me. What if they fall?"

"They're in trouble if they fall," Buster said. "But the adrenaline rush is half of what drives them to do it. They're all pretty experienced and have good gear. I know Ryan said that today was going to be a gentle introduction back into it for all of them. I don't think they'll be doing anything too risky."

"Good." Steph moved her gaze back to the valley and lake. "I still don't think I can watch them. Thanks, by the way. I know you'd planned to free solo today. I appreciate you doing this with me. Ryan was going to, but I guess the day turned out differently than planned."

Buster laughed. "I thought today was going to be forgetting everything Holly-related. Not quite the case. It's been one of those weeks, I guess. The universe is telling me I have things to deal with and should meet them head-on rather than avoiding issues as I did with you, and I guess like I was planning to do with Eve."

"Eve?"

Buster nodded. He wasn't sure why he was opening up to Steph, but there was something about her that made him feel safe, like he could tell her anything. Maybe it was just that they shared grief over Holly, he wasn't sure. "Her mom got in touch with mine earlier this week. She wants to see me. She wants to talk to me."

Steph didn't say anything, just nodded gently.

"She's been seeing a psychologist, and whatever stage they're up to is the stage they need to see people from the outside. Apologize or explain, I'm not sure which."

"Probably both," Steph said.

Buster met her eyes. "Do you think that's what she wants?"

Steph nodded. "I would imagine so. She's probably been living a nightmare since the accident. I don't imagine it's been easy for her."

Anger rose within Buster. "And it shouldn't be. She deserves everything she gets."

Steph placed a hand on his arm. "Part of me agrees with you, but another part of me has spent hours wondering about Eve. Putting myself in her shoes, trying to come to terms with what happened and how responsible she'd feel. I wouldn't wish that on anyone, Buster, not even Eve."

Tears pricked the back of Buster's eyes. He did his best to blink them away.

Steph squeezed his arm. "Sorry. I didn't mean to upset you. You have every reason and every right to hate her. I'm more removed from the situation than you, so I can see it from different perspectives."

Buster closed his eyes momentarily. The discussion he and Steph had had earlier seemed to have unlocked all of his emotions. He was usually good at keeping them squashed down. He opened his eyes and did his best to smile. "You didn't upset me. If anything, you probably convinced me I should go and see Eve. I hate what happened, but as I said earlier, I contributed to this."

He put his hand up when Steph went to object. "No, I did. Marriages rarely end because of the way one person acts. I'm not silly enough to think that. I had a lot of anger and resentment toward Eve stored up and let a lot of it loose in the way I went about fighting for custody and the way I treated her once I'd won. If I could turn back the clock and change that I would."

"Maybe you need to tell her that."

Buster nodded. "Maybe. We both lost out in the cruelest way possible. The difference between us is I get to move on with my life whereas she has the added stress of living in prison."

"I have a feeling with what happened, Eve will be in prison for a very long time," Steph said.

"At least three years."

"I didn't mean the state prison. I meant her personal prison. The hell I imagine she lives in most days…" her eyes met his, "…is probably comparable to the prison you've been living in."

Buster fell silent as Steph stood.

"Come on, let's walk back down to the parking area. I don't know about you, but I'm starving."

Buster took the hand Steph held out to him and allowed her to help him up. He didn't let go of her hand once he was standing. Instead, he squeezed it.

"Thank you. You're making me look at the whole situation differently."

Steph gave a small smile. "At the end of the day, anything we can do to help each other and others move forward is important. Life's hard, Buster. You've been dealt a particularly horrible set of circumstances to deal with, but so have others. It's all about kindness and compassion and trying to live our best lives." She sighed. "Wise words I need to be listening to myself. I'm guilty of having retreated into a shell over the last year or so. I'm going to do more work on me to make sure that doesn't happen again. Both you and I have the chance to live. For Holly's sake, we should both embrace that and make the most of it. None of us knows how long we have to do that. As we've both seen, life can change in an instant." She withdrew her hand from his and began walking along the narrow track that led down the scrubby hill to the parking area. The views of the valley and lake stretched out before them.

Buster watched as she walked away from him. It was hard to believe that the day, which he'd imagined would be an escape from all things Holly, had turned out the way it had. He fell into step behind Steph with mixed feelings as he looked out to Lake Hopeful. He'd renamed it Lake Devastation the previous weekend when he'd driven out and sat by it hoping to feel closer to Holly, but seeing how beautiful it looked today made him wonder if perhaps its name was correct. Maybe there was hope for him. Hope that he could live a happy life. Hope that he could forgive Eve. Hope that he could spend more time with Steph. He jolted to a stop. Nervous energy swirled in the pit of his stomach as he sought out Steph in the distance. Did he really just have that thought?

Steph's legs were shaky as she walked away from Buster and headed down the hill. Their discussion had been cathartic, and a sense of relief had settled over her, but something else had too. Taking Buster's hand had been a completely natural thing to do until a jolt of electricity had shot up her arm. Her body had tingled all over, and her insides turned to mush. It had been an emotional situation, she knew that, and her body had reacted accordingly. She just hoped he hadn't sensed her reaction or her sudden attraction to him. After everything that had happened, it seemed inappropriate.

She was glad when they reached the parking area to find Ryan, Travis, and Matt arriving at the same time. They were all talking excitedly, and Steph smiled, realizing they were adrenaline-fueled.

"How did it go?" Matt asked as he reached them. He looked from Steph to Buster, concern on his face. "Everything okay?"

"Definitely," Steph said. "Today's given us a chance to chat and a chance to move on." Steph was surprised to see Matt's face relax into a smile. His concern had been genuine. After everything that had happened with Asha, it was hard to consider him as anything but a self-absorbed jerk.

"Time for a picnic," Ryan declared, rubbing his stomach. "I'm starving. Margie sends her apologies, by the way. She called as we were walking back and she isn't going to make it. Not that I'm necessarily up for any more climbing after lunch anyway." He flexed his muscles. "These guys are a bit worn out already."

They laughed, and as the men pulled out coolers from their pickups, Steph grabbed the container she'd filled with sandwiches that morning. She had no idea how many of them would be here, so she had made enough food to feed at least ten people.

"What a feast!" Ryan's eyes lit up as they spread out the

containers of cold cuts, macaroni salad, watermelon, and Steph's sandwiches on a blanket Travis had pulled from his truck.

"Did you hear about Bodhi?" Travis asked as they sat down and started eating. "Steph, you'd know what's going on, wouldn't you?"

Steph nodded. "I'm not sure how much is public knowledge yet."

"Is he okay?" Again Matt's face was filled with genuine concern.

"He is," Travis said. "But his dad isn't. He's moving back to Tall Oaks to help his parents out. It sounds like his dad's dementia requires full-time care."

"That's awful," Matt said. He turned to Steph. "What does that mean for you and Heat Wave?"

"I'm not sure. You'll probably hear from Bodhi yourself. He was going to approach you before he puts the business and land on the market."

Matt's eyes widened. "He's going to sell?"

Steph nodded. "He has to. He'll need the money for the care his father needs."

Matt let out a low whistle. "The poor guy. He's spent years building up that business. Can you buy him out?"

Steph shook her head. "No, I'm not in a position to. So I have no idea once it sells whether the new owner will continue with yoga or use the property for something else altogether."

"It's the perfect property to set up a retreat," Matt said. "I've thought about it for ages but assumed Bodhi would never sell. You said as much to Zane at the town meeting when I was presenting my plans for the Sandstone Cafe and the Lake Drive development. I have contemplated talking to Bodhi about a joint partnership in the past but discounted it. I think our visions for what we'd see as progress would be very different. I never thought he'd sell."

"And I truly believed that to be the case too," Steph said. "This has come completely out of left field for me." She held out the box of sandwiches, and Matt took a ham, cheese and mustard gratefully.

"If you're interested, you should chat with him," she said.

Matt raised an eyebrow. "The sister of Asha Jones is encouraging me to purchase the business she works for?"

"For Bodhi's benefit, not mine. If you were to buy it, I'd assume you'd turn it into something fancy and modern and my services wouldn't be needed. Even if you kept offering yoga, a fancy new resort wouldn't be my style at all."

"What will you do?" Ryan asked.

"I'm not sure yet," Steph said. "I'm a true believer that having patience leads us to our best path in life. As soon as we try and rush or take shortcuts, things go wrong. So I'll wait and see. Setting up on my own is an option, of course, but again, I'm in no rush to do anything."

Matt watched Steph as she spoke, nodding and chewing his sandwich. She could see he was deep in thought. Knowing Matt, he was probably working out how he could rip off Bodhi if he were to buy the business.

She held his gaze. "I hope if you do discuss buying the property from Bodhi that you'll offer a fair price, Matt. He's giving up a lot for his family, and it would be heartbreaking to see someone take advantage of the years of hard work he's put into Heat Wave."

Matt flinched at Steph's words. He didn't speak as Ryan started joking about him being put in his place, but he did acknowledge Steph with a small nod of his head. Something in Steph's gut told her that Matt had just given her his word. She would be stupid, after everything that had happened with Asha and Charlie, to believe anything this man said, but for some reason, on this occasion, she did.

Buster replayed the discussion between Matt and Steph in his mind as he and Travis drove back to Drayson's Landing. He'd remained silent during their exchange, finding himself watching her, impressed by the way she spoke to Matt. There was something about her energy that had him wanting to say yes to anything she suggested, and he was pretty sure Matt had fallen under her spell too. He shook himself. *Spell?* Was he being ridiculous?

Travis pulled into Buster's driveway, and moments later, Matt's pickup pulled in behind them. They'd decided to come to Buster's for a few drinks to celebrate the success of the day. Ryan and Steph had declined the invitation, Steph declaring herself too sore to do anything but go home and have a hot bath. Both Ryan and Matt had joked that they felt the same and would happily accompany her, but Steph had only laughed and chosen to ignore both of them. She had turned to Buster before they left and mouthed *thank you*, at which he shook his head and pointed at her. He should be thanking her, not the other way around.

"Got any beers?" Matt asked as he climbed out of his pickup and followed Travis and Buster through the front door and into Buster's house.

"A fridge full," Buster answered, leading them into the kitchen. "Grab a seat, and I'll get the drinks. I've got to say, I'm exhausted. I'm going to need to get back into the gym if I want to do that again."

Travis flexed his muscles. "Not feeling it at all. You're getting a bit soft."

Matt laughed. "You're lying. I work out five times a

54

week, yet I'm beat. That was hard work. I think Ryan was showing off taking us up over that ridge. I'll only admit it now, but there was one section where I was kind of worried. If any of us had slipped, the fall would have been nasty."

"Yeah, I think next time I'll join you and Steph," Travis said, accepting the beer Buster handed him. "You two looked pretty cozy when we returned."

Matt laughed. "Yeah, I think Ryan was pretty put out. He probably spent the whole trip back to the Ridge trying to impress Steph."

A ripple of jealousy coursed through Buster. He took a swig of his beer, shocked by the intensity of the feeling. "Ryan's interested in Steph?"

Matt nodded. "Apparently on the day he arrived back in the Ridge she was one of the first people he saw. She threw herself on him, she was so happy to see him."

Buster frowned. "Really? I can't see Steph doing that."

"Matt's teasing," Travis said. "She hugged him to welcome him home, which I'm not sure is the same as throwing yourself on someone."

"But he's still interested in her?"

Matt nodded. "He's had a pretty rough time in New York, which is why he jumped at my offer to come home. My offer was to Margie, not him, but they'll make a good team."

"It'll be great to get the cafe up and running again," Travis said. "Jodi and I often come into the Ridge on the weekend for a change of scenery. Asha's coffee and muffins are nice, but I've got to say, when it's cold like it is now, sitting inside with an open fire is much more appealing than sitting by the food truck."

"It'll have a heated pavilion soon," Buster said. "Then you'll have your pick of the two." He laughed as Matt's face clouded over. "I think you're going to have to accept defeat on this one, Matt. Charlie owns the land, and it's zoned for development. You're probably lucky he's only looking at doing a seating area. He could have built a cafe or developed the entire lakefront if he chose to."

Matt shook his head good-naturedly. "If I could turn back the clock a few months, this would not be happening. Asha would be happily running the Sandstone Cafe, and Charlie would be enjoying his old age, with me hoping to buy all of his land from his nephew once he inherited it."

"It wasn't meant to be," Buster said. "You would have had a lot of objection from the town with what you wanted to do. Developing Lake Drive and the shoreline, if you'd been able to get the land, would have changed the feel of the town."

"Which was my intention. Still, it's a big enough town to consider other projects. I'll keep plugging away. We'll get the cafe running this week and continue with the apartment development. I'll speak to Bodhi too. That could be an unexpected opportunity."

"Steph was pretty clear about being fair with a price if you were to make an offer."

Matt laughed. "She was *very* clear. It's a shame she can't afford to purchase the business. I know from talking to Bodhi in the past that he credits a lot of the success of Heat Wave to Steph. There's something about her, isn't there?" He looked to Travis and Buster for confirmation. "Something engaging."

Travis laughed. "Don't tell me Ryan's got competition in the form of Matt Law!"

Buster tried to ignore his gut clenching. He was not interested in Steph, so why was he reacting like this? He was probably just feeling protective of her after their discussion today. Realizing after everything she'd been through since the accident, he didn't want to see her hurt further.

"God, imagine that. No, I admire Steph, but I'm not attracted to her. Even if I was, there's no way I'd get anywhere near her. Asha would make sure of that."

Travis laughed. "It would keep us all entertained watching her go at you again. Joking," he added when he saw Matt's face. "On a serious note, you're certainly bringing us a lot of work, which we appreciate."

"I'm hoping to inundate you so you don't have time to do anything for anyone else," Matt said. "Like certain lakefront developments. I'd appreciate it if you could find reasons to hold them up."

They all laughed, and Buster was relieved to see Matt was enjoying the joke. This was the side of Matt he liked. The side Zane Larsen had enjoyed working with. But Zane had been burned by Matt. He just hoped that J.R. Construction wouldn't be put in an awkward position or lose a lot of business because of their association with him. Although the sooner his projects were ready for handover, the sooner Buster could leave the area.

After two beers, the boys called it a day. For all of his bragging, even Travis said he needed to go home and slip into bed. The day had taken it out of all of them.

Buster wondered whether Steph was as tired as he was, or whether Ryan had convinced her to go out for dinner or… He wouldn't let his thoughts go there. They'd shared a connection today, nothing more, and anyway, he was a terrible judge of character. Eve had proven that.

Steph closed her eyes as the car maneuvered its way around the tight bends as the road dropped down into Hope's Ridge.

She felt a squeeze on her knee and opened her eyes to see the concern on Ryan's face. "You okay?"

Steph nodded. "I hate this road. It's where, well, where the accident happened."

Ryan left his hand on Steph's knee, squeezing it in sympathy. "I'm so sorry you went through that. You and Buster, of course. It can't be easy."

"It's not. I'd rather not talk about it if you don't mind."

Ryan removed his hand and nodded. "Of course, I won't bring it up again." He smiled. "I've had a great day, Steph. I hope you did too."

Steph's smiled mirrored his. "Honestly, I had one of the best days in a long time. I can't remember the last time I hung out with a bunch of guys. It was nice to see Matt in that environment. He's been the enemy the last few months, and it's great to see that another side of him exists. Asha's boyfriend, Zane, was working for him and attested to the fact that there's a good side to Matt. Unfortunately, the rotten side took over in his dealings with Asha. It was a shame Margie couldn't join us. Has she arrived in Hope's Ridge yet?"

Ryan nodded. "She has, and to be honest, I'm worried about her and this cafe. It's a great opportunity, but she hasn't been a hundred percent honest with Matt."

"In what respect?"

Ryan sighed. "The day I arrived and bumped into you, I mentioned that Margie's marriage recently ended."

Steph nodded. "I remember."

"Well, it did, but not how I probably led you to believe. Aaron, her husband, died a few months ago. She hasn't come to terms with his death or recovered."

"The poor thing," Steph said, her heart instantly contracting. "She's so young to lose her husband. Was he ill, or involved in an accident?"

"Pancreatic cancer. From diagnosis to death, they only had two weeks. It all happened far too quickly. The cancer was advanced, and there were no treatment options. I don't know if Margie will ever recover."

Steph sucked in a breath. "How devastating."

"It is."

"You said she hadn't been honest with Matt. Surely it's none of his business what happened."

"She needed a change, and Matt's offer was a lifeline. She feels she should have told him what she's been through, but instead, she spoke as if she was currently working and would need to give notice. He wanted her so didn't ask for any references. The guilt's kicked in since, and she feels she should have been up-front with him. She has her good days and bad days and would hate to let him down. It's why I came to help out. If she's having a bad day, I'll take over and make sure Matt doesn't know anything about it."

"If there's anything I can do to help, just let me know."

Ryan reached across and squeezed Steph's hand. "I'd love to spend more time with you. That's something that would help."

Steph laughed and pulled her hand away from Ryan's. "I meant help Margie. I'm not sure you and me spending time together is going to do that."

He grinned. "If I'm happy, I'm sure it will help perk her up. I do mean it. It's been so great to get back in touch. Just like old times."

Steph smiled. It was like old times. She'd always felt comfortable around Ryan, and today was like turning back the clock to their teenage years. He'd been a great friend then, and she hoped he would remain a great friend now.

After waving goodbye to Ryan, Steph enjoyed a long hot shower before gratefully accepting the cup of tea Zane had made for her. He and Asha had spent the afternoon at

Steph's, and it was lovely to see her sister. Steph filled them in on her day at the Bluff and Buster's unexpected arrival.

"I'm so happy for you," Asha said.

"Does this mean no more three a.m. chats?" Zane joked. "You might be able to sleep now."

Steph shrugged. "I don't know about that. It doesn't change the fact that a little girl drowned and I wasn't able to do anything. It's a relief to know Buster doesn't blame me or hate me. He's grateful that I tried to help his daughter. But it doesn't change the outcome from that day. Nothing ever will."

A melancholy settled over the kitchen as they all thought about the little girl who'd lost her life far too early.

"It'll make the food truck project a lot easier," Asha said. "Buster's going to be pretty busy with that and in town a lot. You'd be hiding out from him all the time if you hadn't worked things out."

"He'd be here for Matt's projects too," Steph said. "So there'd be no escaping him."

"The Sandstone Cafe reopens tomorrow. Did you know Ryan and Margie will be running it?"

Steph nodded. "Ryan was telling me a bit about it on the drive to the Bluff. He's going to start up some art classes too."

Asha raised an eyebrow. "You went to and from the Bluff with Ryan?"

"He's just a friend."

"A very good-looking and quite famous friend," Asha said. "Sounds like today was a good day. You fixed things with Buster and spent time with a guy like Ryan. I think you'll sleep very well tonight."

Steph rolled her eyes, doing her best to ignore Asha's teasing. She had had a good day, and since arriving home, thoughts of one person had filled her mind. But it wasn't

Ryan. It was Buster. They'd shared an emotional connection today, a connection they'd always have. But it was more than that. As she'd watched him haul himself up the rock face after her, she'd been shocked at her body's reaction to his muscled arms and chiseled chin. Now that she'd stopped running from him, she wasn't sure whether to be excited or dismayed at the attraction she felt.

She pushed away the thought. They had a connection over the death of his daughter, nothing more, and she couldn't imagine after what Buster had been through with his ex, or his daughter, that a relationship was something he'd be looking for.

4

*B*uster stretched his arms as he walked into the kitchen. He wondered if Steph and the guys were as sore as he was this morning. Having not climbed for several years, he'd woken muscles that had forgotten they existed. He tried to remember the last time he had climbed and couldn't. There was a weekend before Holly was born that he'd been invited to join a group of friends for free soloing, but Eve had stopped him. She'd been horrified that he'd put himself in danger when their baby was arriving any day.

He sighed as he thought of his ex. He'd promised his mom he'd call Cora this weekend.

He picked up his phone and scrolled through his contacts, stopping as her details came up. He stared at her name. He hadn't seen Eve's mother since the funeral. She'd contacted him once following Eve's trial, but he hadn't returned her call. He'd seen the pain in her face and eyes at Holly's funeral and knew it extended beyond losing her granddaughter. She'd lost her daughter too. Many years earlier, truth be told.

Eve had changed after Holly's birth. It was Jodi at work who more recently had made him wonder if she'd suffered undiagnosed postpartum depression. She hadn't coped well with a baby and turned to alcohol and other men. It had been devastating for Buster the first time he became aware she'd had an affair. He'd tried to forgive her and move past it, and maybe he would have if she hadn't done it again— with Oscar, one of his friends.

Holly had just turned four when he asked her to leave. He'd planned the conversation carefully, expecting to have a fight on his hands. He hadn't expected her to pack a bag and walk out calmly. It was two months after she and Oscar broke up that he heard from her again. Suddenly she wanted forgiveness, wanted to get back together, and wanted Holly back. That was when he'd retained a lawyer.

He took a deep breath and pressed the call button on his phone. Cora picked up after a few rings. Her voice was hesitant.

"Henry?"

"Yes, it's me, Cora. Mom passed your message on."

"How are you, son?"

Buster closed his eyes. Cora had always made him feel special, but she was also very good at controlling situations. He used to laugh with Eve that whenever Cora called, they should just drop their plans and do what she said. She was lovely and kind but also very good at manipulating situations to work in her favor. He imagined, regardless of Eve, Cora would still be in his life if Holly were still alive.

"I'm doing okay, Cora. How about you?"

Silence met him. He knew her well enough to know she would be struggling not to cry.

"Mom said Eve wants to see me."

Cora cleared her throat. "Yes, she does. I realize she's the last person you probably ever want to see again, but I would appreciate it if you could make the trip. It's important for her recovery. It's important to me."

Buster bit the inside of his lip, emotions tearing through him. He thought back to his conversation with Steph and her words that Eve would be living in her own prison for the rest of her life. He knew she was right. But it was Cora's *it's important to me* that was enough to have him agree. He'd always found it hard to say no to her, and hearing her close to tears pushed him to a quick decision. "I can go this week. How do I arrange a visit?"

This time he knew for sure Cora was crying. "You're a good boy, Henry, a really good boy. I'm so sorry for what my daughter's put you through."

Buster blinked back tears hearing the despair in Cora's voice. Right at this moment, he honestly felt more sorry for what Eve had put her mother through.

Steph was grateful for the warmth of the yoga room to be able to stretch and remove the stiffness the previous day's climbing had injected into her muscles. She'd arrived half an hour before her eleven a.m. class to run through poses in an attempt to relieve the discomfort she'd experienced since she woke that morning.

"Hey, Steph."

Steph looked up from her seated position as the door to the yoga room opened, and Matt stuck his head in. She beckoned him in so that the door could shut and trap the heat in the room. "Don't tell me you've come to try out a Bikram class?"

Matt laughed. "It wasn't my plan. Although if you've got an instant cure for my sore muscles, I'll take it."

Steph raised an eyebrow. "You're sore? You look like you do all sorts of exercise."

"Climbing up cliff faces isn't a regular one. I'd say all of the boys are hurting today."

"Me too," Steph admitted. "It's why I'm here early. The heat of the room helps. I can't guarantee it will be an instant cure, but if you stay and do my class, I guarantee it will help."

Matt hesitated before nodding. "Okay, I will. Do I need anything?"

"Go and ask Bodhi for a mat, towel, and a large water bottle," Steph said. She could hardly believe he'd agree to do yoga. "There's another ten minutes before the class starts, so come back in and lie down in savasana while you wait. It'll help you acclimatize to the room."

Matt grinned. "Okay." He turned to leave and then stopped and faced Steph. "Would you have time to talk after the class? There's something I'd like to run by you."

"Of course. Is it about the sale of the property?"

"Kind of. Just an idea that I'd be interested in getting your take on."

"Sure. Let's sit down after class and talk. I do warn you, you might be a bit sweaty though."

Matt laughed. "I'm sure I can handle some sweat."

Following the ninety-minute class, and Matt's introduction to Bikram yoga, he sat across from her shaking his head. "*A bit* sweaty?"

His clothes were soaked through, and he'd already drunk two large bottles of water.

Steph laughed. "The question is, how do you feel?"

He grinned. "I'm surprised to admit that while the heat nearly killed me, I enjoyed that. Right now, my muscles aren't sore either. I hate to imagine what they'll be like tomorrow."

"They'll be better than they were today. The heat is healing," Steph said. "Now, what did you want to chat about."

"I've made Bodhi an offer on Heat Wave. Both the property and the business."

Steph's gut twisted. It was happening; Bodhi was selling. While she was pleased for her boss and friend if he sold it, she hadn't expected it to happen this quickly.

"You don't look too happy." Matt's forehead creased in confusion. "It was your idea I talk to Bodhi, wasn't it?"

"Yes, of course. It just happened faster than I anticipated. Has he accepted your offer?"

"In principle, yes. There are a few things to iron out, which we'll need to get a lawyer to do."

"And Bodhi's happy with your offer?"

Matt smiled. "If you're asking whether I made him a fair offer, yes, I did. The conversation was more along the lines of Bodhi telling me what he wanted to sell for and me agreeing to his price."

"Really?"

Matt laughed. "You sound surprised."

"I assumed you'd try to knock his price down."

"His price was fair, Steph. And even though I've done a few things I regret, I'm generally up-front and honest in my business dealings." His face reddened as Steph opened her mouth. He put up his hand to stop her from speaking. "If you're about to remind me of Asha and Charlie, don't. Neither situation was my finest hour, and I imagine it will take a very long time for either of them or the town to trust me again. I'm hoping that once the Sandstone Cafe's up and running and people are enjoying it, they'll forget about the Charlie situation. Although I doubt Charlie will let them forget."

Steph agreed with Matt on this. "Okay. So what are your

plans for here, then? When do you anticipate taking over? I'll be happy to work up until then and try and make other arrangements once you take possession."

Matt shook his head. "I don't want you to make any arrangements. I've bought the business too. I want to keep Heat Wave going, and I want you to run it with me. Ideally, I want us to go into partnership."

Steph's mouth dropped open. "What?"

Matt nodded. "My development plans will be for the cottages on the property and the gardens. I'd like to turn the whole place into a wellness retreat. Combine yoga with attractive accommodations and hopefully food and other facilities. It'll all take time, and we'd do it in stages, but the one area that I think you and Bodhi have nailed is the yoga studio. Just walking in here, you feel the change in energy. It's really great, Steph, and Bodhi said this is all you."

Steph blushed. "I'm not sure about that, but we have done our best to make it a nice experience. But as far as a partnership, I don't have much money for investing." And she wasn't sure partnering with someone who'd own recently shown such unethical behavior was a good idea. She could only imagine what Asha would say.

Matt nodded. "I'd like to go into partnership with you for a couple of reasons. If you own part of the business, you have an incentive to make it a success. Also, after the situation with Asha, I don't suddenly want to own a yoga studio and find you setting up your own business somewhere else. During the summer, there's probably enough room in Hope's Ridge for two studios, but for the rest of the year, there's not. I'd rather we work together, exactly like I should have done with Asha to start with."

"It makes sense," Steph said. "But I'm not sure I want to go into debt to finance an investment."

"We could work out a deal you're happy with," Matt

said. "Would you be willing to step up to run the yoga studio and teach in it? Possibly employ another teacher if you need help?"

Steph nodded. "Definitely."

"Okay. So that would mean a raise from whatever you're currently being paid. We could work out some kind of deal where, rather than taking the raise as additional income, you stay on your regular income, and we convert the increase into a percentage ownership of the business. We'd have to work out the details and make sure you're happy, of course. This discussion is just to see if you're interested."

"What would you do if I wasn't?"

Matt grinned. "I'm counting on you being interested. Heat Wave is you, Steph. As sad as I know you are that Bodhi has to sell, it could be an amazing opportunity. Not only for you but for the community. There's so much we could do here to turn it into a retreat." He stood. "Look, I don't need an answer today. Think about it and give me a call during the week. Bodhi and I will work out the exact terms of sale, and then you and I can do the same if you decide you want to be partners."

Steph nodded. "I guess one thing that concerns me straight away would be you owning the majority share and having the final decision on everything. I'm not sure that would work."

Matt laughed. "Steph, I'm asking you to join me in this because I already know you'll take my suggestions and improve them a million times over. I don't think it will be a case of me making the decisions, just the opposite. Look, have a chat with Bodhi too, check that I'm not out to rip him off, and then think about what you want long term. We can always have an out clause in the contract, so if it doesn't work out between us, then I'll buy back your percentage, and you can walk away."

Steph nodded, feeling dazed by the speed at which things were moving. Owning part of Heat Wave would be a dream come true. Partnering with Matt Law, however, was not part of that dream. Nervous energy coursed through her as she thought of telling Asha what he'd proposed. The one thing she knew without a doubt was Asha would kill her.

Buster's mind buzzed after his phone call with Cora. He'd replayed the discussion many times over. Had her tears been an act to get him to agree to visit? He didn't think so. She was genuinely upset, and he understood that. Not only had she lost her granddaughter, but the change to her daughter's life was probably hard to comprehend. She'd given him the information he needed to arrange his prison visit and offered to come with him. As much as he appreciated the gesture, he knew he'd be better off going on his own. He didn't need to be worrying about anyone but himself and Eve.

He stretched, realizing how sore his arm and leg muscles were. He needed to do something about his fitness. He'd always kept himself very fit with running and the gym before Holly's death. He was active with her too, kayaking, biking, and chasing her around, but in the last twelve months, he'd been going through the motions of life. Exercise had been the last thing on his mind.

His thoughts went to Steph. He imagined she'd held up a lot better than he had. She was a walking advertisement for fitness. Her yoga left her lean and toned, and with upper body strength most people would kill for. She might be small, but she was strong. She'd proven that the day before. He wished he had her number. He'd love to give her a call and see if she was okay and thank her for yesterday. She had helped him decide to call Cora and agree to visit Eve. She'd also helped him to open up and talk about Holly. Not that he and Steph chatted about who Holly was, but he could imagine doing that with her. He wished she'd met his daughter.

He pulled himself up off the stool and found himself immediately drawn to Holly's bedroom. Instead of stopping outside like he usually did, he pushed open the door, his eyes taking in the perfect room. The bed was neatly made with her favorite princess bedding: a huge wand on the bedspread with *May all your dreams come true!* printed across it. Her soft toys took up so much room on the bed that it was hard to believe she'd even fit.

He smiled as he looked at her four different-colored walls. Over the summer before her death, he'd suggested they repaint the room. He'd painted a different color sample on each wall, and she'd immediately fallen in love, insisting that each wall be a different color. Now the room was pink, purple, pale blue, and yellow. He hadn't minded; it was her room and her choice.

Her bookshelf was full of books. Both grandmothers loved to read and had insisted on buying her books, and then, of course, there was her collection of rocks. It seemed like a strange thing for a five-year-old to collect, but she was out in the yard most afternoons digging for *special* rocks and had Buster take her all over the area on the weekends so she could dig up new areas. They'd spent a lot of time at the Bluff and down at the rocky end of Lake Hopeful.

Buster sat down on Holly's bed and picked up her beloved cuddly dog as he thought about their trips to the lake. How ironic that a place she'd loved so much was the place that also claimed her life. He closed his eyes and cuddled the dog, wishing with all his might he was cuddling his daughter. But instead of being sad, he remembered her laugh, her long blonde hair flying in the wind as she ran to the next place to search for gems. She'd had a wonderful love of life that had captured his heart. He doubted he could ever love anyone as much as he'd loved his daughter. Her face was suddenly replaced in his mind with Steph's. Steph's brilliant sparkling eyes smiled at him, encouraged him to want to reach out and touch her. His eyes jolted open, and he stood, replacing the dog on the bed. It appeared he was going insane.

He had the same thought a few hours later as he walked the lake trail along the edge of Lake Hopeful. The same lake he'd driven away from only a few days earlier, feeling melancholy and making the decision he needed to leave the area for a fresh start, had called to him today. On an impulse, he'd driven to Hope's Ridge, hoping he might bump into Steph. He'd thought maybe she'd be hanging out with her sister, but he'd been disappointed to find Asha's food truck closed. He was sure she opened on a Sunday, but maybe it was just for the morning.

He decided to take a walk along the lake edge. If he wanted to, he could ask around, find out where she lived, but he didn't want to seem that pushy. Although she and Zane shared a house. Could he think up a reason to need to visit Zane and hope she was home? He passed by the white and gray house that sat in a prime position on the lakefront. It was referred to as "The Lake House," but no one seemed to know anything more about it. A local company maintained the gardens around it and its external white timber cladded walls had recently been painted. Rumor suggested no one had lived in it for over twenty years. It was such a waste of a prime location. He leaned down and picked up a rock and threw it into the lake, thinking back to his current problem of where to find Steph. He sighed, coming up with no answer, and continued walking.

His thoughts turned to Cora and Eve as he rounded a

corner. He was coming to the end of the trail and would have to turn around soon, which was probably a good thing. He pulled his jacket around him; it was cold and getting colder. He wondered what Eve would say to him and how he should respond. Maybe he should make an appointment with Dan before he saw her, get some advice from the area's local shrink. He squashed that idea as quickly as he'd had it. He'd had a couple of sessions with Dan after Holly's death, but it wasn't for him. He couldn't process his feelings on the spot, no matter how many probing questions Dan asked. No, he'd just have to turn up and see what Eve wanted. He rounded the final corner, ready to turn around, and stopped. Steph had her yoga mat rolled out and was on her knees, arms over her head with her face down. His heart rate increased as he waited and watched, not wanting to disturb her.

Steph's breath rumbled in her throat as she practiced her Ujjayi breathing. She'd done a lot of ashtanga yoga in the past that focused on breathing, and while she didn't teach it in her hot yoga classes, she still practiced it herself. It brought heat to her body and calm to her mind that she adored. She wanted to clear her mind and give more thought to Matt's proposal before she discussed it with Asha or anyone else, so she had brought herself to the end of the lake for some yoga. It was a beautiful spot, with the tall trees bordering the lake and the birds calling out from time to time. She rarely saw anyone this far along the track. The last person, and only person, she'd ever seen when practicing here was Zane. She inhaled before pushing her arms and legs out and moving from child's pose into downward dog.

She continued her breathing, then stopped, suddenly conscious of someone standing at the edge of the walking track.

She pushed herself up to standing and turned around, her heart catching in her throat. Buster was watching her.

"Hey," he said.

"Hey, yourself. What are you doing here?"

Buster cleared his throat. "I don't know. But if I'm honest, I was hoping to see you."

Butterflies flitted in Steph's stomach. "Really? How come?"

"To thank you again for yesterday. You made me think about a few things. I called Cora, Eve's mother, this morning, and I've agreed to go and visit Eve this week. I think I owe her that."

Steph nodded and bent down and picked up her yoga mat. "Why don't we go and sit by the lake. It's so beautiful."

"I hate the lake."

Steph jolted back up at his words, her eyes immediately flooding with understanding. "Then let's go somewhere else."

Buster ran his hand through his blonde hair. "Sorry, I don't know why I said that. It just came out. It's only water, of course, I don't hate it. I wouldn't be walking around it if I really believed that."

Steph moved over to him and linked her arm through his, doing her best to ignore the shiver that ran up her spine. "It took your daughter. You can hate it if you want. It's understandable. I hate driving and being a passenger in cars. We all deal with things differently."

They walked in companionable silence back along the track to an area that branched out into a clearing. "How about we sit down behind those rocks." Steph pointed to a large pile of rocks set well back from the water. "Then we can't see the lake at all."

Buster smiled. "You must think I'm crazy. Here I am walking around the lake, and now I don't want to sit by it."

"I don't think anything about you at all."

"Really?"

Steph's skin tingled. Was he flirting with her? No, of course, he wasn't. He'd bumped into her, and the conversation had taken a strange turn.

Buster cleared his throat and sat down on the yoga mat when Steph unrolled it. "What do you mean you don't drive?"

"Since the accident, I haven't been able to get behind the wheel of a car. I just can't. It doesn't matter, since Hope's Ridge is small. I have my bike and either walk or cycle. It keeps me fit."

"But what if you need something from the city or even Drayson's Landing?"

"I go with Asha or Mom if I'm desperate. But to be honest, I prefer to stay out of cars, so I'm quite happy staying here."

"You went with Ryan yesterday."

Steph nodded. "I did, and I'm glad I went. But it's never easy. I have to psych myself up." She hesitated. "And close my eyes during certain sections of the road."

They sat in silence while Buster absorbed this information.

"Speaking of psyching myself up. I went into Holly's room today," Buster said. "I haven't been in for months. It's made me too sad each time I've opened the door. But today was different. I remembered her and enjoyed being around her things. I guess that was why I was thinking of you and wanted to thank you. Something shifted for me yesterday."

"Me too," Steph said. "What a shame we didn't have our

conversation months ago. It was Ryan's return to the Ridge that forced us together. I guess we have him to thank."

"Did you and Ryan go out last night?" Buster asked. "The guys said he was pretty interested in asking you out."

"Really?" Steph thought back to Ryan squeezing her knee and her hand. That was probably just friendship and nothing else.

Buster nodded.

"Ryan and I were friends in high school. Nothing more. I doubt he'd be thinking of me like that. Anyway, I'm not ready for a relationship."

"Why's that?"

Steph took a deep breath. "I was in a relationship before the accident. We'd only been together for a few months, so I guess what happened was a real test. I disappeared into a dark place when it all happened, and he couldn't handle it."

"He left?"

Steph nodded. "A month to the day. Funnily enough, I was relieved. He couldn't handle my grief, and I failed miserably, trying to act as if everything was normal. I shouldn't have had to pretend. If he loved me, he would have tried to help me, not become frustrated that I was going through a difficult time."

"And you haven't dated anyone since?"

Steph shook her head. "No. Overall I'm doing well." Even as the words came out of her mouth, Steph knew they weren't true, but Buster was the last person she wanted to lay her problems on. She didn't want him to feel guilty. "But I do have my ups and downs, and I think it would be unfair to expect someone to put up with that. It's easier to just be on my own."

Buster nodded. "I understand that."

"Have you spoken to Matt today?" Steph changed the subject.

"No, why? Has he done something else to upset Asha or the town?"

Steph laughed. "Not that I know of. He's asked me to be a partner with him in Heat Wave. He and Bodhi have agreed on a price."

"Matt hasn't taken advantage of the situation, has he?"

"No. It's awful to admit this, but I'm surprised. I thought he'd try to get the property for as little as possible. Instead he agreed to pay Bodhi's asking price."

Surprise registered on Buster's face. "Really? Your little chat with him yesterday at the Bluff must have had an impact."

"I'm surprised Matt would listen to anyone," Steph said. "I must admit I am waiting to see whether there's a hidden agenda or underhanded move like there was with the development along Lake Drive."

"I don't blame you," Buster said. "Although I will tell you one thing. Matt, Travis, and I went back to my place for a few beers after the climb yesterday. Matt was very complimentary about you. Said how much he admired you and that it was a shame you weren't in a position to buy Heat Wave yourself."

"He did?"

Buster nodded. "But, like you, I'm not sure whether you can trust him or not. The whole situation with Charlie leaves a sour taste in my mouth. I know I shouldn't say that. He's our biggest client, but I do worry he's out to rip people off. Be careful if you do decide to join him."

Steph nodded. Buster hadn't said anything she hadn't already thought herself. She shivered. The sun had dropped low on the horizon, and the temperature had plummeted.

Buster stood and held out his hand. "Come on. It's freezing. If Asha's business were open, I'd buy you a hot drink, but it's not, and I'm not sure anything will be."

"Come back to my place," Steph said, taking his hand and letting him pull her to her feet. "We can make a pot of tea and sit by the fire pit. Zane and Asha might be home, and I'm sure they'd love to see you." She laughed. "You can be my buffer when I tell Ash about Matt's proposal. I guarantee you she won't be pleased."

on't be pleased was an understatement! Buster half expected Asha's head to explode, she was so angry.

"How can you even consider doing something with Matt after what he did to Charlie and to me? He's an awful person, Steph. You know that."

Steph shook her head. "My gut tells me there's more to Matt than the awful side we've seen of him."

"Be careful," Zane warned. "When I returned to the Ridge and he offered me the job, I genuinely thought he was doing everything for the good of the town. He had me wrapped around his little finger, while at the same time, he was having other plans drawn up that I wasn't aware of. On top of that, he was doing his best to steal Charlie's properties from under him. I agree, there is a side to Matt than can be decent. Unfortunately, his evil side dominates."

"Tell her, Buster," Asha said. "Tell her she's dealing with a shark who'll eat her up and spit her out."

Buster held up his hands. "I shouldn't get involved. I'm aware that Matt did some terrible things, but he's also a client and a friend. I do agree with Zane that he has a decent side. Travis and I have seen it many times."

Asha snorted. "What, when he's giving you kickbacks for getting jobs canceled that interfere with his projects? I imagine the project that Charlie's engaged you for will suddenly fall through because of Matt's influence."

"Asha!" Steph's tone was incredulous. "You owe Buster an apology. He's here as my friend. He didn't come around to be insulted."

Buster stood. "I think it's time I left."

"No," Asha took a deep breath. "Steph's right. That was an awful thing to say, and I'm sorry. It's just Matt Law. He brings out the absolute worst in me."

"But the best in your throwing arm," Zane reminded her, breaking the tension. "Did you see that dent in his Roadster Asha inflicted with a rock?"

Buster nodded, forcing a smile. Coming to see Steph had been a mistake. He still wasn't quite sure what had driven him to Hope's Ridge.

"Okay," Asha said. "You said you and Travis had seen a decent side to Matt. Give us an example."

Buster considered his response. He wasn't sure that Matt would want his business dealings known by everyone, but he also felt it was his responsibility to make Asha aware of Matt's other side.

"Were you aware that Matt funds part of LakeView?"

"What? The long-term care facility?" The surprise on Asha's face confirmed she didn't know this.

Buster nodded. "He allocates a percentage of the profit he makes from select projects to LakeView, which I believe helps with the upkeep of the facility itself and also the minivan that takes the residents on outings."

"Select projects?"

"Ones where he can see the profit quickly. He buys up

quite a lot of properties here and in Drayson's Landing, improves them, and flips them. He gives a percentage of his profit to LakeView."

"Why LakeView?"

Buster could see Asha's curiosity getting the better of her. "His grandfather was a resident for a number of years and hated that he was dependent on family members to go on outings. Matt told me that a lot of the upgrades, including the minivan, were to please his grandfather. He died three years ago but Matt's continued with his donations. Maybe it makes him feel close to someone he loved, I don't know."

Asha nodded. "That's unexpected. It doesn't erase what he tried to do to Charlie. One good deed would never be enough for that."

"I agree," Buster said. "Did you also know he helped out the Jean family after the fire?"

"The one that destroyed their house and their investment property next door?"

Buster nodded. "He had us draw up the plans for the new houses. The Jeans didn't have insurance. Matt offered to finance the rebuild for a percentage ownership in the property."

Asha snorted again. "Let me guess, ninety percent ownership, or was it a hundred?"

"Twenty. If they sold the properties today, Matt would recoup a fraction of what he's invested."

"That's amazing," Steph said. "Why did he do that?"

Buster hesitated. "I feel like I'm sharing far too much of Matt's story. This is the last thing I'll tell you. As you probably remember, Matt's mom died when we were teenagers. Nicole Jean was a friend of his mother's and also a nurse. She'd helped her on and off for years. It was his way of thanking her."

Silence fell among the group.

"It's like he's two completely different people," Asha said. "Why can't he be that Matt all the time?"

Buster shrugged. "Who knows. But I am telling you he can be genuine. Whether or not he is on this occasion with Heat Wave, only he knows. I would advise being careful but also accepting that he can be decent."

"Does he plan to develop the studio?" Zane asked. "He talked about a wellness center when I was working for him."

"Ultimately, that's his long-term plan for Heat Wave," Steph said. "It's all early days for figuring it out, but that's where he'd like to head in the future. Keep the yoga studio but renovate the cottages and the land around the studio and make it a retreat."

"That's good, at least," Asha said.

"Why's that?" Steph asked.

Asha turned to look at Buster. "Because if he's doing any development, he'll employ Buster's company to do it. If he's doing anything that's not aboveboard, you'll be able to tell us, won't you?"

Buster was aware of the three sets of eyes on him. Matt hadn't even discussed the project with him yet, and his agreement with Travis was he'd be leaving the company as soon as the plans for Matt's apartments on Lake Drive and Charlie and Asha's pavilion were approved by the township. Heat Wave was not part of this plan.

"We'd hate to see Steph taken advantage of," Asha said. "She's had an awful year, and I want to see life get better, not worse."

Buster swallowed. Steph's awful year was because of the accident. For which he was responsible. While he was desperate to get out of the area and start again, he had to hang around for a couple of projects. Adding one more to the mix wouldn't add too much time to his stay in the area. And he owed Steph, that was one thing he was sure of.

"Don't feel you have to—" Steph began, but Buster cut her off.

"Don't be silly. Assuming Matt buys Heat Wave and asks us to be involved, of course, I'll keep an eye on him. I should clarify, I had no idea that he was up to no good with Charlie, so I can't guarantee I'll know what he's doing."

"Yes, but he had two sets of building plans going with the Lake Drive development," Zane said. "If you include Steph in all of the meetings, or brief her afterward if Matt meets with you separately, then there's no opportunity for him to do something unscrupulous."

"That's a good way to approach it," Buster said. And it was. But what had he just committed to? A building development could take months, if not years. He felt a connection to Steph and a responsibility to look out for her, but he was planning on leaving the area for a fresh start, wasn't he?

"I can't believe how quickly it's all happened," Bodhi said. "The paperwork still has to be finalized, but that should only take a matter of days. You're sure you're happy with everything?"

Steph nodded. Her head was spinning with the speed at which Matt worked, so she could only imagine how Bodhi was feeling. He was about to pack up and leave Hope's Ridge, something he'd initially thought was a month or two away, at the very earliest.

"Matt's got some amazing plans for the place," Bodhi said. "I wish the situation was different because I would have loved to have done some of these things with him."

"I still get worried," Steph said. "He was so awful in his

dealings with Asha and Charlie. I'm just not sure I'll ever be able to trust him."

"That's understandable, and I hope I'm right when I say this, but I think this project is different. There's more to it than just money for Matt. He's passionate about creating something unique."

"I hope so. Now, when are you going to leave?"

"Next week," Bodhi said. "If all goes as planned, Matt will own Heat Wave as of Friday. Hopefully, you and he can work out your arrangement, and he'll get the paperwork drawn up for that. We're using the lawyers in town, and he advised them, when I was with him, of the plans for you to have a percentage ownership. He said the two of you would go in together to draw up the agreement. I was relieved when he said that, since it means you can ask about anything you don't understand or say something if you think he's doing anything untoward."

Steph smiled. "I feel bad for Matt. Every conversation I have around this comes back to whether he's doing something unscrupulous."

Bodhi shrugged. "He's brought that on himself. I just hope that Heat Wave is the project that confirms we can trust him."

Me too, Steph thought. She was comforted, however, by the knowledge that Buster would be looking out for her. Who would have thought that the man she'd done her best to avoid for the past twelve months was the man she was now happy to have on her side.

Buster took deep calming breaths as he climbed out of his pickup and took in the high fence with the coiled barbed wire at the top. While he knew Eve was in prison, before today, he hadn't given much thought to what that meant. He couldn't begin to imagine what her life had become. He pushed away the flood of guilt the poured down on him.

The security process took longer than he anticipated, but finally, a guard nodded to the doorway that led into a large meeting room. Buster's nerves, on edge in his stomach since he first arrived, magnified. Tables and chairs were set up around the room, and several women in white jumpsuits sat behind the desks. Some wore handcuffs, but most sat staring straight ahead, waiting for their visitors.

Buster hesitated as he saw Eve raise her hand from a table at the far corner of the room. She wasn't cuffed, thank goodness. Regardless of how much he'd hated her at different times, he was relieved that her hands were free.

He walked over to her table, conscious of his own hands shaking. This was his ex-wife, someone he'd once loved deeply. Why was he so nervous to see her?

Eve's smile wobbled, and Buster couldn't help but notice her shaking hand. She quickly withdrew it from the table and buried it in her lap.

He sat down in the chair opposite her, an overload of emotions rushing through him.

"Thank you for coming." Eve's voice was barely a whisper.

Buster nodded, pretty sure his voice wouldn't work. Eve was thinner, a lot thinner than when he'd seen her at the trial. Her skin and eyes were clear, a contrast to what she'd been like in the final months of Holly's life.

He cleared his throat. "How are you?"

Eve gave a small smile. "Coping. Kind of. You?"

His smile reflected her forced effort. "About the same."

Eve nodded. "Thank you for coming." She shook herself. "Sorry, I know I already said that. I'm so nervous." She leaned toward him. "I spent the morning throwing up. I was so scared to face you." She pulled back, her face coloring. "Sorry, I shouldn't have told you that."

Buster wanted to reach across the table and take her hand, but the rules forbade it. His hatred for his ex-wife melted away as he had this thought. Her eyes were clear but haunted. She was clean but living a nightmare. One that he understood all too well. "I should have come to see you earlier, Eve. I'm sorry too. I wanted to forget about you. Push away all the memories. Not that that worked, of course."

Tears filled Eve's eyes. "I've never wanted to forget you. I want to go back and change everything from the day Holly was born. *Everything*. But before that, I wouldn't change a thing. Would you?"

Buster hesitated. There were things about Eve that had worried him before Holly was born. But he'd brushed them aside. Concentrated his hardest on the fact that he had a beautiful, intelligent, funny, and mostly supportive wife. They had been happy. He couldn't deny that. "What happened, Eve? Why did it change?" He held his breath, waiting for her answer. Jodi had made suggestions to him, but he'd never allowed himself to think too much about it. He needed to blame Eve. It was the only way he didn't blame himself.

Eve rubbed the thumb of one hand on the fingers of the other as she considered her answer. They sat in silence for a few minutes, and then she spoke.

"I've seen a lot of psychologists since I've been here. As you can imagine, dealing with what happened has been pretty hard."

Buster nodded and waited for her to continue.

"In talking with them, it's been suggested that following Holly's birth, I suffered postpartum depression. It's no excuse," she was quick to say. "I'm not trying to justify anything that happened, but it is a possibility."

Buster nodded again and waited for her to continue.

"For me, it would explain how I felt after Holly was born. It should have been the happiest time of my life, and instead, it was the worst. I felt like such a failure. You have no idea."

Tears welled in Buster's eyes.

"It was no one's fault, other than my stupid hormones and lack of knowledge that this was what had happened. Mom's a mess now that I've told her. She can't believe she didn't pick up on it. None of us did. Obviously I was pretty good at hiding it. I couldn't understand why I felt so helpless and certainly didn't want to admit to it. The drinking and…" she stopped for a moment "…and the other terrible things I did, were to try to cope. To make me feel better about everything. A pretty horrible way of coping, I know that. It destroyed our marriage, and for that, I'm truly sorry."

Buster wiped the tears from his cheeks. "I don't blame you, Eve. I did to start with, but I was a terrible husband. I promised to love and cherish you and look at what I did. Pushed you to drink, asked you to leave our home, and then fought for custody so aggressively. I loved you so much before Holly was born. I can't believe what happened to us after her birth."

Tears now flowed down Eve's cheeks. "It wasn't your fault, you need to believe that. So many professionals failed us. I tried to get help for my depression, yet none of the doctors I saw linked it to postpartum depression. The legal system for the divorce was geared up for how we could tear each other apart rather than work amicably to move forward in co-parenting roles. We were let down on many different levels."

"Maybe, but I let you and Holly down," Buster said. "You were my women. My loves." Tears rolled freely down his cheeks now. "When your mom asked me to come and visit, I got angry. Thought of all of the reasons as to why you didn't deserve me to visit. I now realize it was all an excuse. To hide from how much I've let you down, from how much I'm responsible for."

Eve's bottom lip wobbled. "I thought you'd be angry and hate me. I can't tell you how much of a relief this is. But no matter what happened after Holly's birth, I went against the court order, and I'd been drinking. There's no excuse for that, and I don't expect your forgiveness. I'm not even asking you for it. We lost the most important thing in our lives. Our love, our joy. I don't even know how to move on from this point."

Buster wiped his cheeks, his eyes locked with Eve's. She was the only other person in the world who felt the loss as deeply as he did. They'd both lost in the worst way possible.

"It's her birthday soon. She would have been seven."

Buster nodded. Holly had died a few months before her sixth birthday. He'd drunk himself into oblivion on that birthday and had planned to do the same this year, and probably every year moving forward.

"Could you come back and see me? I don't think I'll get through the day on my own."

Buster found himself nodding before he even had time to process what Eve had asked of him.

It wasn't unusual for Steph to wake at three in the morning, but it was unusual for her to wake from excitement rather than the terror of a nightmare. She almost felt guilty when she sat up in bed, realizing her reason for not sleeping was the thought of not only improving Heat Wave but becoming a part owner. She would miss Bodhi, that went without saying, but the unexpected chain of events had left her with an opportunity she'd never considered. The only downside to the whole project was Matt. As much as she wanted to trust him, he'd made it very difficult. The main thing she needed to do was safeguard herself against every possible scenario that could leave her in trouble. She got out of bed, made her way to the kitchen, and placed a pot of water on the stove.

"I've got a lawyer you should contact," Zane said, walking into the kitchen. He handed her a piece of paper, and she laughed.

"It's the middle of the night, and you've got a lawyer's details for me. Should I call them now?"

Zane laughed too. "I've been awake for hours. I know you said Bodhi had a lawyer he was using with Matt, but I thought under the circumstances, you might want to get some independent advice."

Steph frowned. "Speaking of independent advice, I think you need to go and see someone else. Dan's a nice guy, but you don't seem to have made any improvement since you've been here. You need to find someone who specializes in PTSD."

"Nope, that's not why I'm awake. It's something else. Something nerve-wracking and exciting all at once, and something I want your opinion on."

Steph raised an eyebrow. "Sounds ominous."

"I'll tell you over tea. Backyard or living room?"

"Living room. The fire is probably still smoldering from earlier."

"Okay, I'll get it going, while you make the tea. And come in with an open mind."

Steph smiled. Zane was uncharacteristically nervous. She wondered what he was going to ask her. Possibly that he wanted to move in with Asha? If that was his question, he should be asking Asha, not her. She was pretty sure Asha wouldn't live with someone before marriage. But perhaps her sister would change her mind for Zane.

A few minutes later, she carried a tray into the living room. Zane had the fire roaring, and the room was already cozy. She poured the tea and handed him a mug, then sat and waited.

"So, I want to ask Asha something, but I'm worried it's too early."

Steph was right. He did want to move in with her.

"I'm also worried about what Jenna will think."

"Jenna? Why would she care? She knows you're both serious."

"So you've guessed what I want to ask Asha?"

Steph sipped her tea and nodded. "I'm not sure she'll say yes though, Zane. She's always been fairly clear about how relationships work for her. She'd never rush into anything."

Zane's face fell. "That's what I was worried about. Maybe I'll leave it a little longer."

Steph shook her head. "No, I mean, she never will. It's just not who she is."

"Really?" Zane pushed his hand through his dark hair. "Wow, okay. I had no idea. I wish she'd said something earlier." He put his tea down on the coffee table. "I don't even know what to think now. We'd talked about having kids and everything. I'm not having kids if I'm not married, so that's never going to work. I guess I need to have a chat with her."

Steph stared at him. "Hold on. I think you need to backtrack. When you said you wanted to ask me something tonight, what exactly was it?"

"Whether you thought it was too early for me to propose to Asha?"

Steph's mouth dropped open. "No, yes, I mean, oh my goodness!"

"Okay, now I'm really confused."

Steph laughed. "I thought you were going to ask her to move in with you. I meant that she wouldn't live with someone before she was married."

"Phew!" Zane pretended to wipe his brow. "So it's not too early to propose?"

Steph thought about it for a moment. "Jenna."

Zane nodded. "Yes, my next problem."

"Honestly, I think it would be good if you waited. This is Jenna's limelight at the moment. The engagement party's only a few weeks away. Could you wait until after then?"

"Yes, I thought you'd say that. It was what I was thinking, but I'm dying to ask her. I love her so much, Steph. I can't believe how lucky I am to have found her."

Steph blinked back tears. She was so happy for her sister. "You know this would make us brother and sister if you guys got married."

Zane grinned. "I already think of you as my sister. Jenna's amazing, but you and I click on a different level. You understand what I've been through."

"Not really," Steph objected. "And I hope I'd never find myself in that situation."

"You know what I mean, though. You understand that as much as I want to forget about the holdup, I can't. It haunts me, and I have no idea whether I'll ever get over it or not."

Steph nodded. It was how she felt about the accident. She doubted she'd ever be able to forget the look on Holly's face before the car took her into the depths of the lake. The question was whether she'd ever be able to live in peace with it.

"This is so exciting," Steph said. "At least you've got plenty of time to plan your proposal."

Zane grinned. "And buy a ring. Would you help me do that?"

"Of course." Excitement rose within Steph at the thought of Zane proposing to Asha. "I know exactly what Asha would like."

"You have to promise you won't say anything to her."

"I'll be too busy planning the yoga studio and keeping an eye on Matt," Steph said. "You don't have to worry about me letting anything slip." She frowned. "One thing though. Are you going to speak to Dad first?"

Zane nodded. "Definitely. I just wanted to get your feel on the timing. If you'd said go for it, I would be chatting with your dad tomorrow and asking his permission. But I agree, I don't want to upstage Jenna, so there's no rush."

Steph sipped her tea, unable to keep the smile from her face. Only a few weeks earlier, Asha was unsure of her future with both her business and her relationship. Now, she had an exciting business venture and the love of an amazing man. Steph couldn't be happier for her.

6

$\mathcal{B}$uster tossed and turned for most of the night following his visit to Eve. He wasn't sure how he thought he'd feel after seeing her, but it wasn't like this. Guilt seeped through him. He'd let her down so badly. How was it he hadn't questioned her behavior after Holly was born? She'd changed so much. Become someone difficult to live with, yet never once had he considered something like postpartum depression. When he'd returned from the prison, he'd spent two hours googling. Eve's behavior fit the diagnosis perfectly.

He'd buried his face in his hands and cried until there were no tears left to shed. He'd failed Eve, and he'd failed Holly. He was not fit to be anyone's husband or father. He'd proven that to both of them. To think Eve was the one trying to apologize to him when it was him who owed her an apology. Eventually, he'd taken himself to bed, exhausted from the emotional upheaval of the day. He'd fallen asleep quickly, but he woke only an hour later from a nightmare and then struggled to sleep the rest of the night.

He climbed out of bed at seven and stood under the jets of the shower for a long time, trying to wake himself. His eyes were bloodshot, and he looked like he'd had a big night out. He hadn't drunk anything or eaten for that matter when he'd returned from visiting Eve, and he looked terrible. He had meetings with Travis and then with Asha and Charlie at Hope's Ridge that morning. He'd need to stop at the pharmacy before he drove to Hope's Ridge and get some eye drops. He couldn't face clients looking like this.

His phone rang as he thought about making himself some coffee and toast. Cora's name flashed on the screen. He hesitated before answering the call.

"Henry, it's Cora."

"How are you?"

"Oh, love, I wanted to thank you. I spoke with Eve last night. She was like a different person. Whatever you said to her has given her the will to live. I'm so grateful."

Buster swallowed the lump that formed in his throat. "You shouldn't be thanking me. I let Eve down. I see that now. I wish I'd realized how Holly's birth impacted her."

"Love, we all let her down. None of us realized. I'm her mother. I should have known. Gosh, I had a friend with postpartum depression, and I still didn't pick it. Eve's talking about it now, but she hid it well back then. We can't turn back time, as much as we'd all love to be able to, and you're not to blame."

"I appreciate you saying that, Cora." Buster did, even if he didn't believe her.

"Eve said you're going back on Holly's birthday to see her."

"I am," Buster said. "It's the one day of the year we should be together."

Cora fell silent for a moment.

"Did you want to come with me?" Buster asked.

"No. I will visit Eve, but not on Holly's birthday. I know it's selfish, but I just can't. It's too hard. Holly was so precious and regardless of the circumstances..." She stopped talking. "I won't continue, but I do appreciate that you'll be there for her. Now, I'd better let you get to work. I just wanted to say thank you."

Buster ended the call, not sure how to feel. He was glad his visit to Eve had made a difference, but he was also aware that he could have made a difference many months ago. Instead, he'd completely abandoned her. He took a deep breath and flicked on the coffee machine. He was going to need a lot of help to get through the day.

An hour later, Buster sat across from Travis. The concern on his business partner's face was evident.

"I think you should cancel your meetings today. You look terrible."

Buster smiled. "No sugarcoating it."

Travis shook his head, and at the same time, Jodi knocked gently on the door.

"Eye drops for Buster." She handed him a package.

"Thanks, Jodi, but you didn't need to get them."

Jodi shook her head. "Put some in now, drink your coffee, and you should be good to go in about thirty minutes."

"See?" Buster said to Travis. "I'll be fine."

Travis nodded, still unconvinced. "What's the deal with this Heat Wave project? I was speaking to Matt, and it sounds like it's something he's going ahead with. He wants us to do the plans and construction."

"It just happened," Buster said. "The sale goes through today, I think, so he'll probably want to meet up next week."

"I assume you're stepping aside with this one?" Travis said. "If you're leaving the business, it doesn't make sense to take this job on."

"No, it doesn't."

"But?" Travis sensed his hesitation.

"But, I kind of promised Asha and Zane that I would look out for Steph's interests. Make sure Matt doesn't do anything underhanded."

"What does that mean for your timing of leaving here?"

"I don't know at the moment. Is that okay? A lot is going on all of a sudden. Yesterday left me drained, and no sleep doesn't help. Can I think about it and get back to you next week?"

"Of course. There's no rush to make a decision. The longer you're here, the better, from my perspective, but if you decide to leave suddenly, I want to make sure I have enough time to replace you. With what we already had in the schedule, plus these new Hope's Ridge jobs, it's going to be busy. Speaking of Hope's Ridge, has the Sandstone Cafe reopened?"

"It opens today. I've scheduled my meeting with Charlie and Asha there."

Travis frowned. "Really? How did that suggestion go down?"

Buster laughed. "I put it to them that they should be checking out the competition. I want to support Ryan and Margie and hopefully show everyone that we can all work together, rather than being fiercely competitive."

Travis rolled his eyes. "You are aware that Matt owns the Sandstone Cafe?"

Buster nodded.

"Fiercely competitive is his middle name. I hope for your sake he's not there this morning, or I can guarantee your meeting won't go well."

Steph found it hard to believe it was Bodhi's last day at Heat Wave. He'd removed all of his possessions and at four o'clock would be teaching his last class. She'd hugged him as soon as she'd arrived that morning.

"I'm going to miss you so much."

"And me you," Bodhi said. "And this place."

"I hope it turns out to be a good move for you."

Bodhi sighed. "I'm sure it will be. It'll be good for Mom, and that's the most important thing. She's done so much for Becca and me. It's time we gave something back. Now, are you meeting with the lawyers today to discuss your agreement with Matt?"

Steph nodded. "Yes, at the Sandstone Cafe. It reopens today, and Matt asked us to meet there at ten. It will be a good chance to wish Ryan and Margie well too. I still haven't seen Margie, have you?"

"No, but I haven't had any reason to go into town, so there's no reason I would have seen her. What about Ryan?"

Steph hadn't seen him, but he had contacted her and invited her out to dinner. She'd declined. She needed to speak to him, make sure he realized she wasn't interested in anything but friendship. She didn't want to give him the wrong idea. "No, I haven't seen him."

Bodhi glanced at the clock. "You'd better get going if your meeting's at ten. It'll take you at least twenty minutes to walk there, unless you'd like me to drive you?"

Steph immediately shook her head. "I'll walk, I could use the fresh air."

Bodhi touched her arm. "Maybe you should think about driving again soon."

Steph pulled her arm back. "What? Why?"

"Because it's holding you back. What are you going to do when it's freezing and raining?"

"Exactly what I have been doing. Wear a coat and carry an umbrella."

"Pushing through something like your fear of driving

and being in the car more frequently could help you." Bodhi held up his hands to stop Steph from objecting. "It's just a suggestion, nothing more."

"Let's go with the *nothing more*," Steph said. "Now, I'd better go. If I don't see you beforehand, I'll be back for your last class."

Bodhi nodded. "See you at four."

Steph did her best to push Bodhi's suggestion of her overcoming her fear of driving from her mind as she wound her way through the backstreets of Hope's Ridge to the lake trail. She followed it around the lake until it met the populated area of Lake Drive and Main Street. She could see the streamers decorating the Sandstone Cafe as she approached. Music was playing, and a huge menu board stood out the front. She smiled to herself; they were up and running.

She walked through the large arched doorway and into the cafe, her eyes instantly drawn to the walls. The previous owner had decorated with small black and white images. Large, vibrant abstract works of art replaced them. Pieces that were very clearly Ryan's work. Steph sucked in a breath as her eyes traveled from one piece to the next.

"Like what you see?"

Steph turned to find Ryan grinning at her.

"It looks amazing. Your artwork completely changes the feel of the cafe. It was lovely before, but kind of sleepy. Now it feels vibrant and full of life." She reached forward and hugged him. "Well done, and congratulations on the opening."

"Come and say hi to Margie," Ryan said, pulling out of her embrace. "She's been a bit hesitant about seeing everyone again, but she's going to need to get used to it."

Steph followed him across the cafe floor to the service

area. Mouth-watering cakes and individual slices filled a large glass display unit.

"Margie," Ryan called through to the kitchen.

Moments later, his sister appeared. She smiled shyly at Steph.

She was a year younger than Steph and yet looked so much older. Her smile was warm and genuine, but lines etched her mouth and forehead. A testament to the stress she'd been through.

"Margie! It's so good to see you. It's been years."

Margie nodded. "It has. Can I get you some coffee or something to eat?"

"I'll wait until Matt arrives if that's okay. We're meeting with the lawyers to discuss a few things."

"Looks like you aren't the only ones having a meeting." Ryan nodded toward the door.

Steph turned to see Asha and Charlie entering the cafe. She almost laughed. They were the last two people she expected to be frequenting the cafe on its opening day...or any day.

"This is a surprise," Steph said. "It's lovely to see you again, Margie. Hopefully, we can catch up properly when you're not working."

Margie nodded noncommittally.

Steph turned back to Asha and Charlie, who were now seated by one of the windows overlooking the shoreline. She walked over to them.

"I wasn't expecting to see either of you in here."

"Checking out the competition," Asha said. "And we have a meeting."

"Who's looking after the food truck?"

"Orla. Just for an hour, so Buster had better hurry up."

Buster? Steph's stomach flipped. She took a deep breath, wishing it would stop doing that.

Charlie tutted. "Why he couldn't have made the meeting at your premises I don't know. This seems very unnecessary."

"It's a good opportunity to support Ryan and Margie," Steph said. "Their cakes look delicious, by the way. You'll need to try them all for market research."

"Exactly." Buster's deep voice greeted them.

Steph turned to him, her smile slipping as she took in his tired eyes and drawn cheeks. It reminded her that he'd met with his ex-wife the previous day. By the looks of him, she could only assume it hadn't gone well. She wanted to take him in her arms and hug him, tell him everything would be okay. She gave herself a mental shake. Where had that come from? He'd think she was crazy if she suddenly did that.

"Come and sit down," Charlie said. "We have lots to discuss, and Asha has to get back to her food truck in an hour."

"I'll leave you to it," Steph said. "But Buster, could I talk to you once you've finished this meeting?"

Buster nodded. "Sure. Matt's asked me to join the two of you once I've finished here, so we can talk then or once you've finished with Matt. Whatever works for you."

Steph didn't elaborate, just smiled and left them to their meeting.

Buster could feel Steph's agitation as he discussed plans for Heat Wave with her and Matt. He'd had to laugh when Matt had arrived at the cafe and immediately came over to welcome, or possibly antagonize, Asha and Charlie. The teasing had appeared to be good-natured, and he'd insisted their coffee and cakes were complimentary. Charlie, however, had refused to accept his generosity, paying the bill and leaving an enormous tip just to make a point, Buster imagined. Matt had just laughed and called out to Ryan and Margie that they shouldn't worry about Matt's popularity, or lack of, affecting sales. If Charlie was anything to go by, they'd be raking in the tips.

Matt and Steph were engrossed in an animated discussion when Buster joined them. Matt had explained that they were ironing out the details of their agreement before meeting with the lawyers after lunch. Steph had announced she was also getting advice from a second lawyer. If this had surprised Matt, he hadn't reacted. Instead he agreed that it was a good idea. "I want you to be a hundred percent invested in our partnership, Steph. If you've got doubts, or a lawyer points out something that's not going to work for you, then we should find that out now. I don't want any surprises down the line, and I'm sure you don't either."

Now the conversation had turned to what could be done with the existing properties, what the council laws for building on the land were, and the anticipated budget Matt had.

"Some ballpark figures are good for me to get a feel for the size of the project," Buster said. "I've had a quick look at the cottages on the property, and they're pretty basic. Solid structures, but if you're targeting an upscale crowd for your retreats, they're going to need considerable work to bring them up to a suitable standard." He pulled out some papers and passed one to each of them. "This is a very rough budget per renovation. It's purely to give you a starting point and something to think about."

Matt's phone rang as they went through the line items on the budget. He glanced at the screen and picked up his phone. "Sorry, I need to take this."

He stood, answered the call, and walked out of the cafe.

"Like I said to you both," Buster continued, "these figures are very rough at this stage. It just gives us a starting point."

Steph locked eyes with him. "Are you okay? You look like you haven't slept at all."

Buster broke eye contact, picked up some papers, and began shuffling them. "I didn't sleep well last night."

"Was it the visit to see Eve?"

Buster nodded. "It was unsettling."

Matt burst back into the cafe before Steph had a chance to continue the discussion. His face had drained of color, and he looked extremely agitated.

"I'm sorry, Steph, Buster, but I have to leave. Family emergency."

"Is everything okay?" Steph asked.

Matt shook his head. "Dad had a heart attack. I need to get to Tall Oaks right away. Hopefully, I won't be too late. I'll cancel the lawyers from the car. I'm sorry."

"Don't be sorry," Steph said. "Your dad's what's important. We can work everything out later."

"Want me to drive you?" Buster asked. "You look pretty shook up."

Matt let out a breath. "Thanks, but no. I'll calm down a bit before I hit the road. I couldn't ask you to drive me that far."

"Of course you could."

"No. I think I need time on my own. Dad and I aren't exactly close, but I'm not ready to lose him either."

Steph jumped up and went over to the counter where Ryan was serving a customer. "Margie," she called. "Can you get some food to go for Matt?"

Margie sprang into action and, within a couple of minutes, had a bag of sandwiches and some cookies packed along with a coffee. Both Steph and Buster walked Matt out to his pickup.

Steph hugged him. "Stay in touch. I hope he's okay, Matt, I really do."

Matt hugged Steph back. His eyes were misty when he pulled away. "After everything I did, you're so nice to me, Steph. Why?"

"You're a good person most of the time, Matt. Be that person. Make yourself and your dad proud."

Buster clapped him on the back. "I think he probably already is proud, but adding some more reasons to that list never hurts."

Matt wiped his eyes and climbed into his pickup. "I'll try. Sometimes my ideas get the better of me." He gave a weak smile. "I might need you two to rein me in a bit in the future."

"We'd be happy to," Steph said. "Now, drive safely, and we'll be sending lots of positive healing vibes your dad's way."

Matt nodded before starting the engine and pulling out of the parking lot.

Steph turned to Buster. "Should we postpone the meeting. Continue once Matt's back?"

"Yes, although I had hoped to have another look around Heat Wave," Buster said. "Bodhi gave me a tour, but it was a quick look to get a feel for what was there. Now that I've had some time to think about its potential, I'd love to have another look. Would you have time to come with me?"

"Definitely. There's no point meeting with the lawyers until Matt's back, so I'm free until Bodhi's four o'clock class."

"Great. I can drive us over, or would you rather walk?"

Steph hesitated for a moment. "Bodhi told me this

morning that I should be pushing through my fears. He believes it might help me."

Buster thought of his visit to Eve the previous day. That had been a case of pushing through his fear. At this moment, he wasn't sure whether it had helped him.

"You look skeptical," Steph said.

Buster shook his head. "Not at all. I don't think you have anything to lose by trying."

Steph smiled. "That's a good point. Okay, let's take your car. It's such a short drive I'm sure I can muster the courage."

Buster turned to Steph once she was sitting in his passenger seat, seat belt fastened. "You okay?"

Steph nodded. "My gut's a jumbled mess of nerves, but otherwise, I'm okay."

"I'll go slow," Buster promised. "We're not going far, so hopefully you'll be okay."

Steph gripped the car seat with her fingers as Buster pulled out onto Main Street. Part of her considered her fear irrational, but another part, the part that constantly relived the accident, knew that it wasn't. Her problem with being in a vehicle wasn't because she thought she was going to crash; the problem was it brought back the feelings that accompanied the accident and its aftermath.

They arrived at Heat Wave a few minutes later, and Buster turned to her as he pulled to a stop. "You hated every second of that, didn't you?"

Steph nodded. "Sorry."

"You don't need to apologize. I didn't realize how hard something like that would be. I'm amazed you came out to the Bluff with Ryan last weekend."

"It was one of the days I felt more empowered to get over it," Steph said. "It didn't help, but it did get me out for the day."

"And us talking."

Steph nodded before she unfastened her seat belt and climbed down from the truck's cab. "That's enough about me for today. How are you doing? Your visit to Eve appears to have affected you."

"That obvious?"

"Only because I know you went, and I'm not used to you looking so pale or tired. How was she?"

Buster fell silent for a moment. How could he even put into words what the visit to Eve had been like?

"You don't have to tell me if you'd rather not," Steph said. "I get that it's personal and probably pretty emotional."

"No, I would like to tell you. Let's look at Heat Wave while I think of how to work out what I want to say."

They spent the next forty minutes exploring the property and buildings. Buster made numerous notes as they went, pausing from time to time to explain more about his visit.

"In one way, it was like I was visiting the old Eve. The Eve before Holly was born. But in another, it was a very damaged version of that Eve." He went on to explain the postpartum depression diagnosis and his guilt in not realizing she had a medical problem.

"You couldn't be expected to know, Buster, any more than Eve could have. Nothing prepares you for having a baby, and very few people realize their feelings aren't what is considered *normal*. It's overwhelming having a newborn, and a lot of women feel that they have to pretend everything is okay. It's often down the road when they fall apart, not always right after the birth."

Buster nodded. "Eve was fine to start with. She handled everything well, probably too well, if I look back on it. But I felt the distance between her and me immediately. I thought it was that her love for Holly was all-consuming, and she didn't have enough left for me. Now I'm thinking she was putting on such an amazing act that just getting through each day was a challenge."

"Very likely," Steph said. "Do you think her time in prison has helped her?"

"I think getting sober and having the psychologist's help has. Prison, however, probably isn't the right place for her to be doing that. I think that's what kept me up most of the night. There's the part about our relationship falling apart, but then there's also the fact that the mother of my child is in prison, and I'm no longer sure she should be."

"How much longer has she got to serve?"

"Her original sentence was five years, released on probation after three. She's been in for just over a year, and she told me she has the possibility of an appeal. She wanted to know what I thought about her pursuing it. She didn't ask for an answer right then; she just wanted me to think about it and let her know. She said if I felt strongly against her appeal, she wouldn't pursue it."

"Really?"

Buster nodded. "Imagine if I said no. What kind of person would that make me?"

"The kind who blamed her for an accident that took his daughter from him. The kind that didn't have compassion for the woman who was his wife. It sounds like you do have that compassion still."

"Yes, I do. Which I guess is her answer. As I said, I'm not sure prison is the right place for her, but that's not for me to decide. She'll need help moving forward, and she'll need a support system around her to make sure that happens. At the moment, it's the prison. If she was released, it would need to be on the outside."

Steph fell silent. She wondered whether Buster imagined himself as part of that support system, but she didn't want to ask. Instead, she moved the conversation along. "Are you going back to see her?"

"It's Holly's birthday on Tuesday. I said I'd go back to be with her. I'll let her know what I think about the appeal then."

Steph nodded. It was an incredibly difficult position. One that she wouldn't wish on her worst enemy.

"Now, enough about that," Buster said. "I have an idea for the development, and I'd love your opinion on it."

"Before we do that, I'm here if you ever want to talk, Buster. I mean it. I won't necessarily have the answers or even any good advice, but I'm always available to listen."

"Thank you." Buster's voice was hoarse, and he cleared his throat quickly, moving on to the discussion about the development.

Time disappeared as Buster spoke about his idea for transforming the grounds surrounding the existing Heat Wave studio into a lush, zen paradise. His vision was to create a tranquil oasis with a small lake as the central point that the luxury guest houses sat around.

"Look at where they're currently positioned." He pointed to the rundown cottages. They sit in a horseshoe shape around a whole lot of bushes. We bring in a digger, get rid of the bushes, shrubs, and undergrowth, and dig out a small lake. Line it with rocks, plants, and water lilies, and suddenly we have a feature. The existing studio sits in front of it as the flagship of the resort. That will need a bit of a facelift as well to blend in with the luxury of the development."

"What about the rest of the gardens?"

"Having been to your house, I'm assuming you have a lot of ideas already for that."

Steph smiled. "The foliage is so thick in places I was wondering if it would be possible to link the cottages with a raised boardwalk? I'd love it to feature wood carvings and lots of places to burn torches at night and sandalwood throughout the day. It would create an amazing energy."

Buster nodded. "Sounds beautiful. The boardwalk won't be cheap, but we'll work out the budget for everything. Zane's been great with supplying materials from the Mill at good prices. We're lucky he decided to continue working there after the month he agreed to do was up. Although, I'm sure his dad would help us out too. Leave it with me for a few days, and I'll throw an initial estimate together. Matt probably has a ton of ideas that will vary from what we've discussed, so we'll need to allow for them too."

Steph laughed. "Knowing Matt, none of our ideas will make the cut."

Buster raised an eyebrow. "Would that worry you?"

Steph's smiled slipped. "Definitely. This first phase will be a test to see what control Matt's planning to have and whether he'll listen to my ideas. History suggests he won't, but we'll see."

"Although," Buster said, "the Sandstone Cafe has Ryan's touch. I believe Matt let him design the look completely. Who knows, he might surprise you."

Buster found himself whistling as the pickup wound up the road that took him out of Hope's Ridge and in the direction of Drayson's Landing. He stopped himself. What was he thinking, whistling as if he didn't have a care in the world? He'd just driven past Holly's corner. The cross and small roadside grave marked the exact spot Eve's car plowed through the broken barrier. How could he be whistling and feeling happy?

He frowned, his thoughts moving to Steph. It had been so freeing talking to her about Eve and what he was going through. She was a good listener and asked questions that made him think about the situation, but never forced her opinion on him. His lips curled at the edges as he pictured her. Her hair hung loosely around her shoulders today, and her eyes were bright and warm. Her cheeks glowed with good health, and he had to admit, she was gorgeous. Physically, definitely, but more importantly, in her kind nature.

Buster gave himself a mental shake. He had a connection with Steph because of Holly. She felt sorry for him and was being extremely kind. Nothing more. She needed someone who'd look out for her, communicate if difficult situations arose, and most importantly, love her in all of his words and actions. She didn't need someone like Buster. Someone who, when things got tough, turned his back on his wife rather than stepping up to help her.

His thoughts quickly turned to Eve as he rounded the last bend on the mountain and reached the county highway leading to Drayson's Landing. That's who he should be concentrating on, not Steph. In talking to Steph, he knew he needed to encourage Eve's appeal. But what would it mean if she got out? Would she come back to Drayson's Landing? Her parents lived in Tall Oaks, quite close to his. He was considering moving back to Tall Oaks once he packed up his life and left the business. Did that mean Eve would be in his life again? Would he want that? Would she?

He eased his foot off the accelerator, realizing his muddled thoughts were causing him to speed. It wasn't Eve's image that flooded his mind as he thought of his ex; it was Steph's.

Buster started whistling again as his thoughts reverted to Steph and he neared Drayson's Landing. For everything difficult that was going on at the moment, just thinking of her brought a lightness to him. Neither of them was looking for a relationship, and even though only moments earlier, he'd listed the reasons why a relationship between them could never work, it didn't mean it was entirely out of the question, did it?

Who knows, he might surprise you. Buster's words had played over in Steph's head as she'd walked back to the Sandstone Cafe after they'd said their goodbyes. She wanted to find out if there'd been any news from Matt and had been relieved to speak to him shortly after she arrived.

Now she sat nursing the cup of peppermint tea Margie had insisted she have.

"Is it true you're a technophobe?" Margie asked after Steph had finished speaking on the Sandstone Cafe's phone to Matt.

Steph laughed. "Who told you that?"

"Matt, when he was trying to track you down. He called earlier too. He said no one seemed to have a cell phone number for you and you weren't on social media. He tried Heat Wave, but Bodhi said you and Buster had just left. If you're that hard to get in touch with, then it's true, you're living in a different century than the rest of us."

Steph sighed. "Sometimes I wish I was. I guess with the changes happening at Heat Wave, a cell will probably be necessary."

"It's exciting," Margie said. "I am planning to come to a class at some stage. I'm just trying to get used to running the cafe first. Once I settle in, I'll come and try it out. I've been in a bit of a rut and need to be jolted out of it. The move here has already helped."

Steph wasn't sure whether to admit that Ryan had told her about Margie's husband or not. She felt awful not acknowledging the situation but didn't want Margie to think she was prying either. Ryan appeared, deciding for her.

"I told Steph about Aaron," Ryan said, putting his arm around his sister's shoulder and giving her a gentle hug. "Steph's suffered from issues recently, so she'll understand if you don't want to talk about it."

Steph's cheeks flooded with heat. "I wasn't sure whether or not to say anything, Margie. I'm very sorry for what you've been through."

Margie nodded. "Thanks. This is a fresh start, so let's move on and talk about something else." She plastered a smile on her face but was unable to disguise the pain in her eyes. "How's Matt's dad? Did he say?"

"He's doing okay," Steph said and relayed parts of the conversation she just had with Matt. "He's going to stay in the city until his dad's out of the hospital and possibly a few weeks more to help him once he gets home. He's had four stents put in, and the surgery went well."

Ryan gave a low whistle. "Four. That's not good."

"Better that they're in and he's doing well than the other scenario," Margie said.

Ryan nodded. "Of course. It will have given Matt quite a shock. I imagine it will hold up all of his development plans. He messaged me this morning to let me know he put his full trust in us to run the cafe but to contact him if we have any questions."

"He did the same with me just now on our call," Steph said. "The problem is, we haven't finalized an arrangement between us. I'm not sure I can move forward with anything until that's in place."

"Maybe just scale back to basics for the moment," Ryan said. "Keep Heat Wave running, but nothing else. You hadn't started on the development, had you?"

Steph shook her head. "No, other than showing Buster around and throwing some ideas about. I doubt Matt will like any of them anyway. I have a feeling he'll want flashy, whereas I would want the resort to have more of a rustic feel."

"I don't see Matt as flashy," Margie said.

Ryan and Steph both laughed. Steph raised an eyebrow. "Sorry, but that's all I think of him. Have you seen his car? His clothes?"

Margie nodded. "I have, but I've also seen this cafe," she spread her hands as her eyes grazed the walls, "and I've seen his plans for the apartment development. Yes, the insides are quite modern and stylish, but the outside is being built to carry through the sandstone look and feel that the cafe has. When it's finished, the corner will look like it's always been here. He's renovated and flipped quite a few houses here and in Drayson's Landing too," Margie added. "They all fit in with the surrounding area. Yes, beautiful inside, but tasteful and appropriate. I think you might be surprised."

Steph considered Margie's words. It was a shame Matt's recent dealings had left her wary and suspicious of him. Heat crept along her neck. She'd even had the thought that she should just close Heat Wave until he returned and they had an agreement; she wasn't sure she'd be paid. It was an awful way think when his father had just had a heart attack. Whether she was paid or not, she would typically be the first to help out a friend. She sighed.

"That sounded ominous," Ryan said. "Everything okay?"

"Just realizing I'm not very generous toward Matt. In theory, he's offering me a life-changing opportunity, and I'm suspicious of all of his motives. I need to change my mindset and take him at face value to try to make Heat Wave work. If it turns out I'm mistaken, then I'll deal with that later."

"Is Buster working on the project with you?" Margie asked.

Steph nodded. "It's early days, but yes, that's the plan."

Ryan raised his eyebrows at Margie. "Why would you want to know that?"

"No reason. I saw him in here earlier and wondered. We were friends in school, that's all."

"Friends? You were madly in love with him."

Margie punched Ryan playfully on the arm. "I was not. I thought he was cute, that was all. And don't you dare tell him that. I'm certainly not looking for a relationship with Buster or anyone else. It's way too soon."

Ryan pulled Margie to him again, squeezing her to him in a brotherly show of love and compassion. It was how Steph should be reacting too. She was glad that Margie couldn't tell just how tightly her jaw was clenched.

"Now," Ryan said, breaking the more somber mood that had settled over them. "I'm arranging a night out next weekend, and I need a date. You up for it, Steph?"

Steph stared at him. Was he asking her on an actual date, or was that just a friendly invite to hang out with friends?

Ryan laughed. "You don't have to rush to accept, but some indication that you heard my question would be nice."

Steph shifted uncomfortably. "Sorry. I just wasn't sure if you meant a real date just the two of us or a group thing with lots of people."

Ryan raised an eyebrow. "Would it matter?"

Yes, it would. But Steph didn't voice her thought. She didn't want to embarrass Ryan, but she was also aware that he might have different feelings for her than she had for him.

"There's a group of us going, Steph," Margie said, saving

her from having to ask more questions. "Ryan's trying to get me back into the land of the living. We're meeting at Traders for drinks at seven next Friday. He's inviting Zane and Asha, and Zane mentioned his sister might be in town. He had planned to invite Matt and the guys he works with, but that's probably not relevant anymore."

"I'll mention it to Buster when I see him," Ryan said. "Travis and Jodi might want to come down from Drayson's too. Get everyone together."

Steph's stomach flipped at the thought of a night out with Buster. She quickly reminded herself it was a group date, and again, she shouldn't be thinking like that. From the way he'd spoken, there was a possibility Buster might get back together with Eve. She certainly couldn't come between a marriage reconciliation. But if he didn't? She left the thought hanging.

"Well?"

"Of course I'll come," Steph said. "It sounds like a lovely idea."

"Excellent." Ryan winked. "I'll consider myself fortunate enough to have a date. Now, we'd better get back to work."

Steph took it as her cue to leave. She needed to get back to the studio for Bodhi's final class and also work out how she was going to run classes over the next few weeks. She would need to cancel a few from the schedule with Bodhi no longer teaching. She also wanted to look around the property more and give thought to her ideas for the retreat. She liked Buster's plans to have a lake as a feature for the cottages and wanted to work through some ideas of her own. She was annoyed that something still squirmed in her gut, telling her to be careful of Matt, but as long as she was cautious, she hopefully wouldn't be blindsided or disappointed as Asha had been.

 $\mathscr{B}$ uster woke on Saturday morning, dreading the silence that a weekend usually brought with it. He'd enjoyed the previous weekend with the rock climbing and then the trip out to Hope's Ridge, but he didn't feel he had an excuse to turn up there again, and part of him knew he shouldn't. He'd arrived home upbeat the previous night. The time spent with Steph had given him a lift, as it did each time he was with her. But then his phone had rung, and he'd been brought back to reality. It was the prison asking if he would accept a call from Eve.

He moved into the kitchen, replaying in his head the conversation they'd had.

"I'll understand if you can't come on Tuesday," Eve had said. "It's a big day for both of us, and if you'd prefer to spend it on your own, then I do understand."

Nervous energy coursed through Buster as he spoke with his ex-wife. Her words were at complete odds with what her tone conveyed. She was saying the right thing, but he could hear the combination of hope and fear in her voice. She needed him with her on Tuesday but was afraid to ask outright. Had she done this when they were married? Given him an out before he even answered? Did he let her down so often that she felt she needed to tread carefully?

"Of course I'll be there on Tuesday," Buster said. "Am I allowed to bring anything with me? Photos, maybe?"

Silence greeted him, but he could still hear the faint sound of Eve's breathing.

"Eve?"

"Sorry. No, just bring yourself. You're not allowed to bring anything in."

"Okay. What time would you like me to come?"

Eve gave a little laugh. "I don't have any plans for the day. Visiting hours are between nine and two. But they won't let you in after twelve-thirty so before then."

Buster knew he'd be up early that morning. He wouldn't sleep much the night before Holly's birthday, that he was sure of. It was a four-hour drive to the prison, and he could be on the road early. "How about I aim for ten?"

"Perfect. And Henry, thank you."

Buster had hung up realizing the fear and worry he'd heard in Eve's voice when the conversation started had disappeared the moment he'd said he would be visiting.

He put a pot of water on the stove to boil and sat down at the kitchen counter. He'd always considered himself a good person, but right now, there were many indicators he was a terrible person. His ex-wife was in prison, for which he was partially responsible, and he was feeling happy in the presence of another woman. A woman part of him would like to get to know better, but another part forbade him to. Imagine if he put Steph through anything like the trauma he'd put Eve through. He closed his eyes and buried his head in his hands. How had life become so complicated?

The weekend classes reached capacity. Steph hadn't been sure how their regular clientele would react to Bodhi's departure, but other than the hugs, tears, and well wishes from those who'd attended his last class on Friday, it was business as usual. She hadn't had time to scale back the weekend classes, so she had taught three classes back to back both Saturday morning and late afternoon and the same again on Sunday. By Sunday night, she was exhausted.

She arrived home, grateful to find Zane in the kitchen and a large pot of lentil soup simmering on the cooktop.

"Ash's coming over soon," Zane said. "Hope that's okay."

Steph smiled. "She's my sister. I'd love to see her. It's more whether I cramp your style if you want it to be the two of you."

"Of course you don't. And she's got something for you."

Steph frowned. "What is it?"

Zane opened the oven and put in the loaf pan he'd prepared earlier. "I have no idea. Something was sent to your parents' place, and she's delivering it." He turned back to her, his face becoming more serious. "Did you speak to Matt today?"

Steph nodded. "Yes, his dad's doing as well as can be expected. He sounded pretty stressed. The Lake Drive development was about to start construction and now will need to be delayed. Plus, having just bought Heat Wave and having the cafe open, he's under a lot of pressure."

"I should probably call him," Zane said. "See if he wants me to do anything to help."

"Help who?"

Zane and Steph turned as Asha walked into the kitchen. She grinned. "You always say come on in, so this time I did."

"Good, it's about time," Steph said. "I'd give you a hug, except I'm still sweaty from the last class."

Asha put a large box on the counter. "Who needs help?"

Steph hesitated and looked at Zane.

"Matt," Zane said. "He's got a lot happening here but won't be back for a few weeks. Steph was saying he sounded pretty stressed."

"Yes, we should do whatever we can to help," Asha said.

Zane put an arm around her and pulled her close. "Another reason why I love you, Ms. Jones. Willing to help the enemy."

Asha shrugged. "Some things are bigger than everything that happened. Family and health are much more important. I'm happy to do anything he needs, other than shut down the food truck or stop the development at Irresistables."

"I'll give him a call tomorrow," Zane said.

"Now," Asha pushed the box in Steph's direction, "speaking of Matt, this arrived at Mom and Dad's this morning. They were going to drop it by for you, but I said I was coming your way, so here it is."

"Matt sent something to Mom and Dad's?"

Asha nodded. "Guess he knows their address from years ago but not your address now."

Steph took a knife from a drawer and slit open the box. She took two boxes from inside, her mouth dropping open. "A phone and a computer?"

Asha laughed. "He doesn't know you at all, does he?"

Steph put the boxes on the counter and reached back inside the box. "There's a note." She smiled as she read Matt's neat scrawl. "Steph! Here's to our partnership and me being able to contact you. Please learn how to use both of these ASAP so I can at least call and email you! Both the phone and computer are set up and ready to use. I'm sure Zane will give you a quick lesson. I've asked my lawyer to draw up a temporary agreement, so you know you'll be paid for the work you do between now and when we finalize everything. Copy attached. Matt." Steph flipped over to the next page and read through the agreement. Her eyes widened as she read the terms.

"If he's trying to rip you off," Asha began, her hands balled into fists.

Steph shook her head and handed Asha the agreement. "He's not. Reading this, I think he might have had a head injury."

Asha stared at the document before handing it to Zane.

He looked to Steph for approval before reading through. He gave a low whistle. "Well, I don't know what you were earning before, but this looks very generous."

"I can't accept that. He has no idea what yoga teachers earn."

"You won't just be a teacher," Asha reminded her. "You'll be running the business, and I assume planning the new development with Buster. According to Matt's agreement, he wants everything to keep running as if he was here."

The box containing the new mobile phone rang, causing them all to jump.

Zane laughed. "That has to be Matt. Nothing like a grand entrance."

Steph opened the box and took the phone from it. She was relieved to see a green button to accept the call. While she had never owned an iPhone, she'd used enough to know the basics.

"Matt?"

"Phew! Not only did you get it, but you answered it."

"I don't know what to say."

"Just tell me you'll keep the phone charged and answer it when I call. And before you even ask, no, I'm not going to call you every five minutes, but with the studio and the development, you need to be easier to reach."

"The phone's easy enough, but my computer usage is limited to the system at Heat Wave."

"It has email and the web, doesn't it?"

"Of course."

"Then you're set. I'm calling to see if you're okay with the temporary contract I had drawn up?"

Steph hesitated. Should she tell him it was too much?

"I realize with what's happened with Dad that we haven't had a chance to discuss the terms, and I'm open to changing things if you think it isn't fair."

"It's more than fair, Matt. I was going to ask you what else we can do to help."

"We?"

"Asha and Zane are offering their help too. Anything you need with the other developments or your business in general."

Silence greeted her. She took the phone from her ear and looked from Asha and Zane. "I think I hung up on him."

"Steph?"

She put the phone back to her ear.

"Sorry, I was just a bit overwhelmed. I've had so many messages of support from people. I'm finding it hard to believe, to be honest."

"Both Asha and Zane are with me now, and the offers are genuine. I think Zane planned to call you tomorrow to see if you need any help with the Lake Drive development."

"Tell him I appreciate the offer, but I've put another foreman on the job today. He'll be in touch with Buster in the morning, and I'm hoping we won't lose any time on that project."

"That's great, Matt. Any more news on your dad?"

"He's recovering well, and I should be able to bring him home midweek."

"Well, if there's anything you need, just let me know."

Matt laughed. "Now that I can reach you, I will. And Steph, thanks."

The call ended, and Steph turned to Asha and Zane. "His dad's doing well, and he's appreciative of everyone's offers to help. He's got a foreman starting tomorrow on the Lake Drive development, so he won't need your help, Zane."

"Probably someone from Drayson's Landing," Asha said. "There's no one else in town that I know of who would be suitable for that."

"Guess you'll find out tomorrow if you keep your eyes open," Steph said. "Whoever it is will be working right across the road from Irresistables. Now, I'm going to go have a shower, and then if you've got time, I might need a quick lesson on how to use this computer."

Steph smiled as she walked toward the bathroom, listening to Asha laughing with Zane.

"I've wanted to drag Steph out of the dark ages for years, and it's Matt Law who manages to do it. Of all people."

She didn't hear Zane's reply but could picture Asha's eye-rolling. She was proud of Asha's response to the Matt situation. Matt had treated Asha and Charlie terribly, but seeing Asha rise above their past issues and show genuine compassion and care for Matt said a lot about who her sister was. And Zane too. He wasn't immune to Matt's poor treatment. They were both good people, and she couldn't be happier to think that marriage was a possibility.

Buster pulled up outside the Sandstone Cafe at ten to eight. He'd received a message from Matt that he'd appointed a new foreman who wanted to walk through the plans and schedule for the apartment development with him. The three properties adjoining the Sandstone Cafe were in their final stages of being cleared, and work would begin later in the week.

Buster had been relieved to get Matt's message and realize that the project would continue as planned. With ten minutes to spare before meeting the new foreman, he decided to duck across the road for coffee from Asha's food truck. He'd need to alternate his purchases between Asha and the Sandstone Cafe to keep everyone happy.

He grinned as he approached the food truck. Charlie Li was deep in conversation with Asha. They looked up as he approached.

"Coffee?" Asha asked.

"Yes, please. How are you both?"

"Excellent," Charlie said. "Today is a very good day. How are your ideas for our development coming along?"

"I'll have something to you both by the middle of the week," Buster said. "It's exciting."

He took some money from his wallet and passed it across to Asha when she held out a coffee cup to him. "Thanks, I'd better hurry. I'm meeting Matt's new foreman in a few minutes."

"He mentioned to Steph last night that he'd appointed someone," Asha said. "I guess that's a good thing for you and Travis, no holdups with the project."

Matt nodded. "As long as this foreman knows what he's doing. Matt's usually really involved with his projects. I just hope this one doesn't go off the rails without him here."

"I'll walk with you," Charlie said, ushering Buster from the food truck. "You don't want to keep Matt's man waiting."

Buster smiled at Asha and followed the older man. "How are you doing, Mr. Li?"

"Very well," Charlie said. They crossed the road, and

Charlie stopped outside the development site. He checked his watch. "Eight o'clock."

"No sign of Matt's guy," Buster said. "I hope whoever he's got is going to be reliable. Matt doesn't need extra stress right now."

Charlie shook his head. "No he does not, and we will make sure things run like clockwork."

"We?"

Charlie held out his hand. "Yes, we. I am Matt's new foreman."

Buster choked on his coffee. "You? Are you kidding?"

"You think an old man can't do the job?"

"No, that's not it at all. It's just that Matt hasn't treated you well, Mr. Li. Are you sure you're the right person to do this?" *And do you have any idea of what this job entails?* Buster couldn't believe Matt would give the job to a ninety-six-year-old. This was ridiculous. Was he messing with them? He couldn't imagine any other explanation.

"I see the look in your eyes, Buster. *An old man cannot do this job.* Yes, Matthew treated me badly, but he has also apologized. An apology that was more sincere than I would ever have expected from Matthew." Charlie held up his hands. "And before you ask, no the apology was not just to get me to be his foreman. It was genuine and very heartfelt. Me agreeing to the position confirms a truce between us and shows the town that we have put everything behind us."

"I'm glad he's apologized, Mr. Li. But doesn't he need a foreman with experience?"

"His father reminded him of my background and suggested I oversee the job in Matthew's absence."

"Your background?"

"I was an architect for many years and have managed plenty of construction projects. I can't do the fancy computer designs you do these days, but I can draw up plans, read

122

plans, and have a team implement plans. It will be no problem. Now, where are the plans, I would like to review them. I've already spoken with the demolition team this morning. They will be finished by lunchtime tomorrow, and the first stage of the project can begin. I will ensure the plans have my sign off by then."

"Matt's already signed off on the plans," Buster said. "I have copies in my truck to show you."

"Very good. The plans, however, will need my sign off too. Feel free to contact Matt if you would like to know how we will work."

Buster shook his head slowly. "No need. Matt's message was very clear that what you say goes. I just..." Buster's words trailed off. He just what? Just didn't expect a man in his nineties who probably hadn't worked for close to thirty years to be in charge of this project? "I guess I'm still surprised you would do something to help Matt. He treated you so badly, and while I know I'm speaking out of turn, he has asked Travis and me whether there's any way we can stop Asha's project."

Charlie laughed. "I would expect no less of any businessman who wants that land for himself. I would hope that helping Matt now will help make him a better man when it comes to his business dealings moving forward."

"I would like to think so too, Charlie, but I wouldn't count on it."

Charlie's smile slipped. "I'm not counting on anything, but I do believe in helping a man when he's facing difficult circumstances. Whether Matt would do the same is not the point, the point is that others have been there for me when I needed it, and I will pay that forward. Look at how both Zane and Asha helped me."

Buster nodded. It was an admirable way of behaving. He

still had his concerns about Charlie running this project, however, and realized it must have shown on his face.

Charlie tapped his arm lightly. "Consider this a trial run for Asha's project. I'll be the foreman on that development too." He winked. "This gives me a chance to practice at Matt's expense. Now, let's look at those plans."

Steph groaned as the email she'd spent the last ten minutes one-finger typing disappeared from the screen. It wasn't the first time it had happened and probably wouldn't be the last. She was trying to reply to Matt's questions about Heat Wave, but it was taking so long. This was one of the many reasons she didn't do computers. It would be much quicker to speak to him.

While the computer felt like an annoyance, she did have to admit that the phone was already coming in handy. She'd worked out how to divert Heat Wave's phone to her number so that there was no reason for her to be at the studio unless a class was on. Bodhi had always done this. She was surprised at how many phone call inquiries the studio received each day. She generally knew who was calling— after all, it was a small town—and it allowed her to chat with them and encourage them to try out a class.

She closed the lid of the computer, deciding she'd message Matt later. She was sure he was busy with his dad and unlikely to have time to reply. What Steph wanted to do was write up all of her ideas for Heat Wave in the notebook she'd bought especially for the project. She'd lain awake in the early hours of the morning, her usual awake time, thinking through a range of ideas. She planned to go back to Heat Wave after lunch and spend the afternoon in the gardens and around the cottages making plans. The quicker she did this, the faster she'd have an excuse to speak to Buster. She shook herself. She didn't need an excuse to speak to him. She was going to be his client. It was crazy to think about how much time he now needed to spend in Hope's Ridge. If she were still trying to avoid him, she would have found it very difficult. With Matt's apartment project, Asha and Charlie's development, and now Heat Wave, Buster was going to be a regular fixture in town.

She leaned back on the couch. If it wasn't for the accident, it was unlikely she would have had an opportunity to get to know him. Not that she really knew him, but they had an undeniable connection. She shook her head and stood. She kept thinking about Buster, and it was scaring her. She wasn't looking for a relationship, she knew he *definitely* wasn't ready for a relationship, yet her mind kept going there.

She was about to make a cup of tea when she stopped. A small smile played on her lips. It was *change.* For all of her spouting to Asha, that life unfolded as it was meant to, to live in the moment, and to be patient, she had trouble with change. It unsettled her, rattled her even. And this was what was happening now. She was clinging to the idea of Buster because it seemed stable. Whereas Bodhi had suddenly left, she might be going into business with Matt Law; Ryan and Margie had returned to the Ridge; and if Asha accepted Zane's proposal, which Steph was sure she would, Steph would probably need to find a new roommate. For someone who didn't cope well with change, it was no wonder her thoughts were all over the place at the moment.

She let out a long breath, relieved she'd had this realization. Buster would make a good friend, nothing more. He had enough problems to deal with, including his little girl's birthday on Tuesday. Her mind wandered briefly to thinking of his ex and how the visit would go, but she quickly shut it down. No more thoughts of Buster. She needed to focus on Heat Wave and the excitement the new business could bring.

Buster had returned to the office in Drayson's Landing shaking his head following the meeting with Charlie.

"You okay?" Travis asked, poking his head around the door of Buster's office.

Buster indicated for him to come in and take a seat. He then went on to explain the strange turn of events with Charlie now working for Matt. "I get what he was saying," Buster said, "about paying good deeds forward, but I'm not sure Matt falls into that category."

Travis laughed. "Be careful what you say about one of our best clients."

Buster sighed. "I know I should be more generous in my thinking about him. It's a bit hard when I'm double-checking everything he's asking us to do for him just in case he's trying to do something underhanded again."

"There's nothing to worry about now with the Lake Drive apartments," Travis said. "Plans are all approved, and the team is in place. The demolition should be complete by the end of the day, and we have the pre-build meeting on Thursday with the construction crew to go through the site plan. Matt usually claims the role of foreman, but he does share the responsibility with Jerry. He's working on this project so that it will be a similar setup. Having Charlie as an extra pair of eyes won't hurt. But I do agree, it is a strange decision. I would have thought he would have checked Zane's availability rather than one of the town's seniors."

"Knock, knock."

Buster and Travis turned to the door, where Jodi stood

holding two to-go cups. "Thought you might both like an afternoon pick-me-up."

Buster smiled. "Thanks, Jodi. You're the best."

She stepped into the office and gave Buster his drink and held out the other one for Travis. Buster noticed a look pass between the two of them before Jodi turned to him.

"We know tomorrow's going to be a hard day, Buster. Is there anything we can do to help?"

Buster dropped his gaze to his coffee cup.

"Really," Travis added. "Anything at all, you just let us know."

He raised his gaze to meet their concerned looks. "Thanks. I'm going to see Eve. Being together might help, I'm not sure."

Jodi's eyes widened in surprise. "Eve?"

Buster nodded. "I saw her last week for the first time. You were right, Jodi, about her suffering postpartum depression. I should have done something a lot earlier to help her."

"I didn't know for sure, Buster. I just said it was a possibility. Give her our love, please. And," she hesitated for a moment before clearing her throat, "if you're okay with me visiting her, and she'd like to see me, please tell her I'll visit. I haven't suggested it before out of respect for our friendship with you."

"I appreciate that, Jodi, I do. And I think Eve needs our support. I'll ask her, but I'm sure she'd love to see you."

He was right.

Operating on very little sleep but a lot of coffee, Buster arrived at the prison at nine-thirty, allowing plenty of time for processing before seeing Eve at ten. His heart contracted the moment he saw her red-rimmed eyes. He'd had the benefit of the eye drops Jodi had given him the previous week to help mask the emotions he'd been through that morning. Waking to a silent house on the morning of what should have been his daughter's seventh birthday. His mom had rung him to tell him she loved him. As much as he appreciated the call, he could tell that she was doing her best not to cry. There were certain days that he didn't have the emotional capacity to take on anyone else's grief. Today was one of those days, but he would make an effort to be there for Eve.

He reached across the table and quickly squeezed her hand, releasing it before any of the guards noticed or reprimanded him. They sat in silence for a few moments, their eyes and faces saying everything. They had both lost so much.

Buster cleared his throat. "I'm not going to ask you how you are. I can see exactly. It's a hard day, Eve, and it will be every year. But we'll get through it." He forced a smile. "Holly would have been seven today, and I thought of seven memories I want to share with you."

"Oh, Henry." Eve buried her face in her hands, her shoulders shaking as tears racked her body.

Buster twisted his hands together. "I wish I could hug you right now. Do something to help." He meant it.

Eve calmed her crying, wiped her eyes on her sleeve, and looked at him. "Do something to help? You have no idea what you being here has done for me. You've helped me more than anyone. I'm not crying because I don't want to hear the memories, I'm crying because you thought to do that for me and I'm crying because that's all we have. Memories."

Buster blinked back tears. "At least we do have memories, Eve. We had a beautiful little girl, and we both adored her." He cleared his throat. "Memory number one." He smiled as he launched into his memory of Eve's pregnancy, and Holly kicking her like she was practicing soccer every time Eve ate an olive. The second memory took them to Holly's birth, and the rest of the memories Buster had decided to share all depicted their happy times as a family. They were both crying by the time he spoke of her fourth birthday party. It was the last birthday they'd shared with Holly as a married couple. The separation and divorce proceedings had occurred in the eighteen months following that birthday.

"I still can't believe you rescued that one," Eve said, smiling through her tears.

Buster chuckled. "Your face when you dropped the cake. I thought you were going to have a heart attack."

"And you fixed it."

"We were just lucky we had so much frosting left over, and only the top hit the floor. Other than you and I, no one even realized we sliced the top off and redid it."

Eve laughed. "Holly loved it, and her present. Remember her bike?"

Remember it? Buster saw it every time he drove into his garage. He didn't tell Eve this, just nodded.

They continued reminiscing about Holly, sharing both laughter and tears. Buster was glad he'd come. For all of the horrible things that had resulted in his marriage breakdown, to be able to share this part of him with Eve was special. No one else knew how he felt. Sure, if he chatted with any of his friends or family, he'd see their sympathy, but that wasn't what he needed. He needed to talk about Holly with someone who wanted to hear the stories and remember her as badly as he did.

Buster glanced at the clock high up on the wall, realizing he only had another five minutes before his hour would come to an end. "I think you should pursue the appeal," he said.

Eve's eyes widened at the sudden change of topic. "I wasn't sure you'd want me to get out."

"Of course I do, Eve. I'm not sure you should even be here. Regardless, you've been punished, and the reality is neither of us will ever get over Holly's death. I hope we'll both learn to live with it and be able to move on and find happiness again, but it will always be part of us. Being locked away from your mom and family when you need their love and support isn't exactly helping."

Eve nodded. "If the appeal is successful, it means I'd be able to go home."

"You would."

Eve closed her eyes and took a deep breath. She opened them and looked directly at Buster. "Is there any chance that home could be our home?"

Buster was silent. What did she mean by that? That she wanted to buy the house from him to feel closer to Holly? Or did she want him in the house too? "Together?"

She nodded. "Don't answer now. I'm just putting it out there. Mom and I were talking, and she reminded me of how much you and I have shared, and how much we've both lost. It appears illness on my part played a big role in it. It's no excuse, but it does help explain to me why I felt the way I did and why I acted how I did." She held her hand up as he opened his mouth to speak. "Think about it. Mom's advice was good, I think. To take things very slowly. See if we have any chemistry or connection left."

Buster wasn't sure what to say. She was right that they'd shared a past and shared a loss, but he wasn't sure that that was something that would bring them together now. "I'll think about it and try to come back and visit next week. It might need to be over the weekend. I'm getting busier during the week." *And trying to finish projects so I can leave the area.* He didn't say that, but it was true, wasn't it?

Buster's mind raced as he drove back to Drayson's Landing. Was Eve suggesting they get back together? Or was it Cora suggesting this? Whoever was suggesting it, it wasn't a scenario he'd considered. If she hadn't had postpartum depression, where would they be today? In love, celebrating their seven-year old's birthday? His gut churned at that thought. Their marriage had cracks in it before Holly's birth. As much as he hated that postpartum depression had played a role in her death, he wasn't sure it was what had ended his marriage.

He thought of Steph's words that everything was predestined. If that were true, would he have lost Eve and Holly anyway? He pushed the thought from his head. The question now was whether he had feelings for Eve. And if not, did he owe her to try to develop some?

Steph gratefully accepted the coffee Asha passed her from the serving window of the food truck. The raised eyebrows didn't go unnoticed.

"I know, I know, I say I don't drink coffee and then I do. I'm a terrible example to the yoga community."

Asha laughed. "I'm not complaining. What you're saying is the coffee I serve is so good that you can't go without it."

Steph smiled. "I wish that was the only reason."

"Nightmares?"

Steph nodded. "You'd think after this many months, I'd be used to them. I had a week or so without any dreams. I thought things were getting better. But last night was probably the worst one yet."

"Oh Steph, I'm so sorry."

Steph blinked back tears. "Don't be. I'm just tired and

emotional. I've never been that great with change, and with everything going on right now, I'm stressed."

"Did you want to talk about the stress or the dream?"

Steph shook her head. She didn't want to let on to Asha that it wasn't just Holly in her dream last night, Buster was in the car with her. She'd watched them both being pulled under the lake's surface when the car sank. Her heart always raced whenever she remembered the scene of the accident or dreamt about it, but last night she'd woken feeling like it was breaking.

"If you need any help with Heat Wave, you'll speak up, won't you? Especially with the technology side of things. That's something I can help you with."

"I was going to ask you about that. We never did much online with Heat Wave. With the community being so small, we've never really needed to promote the business or advertise."

"You're thinking of doing that now?"

Steph nodded. "I wondered if we should be doing something now to get ready for when the retreat's ready. Maybe a Facebook page and Instagram. I know I've hardly spent any time on either of those, but I thought putting up photos of what Heat Wave's like now and documenting the construction and transformation phase might be a good way to get people's attention and hold their interest. We have to keep in mind that our target market for the retreat isn't Hope's Ridge residents. It's people from outside our community."

"You sound like a real business owner," Asha said. "Planning so far in advance."

Steph sipped her coffee. "I need to. Hopefully Matt's dad will recover quickly, and he'll come back so we can finalize the partnership arrangement."

"He's coming back this afternoon for twenty-four hours,"

Asha said. "Ryan popped over about an hour ago to check that we're still on for drinks tonight. He'd just heard from Matt. He left in such a hurry when he got the call about his dad that he didn't have time to bring everything he needed."

Steph frowned. "I can't imagine he'll have time during his visit to discuss our arrangement. There's no real hurry. I'm fine with the conditions set out in the temporary contract."

"He said he'd join us for drinks, so you might have a chance to talk to him then." Asha's eyes drilled into Steph's. "You are coming, aren't you?"

"I…" Steph's voice trailed off.

"Steph, you have to come. Jenna's arriving any minute, and it's an opportunity to welcome Ryan and Margie back to town. Margie especially needs our support. You've heard what happened to her husband, haven't you?"

Steph nodded. "Yes, of course, I'll come for drinks."

Asha grinned. "Great, it'll be like old times. Like before everyone moved away. Now, I'd better get ready. It looks like I'm about to be inundated."

Steph turned in the direction Asha had just nodded. Five workmen from Matt's building site had crossed the road and were walking toward the food truck.

Asha laughed. "Good thing Matt's not here to see this. I might need to remind them that they should be getting their supplies from the Sandstone Cafe. Matt will probably fire them if he sees them here."

Steph shook her head in disbelief. "Take another look. It appears they're being directed this way."

Both sisters watched as another workman stood talking to Charlie. Charlie had his hand up like a stop sign, preventing the worker's access to the path that led to the Sandstone Cafe. He pointed at the food truck, and the worker turned and crossed the road.

"Now that's what I'd call a conflict of interest," Steph said. "And I think you're right; Matt will hit the roof if he realizes Charlie's costing him business."

Asha shrugged. "As much as I'm all for helping Matt, Steph, karma has to catch up with him at some stage. He can't have us all rushing about doing nice things for him without paying in some way for his awful behavior. If it's in the form of a few coffees and muffins, then I'm in favor of Charlie stirring things up."

8

$\mathcal{I}$f Travis and Jodi hadn't insisted he come with them to Hope's Ridge, there was no way Buster would be standing at the bar in Traders placing his drink order.

"You need a break from your thoughts," Travis had insisted. "You've had a rough week. Come out with us tonight and spend time with your friends."

Buster had declined the invite. "I won't be great company. I'll come another night, okay?"

"There won't be another night to welcome Ryan and Margie back to the area, and we should be there for Matt, see how he's doing. He's heading back to the city sometime on Saturday, so it's our only chance to see him in person. We have a lot of jobs running for him right now, and I think it would be good to make sure he knows we're doing everything to keep them on track."

"I'm sure you can manage that," Buster said.

"Not if he has specific questions about your jobs," Travis said.

"So, it's a job requirement to go to Traders for drinks tonight?"

Travis grinned. "Exactly. I should have phrased it like that to start with. We'll pick you up at six. Make sure you shower, shave, and look respectable. You're looking a bit rough this morning, if you don't mind me saying."

Buster nodded, not bothering to reply. He knew he looked rough. A sleepless night, this time not just thinking about Holly. Eve's suggestion that she could move back in with him, assuming her appeal went through and was successful, had thrown him. He'd known he wouldn't be meeting with clients, so he'd thrown on the previous day's clothes and turned up to work.

Now, clean-shaven, showered, and dressed in his favorite black button-down Oxford shirt and jeans, his eyes traveled the length of the bar as he conceded that Travis might be right—a night out would take his mind off everything. He waited while Isaak prepared his drink, grateful for the large measure of bourbon the bartender poured. He was going to need a few of those tonight.

He returned to the table, where Ryan, Margie, Travis, and Jodi were deep in conversation about Ryan's artwork. Buster sat down, surprised by how humble Ryan was. He'd had huge success with his artwork but played it down.

"Are you still painting?" Jodi asked.

Ryan nodded, nursing his beer. "I've got a few commissions to complete at the moment. Once they're done, I'm thinking of running some classes from the cafe. See if I can get some locals interested."

"Would Matt be okay with you doing that?"

"He sure would!" Matt appeared at the head of the table, a wide smile on his face.

Buster couldn't help but notice an unusual weariness in Matt's eyes as he stood and clapped him on the back. "Great to see you, Matt. How's your dad doing?"

"Much better. He's home, and my aunt, his sister, has

moved in to help. I'm going to go back for the next couple of weeks, since he has quite a few appointments. But at least with her there now, I was able to come back tonight. I need more clothes and a few other bits and pieces."

"Can I get you a drink?" Travis asked.

"No, I'm good. I want to talk to Isaak for a second, so I'll order one myself." He glanced at the empty chairs. "Who else is coming?"

"Asha, Zane, and Steph," Ryan said. "Although I'm starting to wonder if I've been stood up."

Margie slapped his shoulder playfully. "I don't think Steph considered this a real date."

Buster watched Ryan with interest. So it was true, he was interested in Steph. Buster's gut churned uncomfortably.

Ryan sighed. "Well, I wish she would. Each time I ask her out, she seems to think I'm joking."

"She sees you as an old friend, that's all," Margie said. "You'll need a bigger gesture if you want her to take you seriously."

"Take who seriously?" Zane appeared hand-in-hand with Asha. Steph was a few steps behind.

"No one," Margie was quick to say.

"How about I get some drinks," Matt said. "Zane, Asha, Steph, what are you all having?"

With their drink order placed, Matt headed for the bar, and the others sat down at the table. Buster did his best to force a friendly smile and nodded in greeting to each of them. He saw the concern in Steph's eyes when he finally looked her way. He averted his eyes, but she got up, moved around the table, and sat next to him.

"I was thinking of you on Tuesday. Did it go okay?"

"Yup."

Steph fell silent. He hadn't meant to sound so curt, but he

didn't want to talk about it. He threw the rest of his drink back and stood. "Anyone else need a refill?"

"We just got started," Jodi said. "Don't forget how strong that stuff is."

"Yes, Mom."

Buster did his best to laugh as the table fell silent. "Sorry," he mumbled and walked toward the bar. That had fallen flat. He sat down on one of the stools, the beat of the music thumping in his chest. Matt appeared from the side of the bar, sat next to him, and let out a long breath.

"It's been a hard week," Matt said. He motioned to Isaak for two drinks. Isaak was quick to place two whiskeys in front of the men. Matt picked his up and knocked it back in one go. Buster did the same.

"Amazing how you have everything planned, and then life can change so quickly." Matt turned to face him, his eyes suddenly darkening. "Oh, sorry, Buster. I wasn't thinking. You of all people don't need this."

"Don't be silly. You've had a massive upheaval this week. My situation shouldn't come into play at all. Your dad's going to be okay, isn't he?"

"I hope so, but I can already see he's not the same. He thought he was invincible. The big man, the big property developer. It's given him a real shock. He nearly died before they did the stents. Amazing that he's still with us."

"What will you do?" Buster asked. "Move back to the city or stay around here?"

Matt ran his finger around the rim of the glass. "I've given serious thought to moving to be closer to him, but I have so much going on around here. My dreams are here, and I'd hate to give them up. I suggested to Dad that he move back with me, but he just laughed. Said he'd never set foot in this place again. He's still pretty bitter that he feels he was run out of town."

Buster nodded. Everyone was well aware of Walter Law's history in Hope's Ridge. He'd had some good ideas for the town, but many building applications had been rejected due to objections, and eventually, he'd left town, completely fed up.

"We're also not that close, which is another issue." Matt sighed. "There's no rush to make any decisions. I'll see what happens over the next few weeks. Now, tell me, how are my developments going?"

It was ten minutes before Matt and Buster returned to the table. Ryan had moved into his seat and was now talking with Steph while the rest of the party chatted.

A stab of jealousy ripped through Buster as Ryan placed his arm possessively on the back of Steph's chair, laughing at something she was saying.

"Jenna!"

Asha's exclamation had all heads turning, including his. Zane's sister appeared to be making her grand entrance. Buster hadn't seen Jenna in at least three years. She'd moved away from Hope's Ridge right after high school and, from what Zane had told him, preferred city life over sleepy small-town life. Buster had bumped into her unexpectedly in the city one weekend when he had Holly with him. Jenna had insisted they have coffee, and Holly had loved sitting with them, sipping a chocolate milkshake.

Jenna finished hugging Asha and moved around the table, greeting everyone as long lost friends. Which Buster guessed they all were. He stood when she reached him, ready to receive his hug. What he didn't expect was the warmth in her eyes. She was genuinely delighted to see him.

She squeezed him twice before pulling away, a simple gesture that caused him to blink back tears. The one simple movement transported him back three years to the day in the city when he and Holly had bumped into Jenna. Holly had fallen in love with Jenna instantly.

"She's like a doll," Holly had said as they drove back to Drayson's Landing after the impromptu catch up.

"She loved you, pumpkin," Buster said to his daughter. "And I think you even taught her something."

"I know," Holly said, "my double hug. She loved it. She said it was the nicest hug she'd ever had."

Buster was brought out of his thoughts by a gentle squeeze of his arm. Jenna didn't say anything. She didn't need to; the hug conveyed so much.

Buster sat down as the group started firing questions at Jenna about the engagement party. He was incredibly happy for her. She'd fled Hope's Ridge after school ended, wanting to get away from the expectations her father had for her to work at the family's mill. She was a talented graphic designer and worked predominately with advertising companies. She was making her mark in the industry and should be incredibly proud of herself. When he and Holly had seen her, she'd mentioned how happy she was in the city and how she could never imagine returning to Hope's Ridge. He was beginning to think perhaps it was the change he needed too. Disappear into the anonymity a city could offer. But then, of course, there was Eve to consider.

He gratefully accepted another drink from Zane, glad he didn't need to make any decisions tonight. He would sit and listen to Jenna and the others and pretend his life was just as normal as all of theirs.

Steph found herself glancing across the table at Buster. She couldn't help it. He'd cut her off so abruptly. She understood he didn't want to talk about Holly's birthday or the visit to

Eve, but it was unlike him to be rude. He was also throwing whiskey back like it was water. Her heart contracted as she looked at him. He was doing his best to appear to be listening and interested as Jenna talked about the venue for what was sounding like a massive event for her engagement, but Steph could tell his thoughts were miles away.

"Steph?"

She turned to Ryan, who was seated beside her.

"Do you have plans for tomorrow?"

"I'm teaching a few classes at either end of the day." She looked across at Matt, who was deep in discussion with Travis and Zane. "I'm assuming Matt might want to meet up at some point too. Why?"

"I was thinking of driving up to Periwinkle. I haven't hiked the ghost trail in years. Asha was telling me that you and she did it recently. We could go on Sunday if tomorrow's no good."

Steph considered the invitation. "Let's we see if anyone else is free and wants to come."

Ryan shook his head. "I thought we could take lunch, make a date of it."

Date. There was that word again.

Buster cleared his throat from the other side of the table, making Steph realize he'd been listening. His eyes bored into hers. She had no idea what he was trying to tell her, if anything. He'd been rude and was now acting strangely.

"What do you think?" Ryan asked, engaging her again.

"Steph won't want to drive up to Periwinkle," Buster said. "You should get to know her better before you ask her out."

Heat flooded Steph's cheeks. The slur in Buster's voice confirmed he'd drunk too much. The rest of the table quieted, turning their attention to Buster and Steph.

"Everything okay?" Asha asked Steph.

Steph didn't answer. If Buster stopped talking, it would be, but if he didn't, she had no idea.

He didn't.

"A lot's happened since you last lived here Ryan. Lots of horrible things that have left some of us damaged. Cars are no longer Steph's thing."

Steph pushed back her chair and stood. "Buster, I'll answer for myself, thank you, and I'd appreciate you staying out of my business." She turned to Ryan. "I'd love to come on Sunday. I'm free after my nine o'clock class. Now, if you'll excuse me, I'm going to the bathroom."

She didn't wait for any of them to respond, just turned from the table and walked toward the bathroom. She sidestepped the bathroom door and headed out of the side entry of Traders. She wasn't interested in watching Buster drink himself into a coma, stirring up trouble as he did. He was out of line. She pulled her jacket around her as she stepped into the cold night air. She needed to clear her head. Not only had Buster upset her, but now she'd agreed to a date with Ryan. She should have listened to her gut about tonight and not come. She had enough pressure on her without adding unnecessary social stress.

"Thanks a lot," Ryan said, turning to Buster. "What's your problem tonight anyway?"

Buster saw Travis shaking his head at Ryan, trying to convey a message. He stood, realizing he was a little wobbly on his feet.

"I mean it, Buster, what's your problem? Steph's only ever nice to you, and you make her uncomfortable like that."

Buster held up his hands, his head spinning slightly. Drinking whiskey on an empty stomach was not a good idea. "Sorry I shouldn't have come tonight. I wasn't trying to be mean to Steph. I'll apologize when she returns."

"She's fine, Buster," Asha assured him. "She knows you're having a tough time."

"No," Ryan said. "It doesn't matter what anyone's going through. There's no need to be rude."

"Let's change the subject," Jenna suggested. She gave a little laugh. "I think I've bored you all enough now about the engagement party. How about you fill me in on the town's developments." She turned to Matt. "I hear rumors you employed Charlie Li as your foreman. Were you struck by lightning recently by any chance?"

Matt laughed, as did the others, and the conversation quickly changed direction.

A tremor rushed through Buster's body. His face heated, and he knew he needed to leave. His emotions were getting the better of him. He moved over to where Jodi was talking with Margie.

"I'm going for a walk. Get some fresh air and sober up. I'll come back in a couple of hours. I assume you'll be here for at least that long?"

Jodi nodded. "We're going to order some food a bit later. Why don't you come back in an hour or so for that? I told Travis that eleven is the latest I'm staying till. I'm happy to be designated driver, but not at two in the morning."

Buster nodded. "I'll be back before eleven."

"Ignore Ryan," Margie said. "I think he's interested in Steph, and every time he tries to ask her out, something gets in his way."

"Well, he got a yes from her tonight," Buster said, trying to ignore the sinking feeling in his stomach. "I'll see you both soon."

He turned and walked out of the bar, the cold night air hitting him the moment he stepped outside. The icy blast was exactly what he needed to sober up. He shoved his hands in his pockets and walked toward the main street in the direction of the lake.

Steph shivered as she stood by the lake, the full moon casting long shadows across it. She pulled her coat tighter around her. Tonight had been a disaster. From the moment Ryan asked her to be his date, she hadn't felt good about it. On top of that, Buster looked like he'd hardly slept and was drowning his feelings with alcohol. None of it was a good combination.

Her thoughts shifted to Matt and Heat Wave. It was an excellent opportunity, but was it what she wanted? She hadn't had any time to consider whether the opportunity was really for her. The one thing she'd loved about teaching yoga was the flexibility it gave her. She turned up, taught the class, then left. She was only responsible for the time in the yoga room, not the running of the business, a new development, or anything else. If the last year had taught her anything, it was to avoid stress if she could. She didn't cope well with it. Granted, she knew her situation after the accident was more stressful than anything she'd ever had to deal with, but adding all of these extra responsibilities on top of that might be something she'd regret. She sighed. She wasn't sure what to do.

"Steph?"

She turned, her teeth clenching as soon as she saw Buster approaching. She pushed her hands deeper into her pockets and started walking along the lake trail. She wanted to be alone, and she didn't want to listen to anything Buster had to say. He could apologize to her when he'd sobered up.

"Steph!" he called out again, and she continued walking. He needed to take the hint.

The pounding footsteps behind her caused her to spin around. "Leave me alone, Buster. I've had enough of you tonight."

He stopped in front of her, slightly out of breath. "I was completely out of line. I'm so sorry. You're the last person I'd ever want to hurt."

Steph stared at him. "I understand you're hurting, Buster. I imagine you've had a horrible week, but there's no excuse for taking it out on anyone else."

Buster hung his head. "I truly am sorry, Steph. You're right. There is no excuse. I didn't want to come tonight but allowed Travis to talk me into it. I knew I'd be rotten company, and I also know from experience that drinking is the worst thing I can do when I feel like this. Next time I'll listen to my gut."

Steph couldn't help but smile. "I was thinking the same thing myself only a few minutes ago. That I should have listened to my gut."

Buster met her gaze. "You didn't want to come tonight?"

She shook her head. "No, I was talked into it too. I'm feeling very stressed and unsure of what I want to do at the moment, and a hot bath and evening of meditation would have suited me much better."

"Ryan would have been disappointed if you hadn't come."

Steph frowned. "I've got you to thank for that too. Now I have to tell him I don't want to go out with him on a date."

"Really?"

Steph couldn't help but notice the relief in Buster's eyes. Her heart flipped when she saw it. Was he happy she wasn't going out with Ryan? But where did that leave them? Neither of them was relationship ready. Perhaps that was

Buster's appeal—not being in a position to date allowed her to look but not touch, which was a much safer place for her too.

"Let's walk." Buster shivered. "It's freezing."

Steph fell into step beside him. "In answer to your question, yes, really. I'm not good relationship material right now and would hate to lose Ryan's friendship. He's a good friend, a really good one. I don't want him getting the wrong idea."

"You should tell him," Buster said. "Let the poor guy down."

Steph almost laughed at the smile she heard in Buster's voice. Instead, she sucked in a breath and shivered. It *was* freezing.

"Here," Buster said, moving as if to take off his jacket.

"Don't be crazy," Steph said. "You'll freeze to death. I'll be fine; we might just need to walk a bit faster."

"Or," Buster said, putting an arm around Steph and pulling him into her, "we could keep each other warm."

Warm tingles spread throughout Steph's body as she felt Buster's sturdy frame against hers. Her heart rate quickened, and she did her best to keep her breathing calm.

"I did go to the prison on Holly's birthday," Buster said. "It was tough and why I've been in a strange mood."

Steph nodded. "I lit a candle. Seven actually. Hopefully Holly is fussed over in heaven."

"Spoiled rotten, I hope."

They fell into a comfortable silence for a little while before Buster spoke again. "I told Eve I thought she should pursue the appeal. That she didn't belong in prison."

"That was very big of you."

"It's how I feel. She's being punished daily with her memories and regret. The postpartum depression put her on the path that ended in disaster. It's very cruel, and I don't want to be the one to inflict any more hurt on her."

Steph found herself wrapping her arm around Buster's back. She squeezed him gently, letting him know that his words touched her.

"Do you think we should turn back?" Buster said. "It will be warmer at Traders than it is here."

"I don't want to go back there," Steph said. "Not tonight."

Buster nodded. "I'm a bit stuck because Jodi's driving, and they're not leaving until eleven."

"Why don't you come back to my place? I'll make us some tea, and we can sit out on the back. I have patio heaters, and we can get the fire going."

"I'd love to," Buster said. "But only if it's not too much trouble."

Steph laughed. "Definitely not too much trouble. The cold air seems to have sobered you up a lot already, and the tea will help too. Why don't you message Jodi or Travis and get them to pick you up from my place? Save you having to walk back to Traders."

Buster slipped his phone from his pocket and sent the text. His phone chimed seconds later with a message. "See you at eleven," he read out to Steph. "That's not too late for you?"

"Considering I'm likely to be awake half the night, it isn't. Now come on, let's go. I'm freezing and would love some tea. Zane baked some bread today, so we can throw together some sandwiches."

She smiled as Buster pulled her close once again, and they set off companionably for her place.

Buster closed his eyes and inhaled a delicious aroma of sandalwood and something else. Lilies? He opened his eyes and sought out Steph's. "Your home is so nice. I can see why Matt wants you to be the leading designer of the retreat."

"I'm not sure about the leading designer, but I do have some ideas," Steph added a teapot and two mugs to a tray. She'd cut thick slices of bread from Zane's loaf, lavished them with butter, and added them to a plate. "You bring the bread, and I'll bring this," Steph said, nodding at the tea tray. "The patio heater should be warm by now, and the fire's built, so we should be able to just put a match to it."

Buster followed Steph out of the back door into a garden oasis. He placed the bread on a small table where Steph had put the tea tray down.

She picked up a box of matches and passed them to Buster. "Can you light the fire? I'll pour the tea."

Buster struck a match, and within a few seconds, he had the fire lit.

"I built it up earlier," Steph explained, passing Buster a teacup. "When I can't sleep, I'll often come out here in the middle of the night and stargaze. It's not as appealing if I have to build the whole fire first. Knowing I just have to throw a match on it gets me out here most nights, even though it's freezing."

"You're up in the middle of the night, most nights?"

Steph nursed her teacup and shrugged. "It varies. I seem to go through stages. When things are particularly stressful, I seem to sleep for a few hours, and then I'm wide awake. My mind is racing so fast there's no way I'll get back to sleep."

"Was it like that before Holly died?"

Steph fell silent.

"Steph?"

She shook her head. "No, it's been since then. Nothing's been quite right since the accident. But it's not always because of Holly that I don't sleep. Sometimes she's not in my dreams at all. I know at the moment I'm particularly stressed. There's just so much change happening, and it only really occurred to me tonight that I didn't ask for any of this. Bodhi leaving so quickly and selling to Matt set off a chain of events that makes sense on paper, but I'm not sure if they make sense in here." She tapped her chest. "Margie called me a technophobe the other day, which is pretty accurate. It's not that I'm scared of computers and technology; I've just never had any desire to use them. I like living a simpler life. I don't want to be involved with social media and know what people are doing all the time. I'd rather chat with those I'm interested in to find out. Suddenly Matt's sending me phones and computers and telling me to get up to speed."

Buster nodded. "I kind of understand where he's coming from."

"So do I," Steph said. "And so far, I've been whisked along by the excitement of everything. But today, I realized the one thing I love about my life is disappearing."

Buster waited for Steph to explain.

"I like having very little responsibility. Teaching a class means I'm responsible for sixty or ninety minutes of someone's life. I can manage that. Scheduling classes, enrolling clients, developing the retreat—that requires someone responsible. Someone who can be counted on, trusted, and won't let anyone down."

Buster stared at Steph. The conversation was taking a turn he hadn't expected. Her words mirrored the thoughts that had been building within him since Holly's death and even more so since seeing Eve. He cleared his throat. "Before the accident, did you have plans, or were you happy teaching?"

Steph sipped her tea. "I was planning to travel. I wanted to go to India and Southeast Asia. Practice and hopefully teach yoga. I was hoping the experiences I had would give me enough confidence to open a studio of my own when I returned."

"Really?"

Steph nodded.

"That sounds like something someone looking to take on responsibility would do."

"I didn't worry about things then. I believed life unfolds the way it is supposed to, and you can't control it. I still believe that, kind of. But now, after what's happened, I can't explain it, but I'm not as carefree as I was." Her eyes took on a faraway look. "If I'm more cautious, I should be able to prevent horrible things from happening. I hope, anyway."

Buster put his teacup down and took her hand in his. "Steph, the accident changed you. It changed both of us. But I think your original line of thinking is the truest: that life unfolds as it is supposed to. There's one good thing that I'm realizing has come from all of this."

"What?"

"There's part of me fighting this every step of the way. I shouldn't be allowed to be happy, and I'd never want to let you down. But there's something bigger at play than what I'm telling myself." He searched her eyes. It wasn't just him feeling this, was it? Her eyes reflected his hope, excitement, and desire. She felt it too, he was sure of it. "I have no idea what this all means, or whether there's any chance for us to be happy, but the only time I'm happy lately is when I'm around you or when I'm thinking about you."

He reached out his hand and brushed a stray tear that was rolling down her cheek. "I think you feel the same and are as scared and unsure as I am. Is that true?"

Steph nodded.

He smiled. Cupping her chin in his hands, he kissed her lightly on the lips.

9

_A_fter teaching her morning classes, Steph made her way from Heat Wave to the Sandstone Cafe. She'd arranged to meet Matt there before he returned to the city, and she also needed to speak to Ryan. Only hours after agreeing to go on a date with him to Periwinkle, she'd found herself kissing another man.

She hugged a secret smile to herself as she thought of Buster. The kiss they'd shared had been gentle, delicious, and full of promises to come. They'd spent the remainder of the evening huddled together, talking and laughing. She hadn't felt so happy in months and was disappointed when Travis and Jodi arrived to pick up Buster. He hadn't kissed her again but had hugged her and promised he'd call her this morning. She stopped walking. What if he'd had second thoughts? It was entirely possible. He'd drunk too much the previous night, although by the time they were sitting around her fire, he seemed to have sobered up.

Her phone chimed with a message as doubt crept over her. She pulled it from her pocket and saw Buster's name.

Last night was so special. Can I see you later today or tomorrow? x

Steph smiled, the doubts immediately falling away. Her worry that he was regretting their evening was unfounded. She sent back a message.

I'm teaching afternoon classes today. How about tomorrow? I'm free after my 9 am class, so from 11. x

Aren't you hiking tomorrow? Buster responded immediately.

Not anymore. How about a picnic at Spicer's Peak? Steph sent the text, hoping it would suit Buster. Spicer's Peak was a beautiful spot only a short walk from Hope's Ridge. They could get there without the need to drive anywhere, which suited her as long as he didn't mind coming all the way back to Hope's Ridge again.

Perfect. I'll be at your house at 11 and will be thinking of you today. x

Steph's smile widened as she put the phone back in her pocket. She'd be thinking of him too. After Buster left the previous night, she'd made herself a promise. To try to live in the moment. To not stress and not overthink. Life would unfold as it was supposed to; she had to trust her judgment on that.

"You look happy," Margie commented as Steph entered the cafe. "A lot happier than you looked last night." She raised an eyebrow. "Any reason for this change?"

Steph shrugged noncommittally. "I just taught two classes. I must have absorbed the positive energy in the room."

"Or," Ryan stepped out from the kitchen area into the service area, "you're excited to see me."

Steph smiled. She hoped he wasn't going to be too upset when she told him how she felt. "I'm always happy to see you, Ryan, and I was hoping to talk to you."

Ryan raised an eyebrow. "That sounds ominous. Can it wait until tomorrow?"

Steph shook her head. "No, it's about tomorrow. I need to cancel."

"That's okay. We can do it another time."

Steph looked from Ryan to Margie and back again. Margie didn't need it spelled out for her and slipped away under the pretense of offering table service to a small group of customers.

"Or not do it another time," Ryan added.

"I'd love to go hiking with you another time," Steph said, "but as friends, not as a date. I've always thought of you as a friend, more like a brother than someone I'd date. I'd hate to ruin our friendship by trying to turn it into something else."

Ryan nodded. "I had a feeling you were going to say that. It's Buster, isn't it?"

"Not exactly. I'd say the same thing regardless of having feelings for Buster. I want us to be friends, Ryan, good friends, but without expectations of anything else."

Ryan sighed. "You have no idea how many times I've heard that line. That I'm *more like a brother than someone I'd date*."

"I am sorry."

"No, don't apologize. I'd rather you tell me now than string me along." He leaned forward and hugged her. "All I can say is Buster is one lucky man."

Heat flooded Steph's cheeks. "I hope we'll still be great friends."

"Of course we will," Ryan said. "Although I might have to glare at Buster the next time I see him."

"What's Buster done?"

Steph turned to find Matt approaching the service area.

"Nothing," Ryan said. "We were just joking around. Now, I take it you two have a meeting. What can I get you?"

Steph ordered tea and a bliss ball and Matt asked for coffee and a slice of lemon cake. They chose a table by the window looking out to the lake and sat across from each other.

"I'm sorry about how everything turned out, Steph," Matt said. "It's been manic. I was thinking this morning that there is no rush to do anything with Heat Wave. If you're okay with keeping the studio running, we can discuss the development when I'm not quite so frantic. It would give you a chance to get used to running the studio first."

Steph felt a massive weight lift from her shoulders.

Matt laughed. "You look relieved."

She nodded. "It only really registered with me what was happening yesterday. Bodhi leaving and selling you the property, and then us talking about being business partners is all such a massive change. Being a partner in Heat Wave is something I have considered but never really seriously. I had always planned to travel, see what's out there beyond Hope's Ridge before settling down. Don't get me wrong, I was planning to have my own studio, just not like this."

"You know, it's funny," Matt said. "If we were having this discussion a week ago, I'd be telling you that you're crazy. How often does an opportunity like this land in your lap." He smiled. "I would have been one of two things: either very convincing or, more likely, exceedingly arrogant."

Steph smiled. "You know yourself well."

Matt rolled his eyes and laughed again. "This week has been eye-opening for me. The reality that I could have lost my dad, and still could, has brought a lot of things into perspective for me. The first being I need to slow down. I need to start living in the now a bit more than constantly rushing to make the future happen."

"I imagine in your line of work you do need to do that too."

"Yeah, but not to the extent I have been. Anyway, it's

early days with my dad, and depending on how he shapes up, it's likely I'll be taking over a number of his projects."

"That hardly sounds like you'll be living in the moment. You'll be even busier now."

"Possibly, unless I can learn to let go of controlling everything and employ some good people to take over some of the jobs I normally do. Once again, early days. I haven't worked out what I'll be doing yet but did want to say that I'm fine with slowing down the retreat. It's busy enough with construction starting next door. The only way I can see the retreat moving forward would be having you drive it. If you're not sure that's what you want, let's put it on hold. The business is profitable as it is, and the land is probably worth a fortune. Bodhi had to sell it quickly, and I was happy to pay his asking price, but with the right time and planning, a backup plan would be to subdivide it and split it into lots. I can recoup my investment and more doing that without outlaying too much time or energy."

"Was that your plan all along?" Steph couldn't help but ask the question. A quick profit seemed much more likely than Matt developing a wellness retreat.

He frowned. "No, it wasn't, and it's still my second choice." He studied her face for a minute. "Should I assume you're now considering that I've ripped off Bodhi and plan to make a quick profit and sell it?"

"I hope not, but it's not entirely out of the realm of possibilities."

Matt sighed. "No, I guess if you look at my track record, it's not. I give you my word, Steph. I bought Heat Wave with the idea of creating an amazing wellness retreat. It's what I'd still like to do, but I need a partner. Someone passionate about the project and willing to drive it. If that's you, fantastic. If it's not, then I'll see if I can find someone to fit the role. If that doesn't work, I'll give thought to my backup plan." He glanced at his watch. "I'd better get going. I've got a long drive and a few things to do before I leave."

"Just to clarify," Steph said. "For now, we run the studio as usual and nothing else."

Matt nodded. "And if you decide you want to partner up, we sign the agreement, and you take the lead on the retreat project. You'd work closely with Buster and his construction team to transform what we already have. I'd suggest you get Charlie up to have a look at the cottages too. His architectural design experience is phenomenal. I think a combination of your ideas and his skill would deliver an amazing result."

"I'll give it some more thought," Steph said. "But I do appreciate you slowing things down, Matt. I realize that change and I aren't the best combination, but if I take things slowly, I tend to embrace it easier."

"We'll work at your speed then. Like I said, if you suddenly decide you want to take the leap and do it, then call me and we'll work out the details. If not, we'll review the whole situation in a month or so. Check that you're okay with running the studio, and if you're not, get someone else in so you can go back to teaching as you did with Bodhi."

"So, I could go back to my life exactly as it was?"

Matt stood. "If staying in your comfort zone is what works for you, Steph, then of course you can. As I said, you let me know. I'd better get going. I'll chat with you in the next few days and make sure the studio's all good. If you need anything in the interim, just call me, okay?"

Steph stood and hugged Matt. "Thank you. This meeting has gone so much better than I expected. Give your dad my love, okay?"

Matt laughed. "He'll probably have another heart attack if I tell him someone from Hope's Ridge sent their love. But I will, thanks."

Steph sat back down, sipping her tea while Matt went to talk to Margie and Ryan before leaving. She'd organized a date with Buster, let Ryan down with no hard feelings on either side, and now Matt had given her the breathing space she needed for her work. It was shaping up to be a good day. A very good day.

Buster changed his shirt three times before settling on a simple navy tee. Steph wasn't flashy, and they weren't going anywhere fancy. Jeans and a tee would be perfect. He wasn't sure why he was getting so concerned over a shirt. It was cold outside, and he'd need a fleece pullover and possibly a jacket too. She probably wouldn't even see the tee. He gave himself a mental shake. Where was all of this coming from? T-shirt talk? Really?

His phone rang as he was about to leave the house. He contemplated not answering it, but in checking the screen he saw it was Eve's mom.

"Cora, is everything okay?"

"Henry, love, it is okay, thanks to you. I wanted to let you know how much I appreciate what you've done for Eve."

"I've hardly done anything."

"Oh, but you have. She's agreed to pursue the appeal, which is the first good thing."

Buster smiled. "That's great. I don't think prison is where she needs to be."

"But you've done so much more than just that, Henry. You've given her hope. For the first time since…" she hesitated, still unable to comfortably talk about anything Holly related, "…since we lost our little love."

Buster took a deep breath. "That's wonderful news. I feel

like I have a lot of making up to do to Eve, so I'm glad she's feeling more positive."

"Oh, she is, love, she is. That you are so forgiving is beyond her wildest dreams." She gave a throaty chuckle. "I think she's mentally redecorating the house as we speak."

"The house?"

"Oops. I've probably spoken prematurely, but the fact that you're considering having her move back in with you is just amazing, Henry. Absolutely amazing."

Dread settled in the pit of Buster's stomach. "I haven't agreed to that. As much as I don't want to let Eve down, I'm not sure it's best for either of us."

"Of course it is. You two were like peas in a pod before Holly was born. You can get that back again, I'm sure."

Buster didn't respond. He already knew where his heart lay, and it wasn't with Eve.

"Don't worry, love. I know you'll do the right thing. You said when we last spoke how badly you thought you'd let Eve down. Well, here's your chance to make that up to her. I know you wouldn't dream of breaking her heart twice."

Buster's stomach churned when the call ended. How, in two visits, had Eve escalated the situation so quickly? He had no idea how long he sat in stunned silence, but when he finally jolted out of it, the clock said it was almost eleven. He cursed under his breath. Now, not only had Cora's call put a dampener on his day, but he was going to be half an hour late getting to Steph's. He sent her a quick text message, hoping she used the new phone, before rushing to his pickup.

Cora's words played over and over in his mind as he pulled out of the driveway. Her words had extinguished his previous excitement. Eve was getting through her days thinking there was the possibility of a reconciliation between them. He turned onto the county highway, his foot hitting the gas harder than was needed. He hated, but had to remind himself, that he'd been a key component in Eve's journey of destruction. If he turned around now and said they had no future, how would she react? Would it send her spiraling into despair? The one thing he knew for sure was he couldn't live with himself if he let her down in such an extreme fashion for a second time. An image of Steph popped into his head as he had the thought. He slammed his hand onto the steering wheel, wincing as it connected. Why, when he'd been given a short reprieve from the misery his life had become, did things have to get so complicated?

Steph smiled at the message that appeared on her phone. Buster was running late, which was fine. It gave her a little more time to put the finishing touches on the picnic lunch she'd made for them to take up to Spicer's Peak. It was a short but steep climb up to the peak and provided beautiful views of the valley that stretched out from Hope's Ridge. Knowing Buster's aversion to Lake Hopeful, they would have their choice of plenty of picnic spots that kept the lake from view. While most people sought out views of the lake, today they'd do exactly the opposite.

Steph had two backpacks full of food, water, and a blanket packed and sitting by the front door when Buster's pickup pulled up out front. She smiled as she heard his door slam and footsteps hurrying up the path.

"Hey, Buster," Zane's voice rang out from the garage. He had the door open and was spending the morning putting the finishing touches on one of his carvings.

"Hey," Buster called. "Can't stop. I'm already running late. Steph will probably kill me."

Steph met Buster at the front door with a raised eyebrow.

"Kill you?"

Buster grinned. "I'm so sorry. I got a call just as I was leaving the house. It delayed me. I shouldn't have answered it."

"Of course you should. It's no big deal. I appreciate you texting me. That phone's turning out to be more useful than I ever imagined." She scooped up the backpacks and handed one to Buster. "Ready?"

"Not quite." Buster leaned in and brushed his lips across Steph's before pulling back. "I've been thinking constantly about doing that again since last night."

Steph smiled, her cheeks hot. She'd been thinking about it too. She couldn't help but notice a flash of something cross Buster's face after he pulled away. It was quickly replaced with a smile.

He took her hand. "Now, I assume we're walking?"

"Definitely. Hope you've got your trekking legs on. I thought we'd do our best to avoid the lake today," she added.

Buster nodded. "Thanks. Although I'm spending so much time in town lately that I'm getting used to seeing it more regularly. It is beautiful. I just need to get past what happened."

Steph squeezed his hand. "You're not expected to get past it."

"Maybe not past it," Buster said. "But more willing to live with it and enjoy its beauty. At least Holly's journey to the next part of life happened somewhere stunningly beautiful. Hopefully some of that went with her."

They continued walking, and Buster's grip on Steph's hand was warm and comforting. Butterflies flitted in her stomach from time to time. It was hard to believe she was feeling this close to someone. When Dylan had ended their relationship, she couldn't imagine letting herself feel the emotions she currently felt. Although she did have to remind herself, it wasn't a case of letting herself feel this way. It was just happening. She was letting herself experience and enjoy it, and that was the one thing she did have control over. Steph dropped Buster's hand when they reached the narrow entrance to the trail that wound its way up the hillside to Spicer's Peak.

"I've never been up here," Buster said.

"Really? I often come up here to meditate." Steph blushed as the words left her lips. She usually kept her meditation and spiritual activities to herself.

"I haven't done much meditation," Buster said. "Maybe you could teach me? It might help to calm my mind a bit."

"It does," Steph gave a small laugh. "It's just the rest of the time when you can't meditate that it's hard to keep those thoughts quiet."

Steph led them up the steep track, not stopping at any stage. She was aware of Buster's labored breathing as the incline increased, but she didn't slow. She was enjoying putting him to the test. Testing his fitness, but also testing whether he'd admit he needed to slow down. She wasn't sure why she was testing him, but she was.

"Steph!"

There were still at least another ten minutes of the climb left when Buster called out. She stopped and turned. He was bent double, his breathing even more labored. He looked up at her. "Can you possibly slow down?"

Steph smiled. "Of course. You should have said something."

Buster shook his head, doing his best to catch his breath. Steph took off her backpack and took out two water bottles, handing him one. Buster took a sip. "Thanks." He laughed. "Are you really this fit, or are you testing me?"

Steph shrugged.

"I could have told you right off the bat that I'm not as fit as you. I spend most of my week behind a desk or in the truck visiting clients. Other than the occasional run, I'm really out of condition."

"I wasn't testing your fitness," Steph admitted. "I wanted to see if you'd keep going and try to be a macho man or whether you'd speak up."

Buster's eyes twinkled. "So by failing the fitness test, I passed the Steph test?"

"Exactly." Steph realized it was what she was doing. She didn't want to be with someone who'd do things just to please her. "I guess I want to start off knowing that if something's bothering you, you'll tell me. I don't want secrets or pretense in a relationship. Sure, sometimes I won't like what you have to tell me, but I'd rather hear it and know what I'm dealing with than find out later."

Heat flushed through Steph's body as she realized Buster was staring at her strangely. It was their first real date, and she was laying down rules like a crazy person. She slipped the backpack back onto her shoulders. "Sorry, this is probably too intense for our first date."

Buster shook his head. "No, not at all. I agree. I hate having to guess how someone's feeling or whether I should be doing something a different way. Let's agree to be up-front with our issues and speak up when we need to."

"Deal. Now, why don't you set the pace for the rest of the hike," Steph said. "I'll yell out if I'm struggling."

Buster rolled his eyes. "Yeah, like that's going to happen."

Buster spread the picnic blanket out. "Wow, this view is stunning. I'm so glad you brought me up here."

Steph sat down on the blanket. "It sure is, and I'm glad you came. It's one of my favorite places."

Buster's heart thudded as he sat down next to Steph. That she'd shared one of her favorite places with him was pretty special.

"Do you have a favorite place?"

"I used to," Buster said. "But a lot of my favorite places were tied up with Holly and things she loved or we'd done together. Most of those places I avoid now. It's too painful to go to any of them."

Steph squeezed his arm. "I might be completely out of line saying this, but you seem to have relaxed a bit in the last couple of weeks. Zane mentioned it too. I wondered if it was the visits to Eve. That you've let go of some of your anger."

Buster felt his back stiffen at the mention of Eve. He was doing his best to push Cora's phone call from his mind to allow him to enjoy the day. It certainly wasn't something he could share with Steph. Not until he'd worked out how he was going to deal with the situation. "Possibly," he said in response.

"I'm glad for you. Having all of that inside you, churning around, making you miserable just isn't healthy. It's not just you either; I imagine Eve and her mother and family are incredibly grateful."

Grateful for what? That he'd let her down after Holly's birth and had now provided her with false hope? Was it false hope? He wouldn't be able to live with himself if he said no to trying again, and then she did something drastic. His conscience couldn't handle another death.

Steph fell silent next to him.

He turned and met her gaze. "Let's talk about something else. I want our relationship to be one where we're looking forward, not always rehashing the past."

Steph nodded. "The past does shape us, though."

"I'm not saying we forget about anything." He gave a wry laugh. "It's not likely either of us could anyway, I'm just saying let's try not to get too caught up in it. Let's talk about something more interesting."

"Like?"

"Like you and Heat Wave. Have you given more thought to the development?"

Buster was surprised to hear that Steph was having second thoughts about the development.

"Not second thoughts exactly," she clarified. "It's just that it all happened far too quickly. With Matt away, it's good timing to slow things down and make sure it's what I want to do."

"How does Matt feel about that?"

"Surprisingly, he's cool with it. He's got a lot happening on top of his father's issues and suggested I just run the business for the moment and work out what I want my involvement to be. I couldn't have asked him for a better response to be honest."

"Very un-Matt like."

"I'm wondering if I should be worried by that," Steph said. "But I don't see how I can lose. He's paying me well to keep the business running. I've got two people coming to meet with me this week who are teachers and might take on some of the classes. If they do, I can get the schedule running at full capacity again, possibly even add a few extra classes since one of the potential teachers is an expert in barre."

She laughed, making Buster aware that his expression must have given away his complete ignorance of what barre was.

"Barre is a different kind of workout than traditional yoga. It combines ballet moves with Pilates and yoga. It would be good to be able to offer it, but I'm not trained to teach it. Anyway, it could bring something new to the studio if the person I'm interviewing is any good."

"I don't picture Matt being the owner of a yoga studio," Buster said. "Don't get me wrong, it's a great business, but it doesn't sit in the high-profit type of ventures he normally does. The retreat, of course, would fit his portfolio better."

"He admitted everything happened quicker with Bodhi than he anticipated," Steph said. "His backup plan, if we don't go ahead with the retreat, would be to create a subdivision with the land and sell it off."

Buster gave a low whistle. "I'm pretty sure Bodhi wouldn't have sold the land if he'd know that was the plan."

"He didn't have a choice with regards to selling," Steph said.

"No, but he didn't have to sell it to Matt. He didn't even put it on the market. I think it would be a real shame if that ends up happening."

Steph nodded in agreement. "It would be, but I'm not going to let that side of it shape my decision. I need to do what's right for me. If I base my decision on what's in the best interest of others, I'm likely to end up feeling resentful later on."

Steph's words played over in Buster's mind as he drove back to Drayson's Landing later that afternoon. He'd had a great time with Steph but was beginning to think he was jumping into something before he was ready. She was so smart and knew her mind. She'd made it very clear that honesty was essential to her, and he'd been the one to say that they should agree to be up-front with their issues and speak up when they needed to. He saw from her reaction that she'd loved that he'd said that. That he was committing to being honest. And yet he hadn't mentioned anything about the call from Cora or Eve's hope for reconciliation. It was hardly a good start.

10

———

*S*teph plucked a blueberry from the muffin Asha sat in front of her and popped it in her mouth. She'd come to speak to her sister to get advice after her date the previous day with Buster.

They sat opposite each other at one of the tables Asha had carefully positioned next to the food truck to make the most of the lake view. The sun was pushing the clouds away, and while it was chilly, it had the promise of a beautiful winter's day.

"I'm so happy for you, Steph," Asha said. "Buster's such a nice guy."

Steph nodded, picking at another blueberry.

"But?"

Steph met her sister's penetrating stare. "You know me far too well."

"I do, and I also know that it doesn't matter how perfect Buster is, you're going to have reservations. You're probably going to tell yourself that you don't deserve happiness because of what happened and that you aren't ready to give yourself to someone again after the way Dylan treated you. Am I right?"

Steph laughed. "No, but they are good points. I'd better add them to my list." She wasn't being entirely truthful. Both had crossed her mind. She had already decided she needed to push past the idea that she didn't deserve to enjoy her life because she couldn't help Holly. She was sure Buster's daughter would want to see her father happy, and if she was the one to help with that happiness, then that was a bonus.

"Okay, so what is it then?"

"A feeling."

Asha rolled her eyes. "Here we go. Some deep dark yogi feeling that's going to make you throw away something before you even allow it to start."

Steph's mouth dropped open. "I don't do that. And anyway, my feeling is based on how the day turned out yesterday. Regardless of whether or not I can overcome my issues about relationships and what I do or don't deserve, I don't think Buster's ready."

"Oh."

"Yes, oh."

"Because of his past?"

Steph nodded. "We were having a really nice time yesterday, and I mentioned his visits to the prison and how he seemed more relaxed since he'd been. That maybe forgiving Eve has helped him to release a lot of the anger he was feeling. It was just an observation. He practically froze when I mentioned her. He went from being happy and chatty to speaking in monosyllables. I get that it might be difficult, but he's still so damaged."

"Everyone's got baggage," Asha said. "It just depends on whether you're up for helping him with his."

"That's the problem," Steph said. "We still had a nice day, but a wall went up. One that I knew he didn't want me to cross again." She sighed. "I like him, Ash. I do. But I haven't even figured myself out since the accident. In the sessions I had with Dan, he suggested I need a change of scenery. That I get away from Hope's Ridge and all reminders of the accident. To try to have a fresh start beyond Hope's Ridge and start enjoying life again. I don't think dating the father of the child who was killed was part of that suggestion."

Asha reached across the table and squeezed Steph's arm. "You're the only person who can decide what you think is best for you, Steph. You've got a lot going on at the moment. You've only just started seeing Buster. It's too early to be making any decisions about it."

"I know. I'm jumping way ahead of myself. I guess I suddenly feel like things are crashing down on me. First Heat Wave, now a possible relationship." She gave a wry grin. "I do a lot better when the only decision I have to make is which tea to drink at three a.m."

"Imagine this scenario before the accident," Asha said. "What would you have done if Bodhi had offered you the business then. Or Matt had offered you the same deal. Do you think you would have taken it on?"

"I'm not sure. I was seriously considering traveling. Dylan and I had talked about going to India and parts of Southeast Asia."

"Do you still want to do that now?"

Steph shook her head. "I honestly don't know what I want. I've been so busy just getting through each day up until recently. I haven't been planning ahead."

"Then maybe you should consider reverting to that strategy. Just taking each day as it comes. You've rammed into me for as long as I can remember that I need to be patient, and that I can't control how things are going to unfold. I think maybe you should be taking your own advice."

Steph pretended to pout. "It's so much easier dishing out advice, Ash. You should know that."

Their laughter was interrupted by the arrival of the construction crew at the worksite across the road. Charlie was out front, gesturing with his hands to the driver of a crane.

"I seem to be the only one stuck in the same place," Steph said. "Matt's constantly developing things, you're moving ahead with the Irresistables expansion, Jenna's engaged and will soon be married. Even Charlie, at ninety-six, has embraced a new project. I'm thirty-two and need to work out how to be an adult."

"I think you've worked it out, Steph, but now you need to let it unfold. Don't rush to make decisions or judgments just yet. You need more data. You might have hit a nerve with Buster about his ex. As you get to know him more, you'll learn more about which topics are best to avoid. And to be honest, anything to do with exes is usually a good starting point for avoidance."

———

Buster considered calling in sick on Monday morning. He pulled a pillow over his face when his alarm sounded and groaned. He'd arrived back from his date with Steph feeling considerably less excited than he had before going. He'd loved spending time with her, but there'd been a shift in the energy between them. It was his fault. He knew that. He was rattled before he'd even arrived. He wondered if he'd told Steph about Cora's call how she would have reacted.

He sighed. He probably should have told her. Maybe he still should. He needed advice on what to do, but would she be the best person to ask? *Definitely not.* Jodi's voice was in his head, and he smiled. She was so protective of Buster, which was lovely and could work in his favor today.

He pulled himself out of bed and headed to the shower. He would go to work, and he'd speak to Jodi. He was pretty sure her advice would be better than anything he was currently telling himself.

Jodi's face fell the moment Buster explained the call from Cora and how he'd inadvertently raised Eve's hopes.

"I didn't realize she was so interested in getting back together," Buster said. "I probably would have given more thought to what I said if I'd realized. I don't want to hurt her again."

"I visited her yesterday, Buster. From what I gathered, she's hopeful but not unrealistic. She knows it would be a huge ask to take her back after what's happened."

"I don't think that's the whole problem," Buster said. "Yes, we had a good marriage before Holly was born, but there were cracks in it even back then. On top of that, we've both changed since her birth. Events, whether anyone is to blame or not, have shaped us and changed us. I don't know if I'd ever feel the same way about Eve. If I met the woman she is today, I probably wouldn't pursue anything."

"She's a different Eve, but deep down, I believe she's still your Eve."

Buster sighed. This conversation was not going how he wanted it to. He'd hoped Jodi would give him every reason he needed to walk into the prison and let Eve down gently. *Let her down.* That, unfortunately, was the recurring theme.

"Buster, in saying what I've said. I should also clarify that if you don't love Eve anymore, or if you don't think you can get back to a loving place, then it would be best to end it before it gets started again. Even if the appeal goes ahead, it will be a few months away at the earliest. Sitting in prison clinging on to the hope that you and she might reunite isn't healthy."

"I'm worried that she might not pursue the appeal if she knows I won't be here for her when she gets out. I don't want to be responsible for her slipping back into depression. Her mom made it pretty clear that she's changed considerably in attitude and outlook since I saw her."

"Do you have to make a decision right now? You've only visited her a couple of times after years of hating her."

"I don't know that I ever hated her," Buster said. "In the final stages of our marriage, I hated what she'd done to us, and once we were divorced, I hated what her negativity and drinking was doing to Holly. I guess I felt like I hated her when the accident happened."

"You don't have to explain to me. But is there any rush to make a decision? Can't you spend more time with her and see what happens?"

"I guess I don't want to lead her to believe there's a possibility if I don't feel it."

"Perhaps that's what you need to tell her. That it's too soon and you want to get to know her again before you'll consider anything more permanent." She raised an eyebrow. "You won't have to worry about her stalking you, at least."

Buster managed a small smile. "No, unless she's got good escape skills, that's not a problem." He wavered slightly.

"But?"

"But I had a date with Steph yesterday. And that is a problem."

Jodi's eyes widened. "You swore on the way home from Traders that you were just friends. That nothing was going on."

"I might have bent the truth slightly. I wasn't ready to tell you or Travis."

Jodi shook her head. "Oh, Buster. I don't know what to suggest. What a situation to be in. Does Steph know about Eve?"

"Only that I've visited her a couple of times. She encouraged me to go the first time."

"She's a levelheaded person. I think you should tell her. Possibly suggest the two of you put what you've got on hold until you've figured out the Eve situation. That way, you're not messing around with Steph, and you're not lying by omission either."

Buster nodded. "You're probably right. I think she'll be pretty unimpressed when I tell her."

"Unimpressed that Eve wants you back?"

"No, unimpressed that I didn't tell her already."

"It's only twenty-four hours, Buster. Definitely not long enough for her to get angry. But if you continue seeing her without telling her, I think that's when you'll find yourself in trouble."

As she pulled weeds from one of the garden beds in the backyard, Steph was amazed to think how fast the week had flown past. It had been a productive week. She was on top of the bookkeeping and scheduling that went with her new role at Heat Wave, and she was delighted to have found that both of the yoga instructors she'd interviewed would be perfect additions to the studio. They were a couple, Yani and Fiona, who were looking for a change from city life. Casual teaching suited them both perfectly. Steph had had them both teach a class during the week, which she attended to get a feel for their ability. They were both fantastic. Over cups of tea, they'd told her about their travels through India and Thailand. How much they'd learned from some of the worlds' leading yogis and, more importantly, how much deeper their spiritual beliefs now were. Steph was not only thrilled to have them working at the studio but excited at the prospect of chatting with people who shared the same passions as her.

Matt had touched base the previous day to check that Steph was still happy with the arrangement. Running the studio, teaching, and hiring new staff were big adjustments, and she was enjoying it.

The one dark cloud that had hung over her since their date on Sunday was Buster. She hadn't heard from him. She knew he'd been in town—he'd met with Asha and Charlie to present detailed drawings, and she'd also seen his pickup outside the Sandstone Cafe. She'd been on her way to chat with Margie after teaching a class but found herself making a hasty retreat and going home instead. It was silly. She didn't know why she was avoiding him. It was that gut feeling. It was there, and it was annoying. She almost laughed when she realized she was back in her old routine of trying to avoid Buster. For entirely different reasons, but she was still avoiding him.

The back door to the house opened, and Zane called out to her. "Steph, visitor."

Her heart rate increased. Had Buster turned up without calling first? She looked down at her dirt-covered shirt. She was a mess. She was about to ask Zane to tell him she'd meet him at the cafe in fifteen minutes when Matt stepped out of the house and into the backyard.

"Matt? What are you doing here?" It was a relief that it wasn't Buster, but she was still surprised.

"I'm back for the weekend and wanted to talk to you. I called you a few times this morning but didn't get an answer."

Steph's hand flew to her mouth. "Sorry, I think I left the

phone at Heat Wave after the last class. I'm still not used to remembering to check if I have it with me all the time."

"No drama." He nodded to the seating area that surrounded the fire pit. "Can we sit down and chat for a minute?"

"Sure, let me just wash up. Would you like a drink?"

"No, I'm fine."

Steph hurried inside, washed her hands and face, and was back sitting across from Matt in a matter of minutes. "Is everything okay?"

"Yes and no. I've had a lot of time to think this week." He gave a wry smile. "I'm used to running around all over the place, but being holed up helping Dad, when he's sleeping most of the day, gives me a lot of thinking and planning time. I've been looking into different opportunities too."

Steph continued listening, not sure where she came into all of this.

"I know last weekend I said not to worry about Heat Wave and that we could figure it out over the coming weeks or months, but something's come up, and I need to move my decision forward as to whether I develop it or sell it."

Steph's heart sank. She wasn't prepared to make a decision either way. "When do you need an answer by?"

Matt bit his lip. "I'm sorry, Steph, but I need an answer by Wednesday. I've had another opportunity arise, and if I'm going to commit to it, I'll need to sell the land that Heat Wave's sitting on."

"I thought you were going to subdivide first and make it profitable?"

"I won't have time. I'll need a quick sale. To be honest, I'll be happy to get what I paid for it. The opportunity at Tall Oaks is too good to pass up. I don't think the bank will loan me enough, so I'll need the additional money. I am sorry."

Steph sat silently for a few minutes, considering her

options. "What's your preference, Matt? Would you rather have the funds available for the Tall Oaks project or start on the retreat?"

"Honestly?"

Steph nodded. "There's no point in saying I want to develop the retreat if you want to move forward with the other investment."

"True." Matt sighed. "I see amazing potential in both. The Tall Oaks opportunity will turn around a nice profit in a short space of time, whereas the retreat is a long-term project and more of an altruistic one."

Steph almost snorted. How could a luxury resort, charging *luxury* fees, be altruistic?

"You look skeptical."

"I had assumed the retreat would target an exclusive market, that's all. Not affordable for the average person."

"Possibly." He looked like he was going to explain further but then changed his mind. "As you know, the retreat is a project I've had in the back of my mind for ages. It's the reason I snapped up the property the moment Bodhi mentioned it. But now I'm not sure it's the best timing."

"But if I say yes, you'll continue with it?"

Matt nodded. "You're pretty sensible, Steph. If you think it's the right timing for you, then I'll know it's the right timing for me too. If you say no, then I'll assume it's the universe telling me to move forward with the other opportunity."

"I'm amazed you'd involve me in your decision," Steph said honestly. Matt usually had a plan that he alone devised and followed.

"It's my new foreman," Matt said. "He's doing his best to change my way of thinking on a number of things."

"Who? Charlie?"

Matt nodded. "He seems to have decided he'd be a good

mentor for me. He's sharing all sorts of wisdom, and for the first time in my life, I seem to be listening."

"What does he think about the Tall Oaks opportunity?"

"Very sound investment, Matthew." Matt managed an almost perfect rendition of Charlie's voice.

Steph laughed. "Did he know you'd have to choose between here and Tall Oaks."

Matt bowed in the same manner Charlie often did. "Straightforward decision, Matthew. The retreat will help many people. Tall Oaks will line your back pocket. No brainer. Help others and your fortunes will increase in many different ways."

"And you're listening to him?"

"I'm beginning to think I should. He's been hugely successful, plus he's a well-liked, decent guy. My dad was nothing like him. As much as I admire Dad and what he's achieved, I also recognize that the town hates him, and he's very lonely. The heart attack has really highlighted to me how few friends he has. I don't want that to be my life down the road."

"It is sad."

Matt nodded. "What's the point of amassing fortunes to end up alone? It's not what I want. I'm nearly thirty, and I haven't had a serious relationship. I've dated, but I've never found someone I would want to share my life with. Sure, I've done well financially, but I'm beginning to realize that marriage and kids is something I do want."

Steph did her best not to look too surprised. "I would never have guessed that."

"I know. It's because I'm too busy racing after one opportunity and then the other. It doesn't give me time for relationships or anything else. My priorities are all wrong, and that needs to change. This whole situation with Dad has really made me stop and take a look at my life and think about what I want."

Steph was overwhelmed with everything Matt had shared with her. She couldn't see any loopholes in what he was asking that would prove him to be anything but genuine. "I'd like to think about it, if that's okay."

"Of course. If I haven't heard from you, I'll call you on Wednesday. There's no pressure either way, Steph. I mean it. Both options are good opportunities for me, so it's a win-win. I'm sure we can find you some space in town to set up a new studio if you decide you don't want to continue with Heat Wave. Don't let being employed sway your decision. If we develop Heat Wave into a retreat, it's a passion project. It's one we're both in love with, and that's why we do it. It'll show in every finishing touch. Whereas Tall Oaks will be a profit project." He laughed. "That's what I'm better known for, of course."

"The Sandstone Cafe's looking like a passion project. It's so lovely inside now."

"That's what I call a profitable passion project—the perfect kind. But the passion is mostly Ryan and Margie, not so much me. I'm passionate about it being profitable and providing a lovely place for the town residents. Still, I'm not thinking about it constantly and what I can do to improve it or bring in my business. As far as I'm concerned, that's Ryan's job. He has the artistic eye to make it something special. But with the retreat, I have a personal interest, so I would be more involved." His eyes clouded over for a moment. "Imagine the difference it would make to someone like my dad right now to check into a retreat. Well, maybe not right now, but when he's recovered. It's probably exactly what he needs. And I wish…" He shook his head. "Ignore me. I'm getting carried away."

Steph felt a rush of affection for the man sitting in front of her. She wished he had finished what he was going to say, but she decided not to push him. She also wished Asha, Zane, and the rest of the town could see this decent side of him. If she'd been asked three months earlier whether she would go into business with Matt Law, she would have rolled on the floor laughing. Yet now, she was seriously considering it.

Matt stood. "I'd better get going. I need to drop in on Ryan and then head to Drayson's Landing to meet with Travis and Buster. Lots to go through and discuss. Then back to the city and back to playing nurse." He rolled his eyes as he delivered the last comment, but Steph could see from his pale face that it wasn't a joking matter.

"Your dad should be incredibly proud of you, Matt. You're doing a very noble thing."

Matt shrugged. "No different from what anyone else would do. He's my dad. No matter what his reputation is, I love him, and I'll help him now while he needs my help. Although, if I hear one more complaint that my grilled cheese isn't stretchy enough, I'll have to employ a grilled cheese master to replace me."

Steph laughed as she walked Matt back through the house to his pickup. She hugged him before he got into his truck. "Thank you for being so kind. I know this is ultimately your decision, but involving me has given me a confidence boost."

Matt's forehead creased. "Really? You need a confidence boost? Steph, you're one of the most levelheaded and insightful people in Hope's Ridge. I know the last year or so has been hard on you, but you appear to be managing well, and before that, you always lived life on your own terms, nobody else's."

Steph found herself staring at Matt. "I think you're confusing me with someone else."

"No way. You're probably the only person in this town—well, maybe Charlie fits the bill too—that I've always been in awe of. You know how to be."

"To be?"

"Yes. I'm always rushing around trying to make money, trying to prove myself as important or successful. Then I come across you, and you're calm, happy, and at peace with yourself. Okay," he interrupted before she could object, "maybe not in quite the same way since the accident, but that's understandable. People come to your yoga classes to be inspired. You have a quality that's hard to explain. You ooze health and wisdom."

Steph had to blink back tears. She didn't realize Matt had even noticed her before.

"It's why I wouldn't hesitate to go into business with you. It will be a huge success on many different levels. In my eyes, the opportunity outweighs anything I could gain financially elsewhere."

Steph wiped her eyes on the back of her sleeve. "I think that's the nicest thing anyone's ever said to me."

Matt smiled. "Well, for as awful as I know I can be at times, just know I mean it. There are no hidden agendas or anything else. I'm completely honest with you. I'd love to be partners, but if that doesn't work, it's no problem at all. We'll still be friends, and that's more than enough for me."

Steph hugged herself as she watched Matt climb into his truck and pull away. She had many preconceived ideas about Matt Law, and he'd just crushed every single one of them.

Buster sat at the kitchen counter, staring at his phone. It was nearly a week since he and Steph had been on their date, and they hadn't spoken or messaged. Part of him had hoped she would contact him, but another part felt relief that she hadn't. He planned to visit Eve later that afternoon and knew he needed to get that out of the way before he saw Steph. As much as he hadn't rushed to contact her, he'd missed her during the week—a lot. He typed a message into his phone.

Sorry I haven't been in touch. I'd love to see you tomorrow. Are you free?

He pressed send before he had a chance to talk himself out of sending the message. Based on his lack of contact, he didn't expect an immediate answer. She'd probably make him sweat a bit before responding. He put the phone down, planning to change out of his running gear into something more appropriate for his visit to the prison. After realizing how out of condition he was on the walk to Spicer's Peak the previous weekend, he'd vowed to get into shape and had been running each morning. He doubted he'd be able to keep up with Steph, but given another opportunity, he wanted to at least try.

His phone chimed with a message. He picked it up, surprised she'd replied so quickly.

Yes, free from eleven. Lunch at the Sandstone Cafe?

He sent her a quick text back, suggesting they meet at twelve, and then he headed to the shower. He just hoped his meeting with Eve went okay, and he'd be in a positive frame of mind to see Steph.

After the long drive to Tall Oaks, a guard ushered Buster into the meeting room with several other visitors to the prison. If he turned back the clock to before Holly was born, he would have laughed if anyone suggested Eve would be sentenced to a prison term. It was unthinkable. Seeing her across the room in her white jumpsuit still seemed surreal.

Buster's heart thumped as he reached the table where his

ex-wife sat. He did his best to smile, noticing the nervous twitch in her cheek.

"It's just me, Eve. No need to look so scared."

Eve forced a smile. "I worry each time that you're not going to come, and if you do that you'll yell at me and say all of the horrible things I expected you to say the first visit."

"I'm not going to do that. I think you're an incredible woman, and like I've said before, I just wish circumstances had been different. Now, tell me about your week. What did you get up to?"

Buster listened as Eve told him a little about the work she did in the prison and the bookkeeping course she was taking. "I'm not sure anyone will employ a criminal when I get out, but I figure at least if I've increased my skill base, I might have more of a chance. I could even freelance with bookkeeping, so that would give me more options."

Before Holly's death, Eve had worked as an elementary school teacher. It was unlikely she'd be employed in a similar role again.

Buster nodded as she spoke with enthusiasm about the course. If he was honest, he was only half listening, waiting for the opportunity to interrupt and tell her how he was feeling. Finally, his opportunity came.

"I had a visit from Jodi last Sunday," Eve said. "It was so lovely of her to come all this way. She and Travis are good people, Henry, really good people."

Buster nodded. She was right; they were.

Red spots appeared on Eve's cheeks. "I mentioned how wonderful you've been and that I hoped there might be a chance of us reconciling."

The energy between them shifted as Eve seemed to hold her breath waiting for a response.

"I saw Jodi at work and she told me," Buster said. "It made me realize that I might have given you the wrong impression.

I'm so glad that we're getting along and can consider each other friends again, but I'm not sure if I'm ready for more than that."

"I wouldn't expect you to be," Eve said. "I know I'm not."

"Oh? I had the impression you thought we might get back together."

"Maybe down the road. I'd certainly be open to it, but it's not something I'd want right away." She pushed a loose hair off her face. "Mom's been getting into my head, which we both know she's a master at, trying to plan the future she wants to see."

"But you mentioned coming back to the house. Was that you or your mom talking?"

"Henry, it would be my wildest dream come true to turn back the clock and fix everything between us. I want that and wish it was realistic, but I'm not convinced it is. If you are willing to give us a chance and see if we could rekindle the feelings we had, that would be wonderful. But I'd need to take it slow, and I think you would too."

A massive weight lifted from Buster's shoulders. He couldn't help but laugh. "I've been stressing since I spoke to your mom that you might do something awful to yourself if I said I didn't want a relationship. I forgot how good she is at steering us toward what she wants to happen."

Eve smiled. "Yes, she does it out of love, but I do need to watch her. I also understand that you might not want a relationship with someone who's been in prison."

"No, I don't have a problem with that."

"Really? There aren't many men who would be okay with my situation. What do you have a problem with, then?"

"I think we've both changed a lot since we first got together, and I also have feelings for someone. It wasn't something I planned. It's new and kind of just happened."

Eve looked as if he'd slapped her. It was a quick look that flashed through her eyes but was replaced quickly with a forced smile. "That's great. Is she someone I know?"

Buster shifted uncomfortably in his chair. He didn't want to discuss Steph with Eve. It all felt too weird. "Kind of, but I don't want to talk about her right now. I think I've messed it up anyway."

The relief in Eve's eyes was evident at this admission.

"I'm not expecting anything from you, but it's making a huge difference to my state of mind that you're visiting and that I know you don't hate me."

Buster wished he could reach across the table and take Eve's hand. She looked so vulnerable.

"Whether you and I can work things out or you find happiness elsewhere, I'll be happy for you. I know you didn't mean to let me down the way you did, and I'm certain you wouldn't let it happen again with me or in a new relationship. I know that waiting around for me and trying again would be like going backward. It's probably easier for you to forget about me and move on."

"I'll never forget about you, Eve. I'm just not sure what I want right now. What I had planned to say was I'm not willing to make any kind of commitment to starting over."

Eve nodded. "I agree, and there's no rush. Let's follow Mom's advice and take things slowly. No pressure on either of us. We owe ourselves that I think."

Buster found himself nodding but was replaying her words in his head. Was she still suggesting they try again? He was confused.

Eve gave a little laugh. "I think my priority at the moment is getting released and nothing more than that. Nathan, my lawyer, visited yesterday."

The rest of their session was spent discussing Eve's

appeal and her lawyer's feelings about the approach she needed to take.

"Nathan mentioned that having you on my side could make a big difference in how the appeal is received. Is it okay if he contacts you?"

"Of course. I'll do whatever I can to help."

Eve smiled. "Thanks, Henry. Deep down, I know I can count on you *this* time."

11

———

Steph waved to Orla, the woman who helped out at Irresistables occasionally, as she parked her car outside the Sandstone Cafe.

"Don't let Asha see you buying coffee in there," Orla joked as she shut her car door and started across the road toward Irresistables.

Steph smiled. Once Asha had the seating area set up—with heating in place and more on her menu—she'd definitely get a group together for lunch, but right now, the warmth of the cafe was more appealing. She'd arrived a little early so she could see how Ryan and Margie were doing and hoped that having a conversation with them would rid her of the nerves she was feeling about catching up with Buster. It was ridiculous. A week ago, she'd been nervous with their first date looming, and now she was nervous because it felt like they'd broken up, even though they were never officially going out. The relationship had been fast-tracked in the space of a week.

Ryan was tucked away in a corner, an easel in front of him and paint pots scattered on a nearby table. She waved to

Margie, who was serving behind the counter, and wandered over to look at what he was painting.

"Wow." The word slipped from her lips the moment her eyes locked on the painting. It wasn't complete, but he'd captured the mist hovering over Lake Hopeful with the early morning sun poking over the ridge. "That's beautiful, Ryan. I thought you usually did more abstract pieces?"

Ryan smiled, his blue eyes creasing at the edges. "Thanks. I thought I'd make the most of a quiet Sunday and try something different. I used to do a lot of landscapes but haven't painted one in ages. I'm sorry to hear about Heat Wave, by the way. I know you were excited about running the business and the expansion plans."

Steph frowned. "Sorry? What do you mean?"

Alarm flashed in Ryan's eyes. "Matt came and saw you, didn't he? He said he had."

"Yes, we had a long chat on Friday."

"And you were fine with everything?"

"Definitely. And appreciative of how open he's been with me."

Ryan pretended to wipe his brow. "Phew, thought I'd put my foot in it for a moment. I had a few beers with him last night, and he was talking about the opportunity in Tall Oaks. You already know all this, I know, but he was telling me he's signing the contract tomorrow, and Heat Wave is part of the security for the purchase. He's sure he can sell it quickly so the security will convert to cash, which is both his and the buyer's preference. I think that's what he said, anyway." He grinned. "Possibly one or two beers too many to have the facts completely right. Have you had a chance to think about what you'll do, or has it all happened too quickly?"

Steph stared at Ryan. Why on earth would Matt have made up such an elaborate story if he was planning to sell the property? He could have just told her what he was doing, and she would have had to accept it.

"Are you alright, Steph? You look a little, I don't know, dazed."

Steph snapped back to attention. "I'm fine, and no, I haven't worked out my plans yet. As you said, it's only just happened. I think I'll still have a few more weeks running the studio before it changes hands. I might look for some space in town or do something completely different. A change is as good as a rest, as they say."

Ryan was still looking at her strangely when Buster walked through the front door of the cafe.

"I'll catch up with you later." Steph moved toward Buster. Her nerves of seeing him had vanished entirely. She was pretty sure she was in shock.

He took her arm and led her to a table by the window. "Are you okay? What happened?"

Steph shook her head. "Is it that obvious? I just heard something from Ryan that shocked me."

Buster looked across at Ryan, his mouth set in a hard line. "Do you want me to talk to him?"

Steph managed a smile. "No, it's nothing Ryan did. It's Matt." She went on to fill him in on Matt dropping in to see her on Friday and then what Ryan had disclosed. "I guess he's trying to play me." She shook her head. "I honestly can't believe it. He seemed so genuine on Friday and said some nice things."

Buster shook his head. "That's odd. He met with Travis and me to go over the projects we're doing for him, and he mentioned the Tall Oaks opportunity. He said it was dependent on Heat Wave, and you and he were discussing it further."

"Did he know we went out on a date?"

Buster nodded. "I did mention it."

"He probably knows that anything he tells you would come back to me. Whereas he didn't expect Ryan to say anything. If what Ryan's said is true, he really is a low life."

"I can't see any reason Ryan would make up a story like that," Buster said. "Unfortunately, Matt's reputation means I'd assume the information is true."

Steph sighed. "Me too. I guess it saves me having to make a decision. I've been going over and over it in my mind and hadn't been able to decide. That tells me something in itself. Funnily enough, I realized I would like to own and run Heat Wave. I love the idea of the retreat and expanding, but probably not initially. Until he came and spoke to me on Friday, the one thing that was holding me back was the thought of partnering with Matt. He'd been saying all the right things, but my gut was still undecided. But on Friday, the way he spoke removed all of my reservations. And now, hearing what he said to Ryan, I realize I shouldn't have changed my opinion or dismissed my instincts. I always say to listen to your gut." Steph's words faded as she realized what she'd just said. *Listen to your gut.* She'd told Asha only a few days earlier how her gut was telling her not to pursue anything with Buster.

"You could still set up a studio," Buster said. "I'd be happy to help you find some space in town and do any work that's required to get it up and running. I'm sure your clients would all follow you, so it would be an instant business."

Steph smiled. "Thanks, I appreciate the offer. I'll need to get my head around Matt and his lies and everything else first before I think about my next steps. Now, tell me, what's been happening with you? It feels like a lot longer than a week since I saw you."

Buster decided the easiest way to start the conversation with Steph was not to and instead order lunch. He wanted to put it off as long as possible. He could hardly keep his eyes off her. Even in her distress over the shock of what Matt had done, she was gorgeous. Her blonde hair was loose around her shoulders, her cheeks pink from the crisp air, and her eyes bright and radiant as usual. It was hard to believe someone could look so good so effortlessly. She didn't wear makeup, which he loved about her, dressed very casually, and most importantly, spoke from her heart. She didn't lace her words with other meanings.

His thoughts went back to the conversation with Eve. Her comments about him not meaning to let her down and Eve being sure he wouldn't let her down *this* time hadn't gone unnoticed. If she was trying to lay a guilt trip on him, she'd succeeded. But not in a way that would make him suddenly ask her to come back to him. It was the first sign he'd seen of the Eve he'd broken up with three years earlier. He'd been so busy beating himself up about not noticing her postpartum depression and not being there for her that he'd forgotten how nasty she could be. Manipulating situations and, when she didn't get her way, throwing comments at him that hit like poisonous darts. Sometimes subtle, other times with full force. They'd mostly had a good relationship before Holly's birth, but when this side of Eve appeared, Buster would generally do his best to keep out of her way.

After Holly's birth, it became who she was ninety percent of the time. An angry, bitter person who dealt with her frustrations through alcohol and other men. The subtle digs left her repertoire, and she communicated mainly via screaming and yelling. She made sure Buster knew about every man she cheated with. He hadn't understood that at the time. Wouldn't she want to hide her infidelity? It was his lawyer who, during the divorce, looked at him like he was an idiot. "She didn't hide it because she wanted you to know. She wanted to make you jealous. Get a reaction." Could she have honestly thought his reaction would be anything other than separation?

Margie arrived at their table with two steaming bowls of vegetable soup and a board with freshly baked sourdough bread.

"That smells delicious." Steph smiled at Margie. "Thank you."

Margie returned her smile. "I'm planning to come and try out a class this week, Steph. Any suggestions for which one?"

Buster could almost hear the cogs turning in Steph's mind. No doubt she was thinking something along the lines of *don't bother, we'll be closed*.

"I'm running a beginner's class on Tuesday night," Steph said. "It's introducing people to the hot room and most of the Bikram sequence. I'd start there if you're free. It's at six."

"Great, I'll see you then."

Buster waited until Margie retreated to the counter. "I wasn't sure what your response was going to be."

"Me either," Steph said. "Anyway, enough about all of that. Let's talk about you."

Buster felt the heat rise in his cheeks. "This is the bit I've kind of been dreading. And it's why you haven't heard from me all week."

Steph raised an eyebrow. "Has something happened?"

"Something happened before our date last Sunday." Buster went on to explain that Cora had rung, suggesting Eve was expecting him to take her back.

Steph's mouth dropped open as she listened. "Why didn't you say something?"

"I couldn't. She called as I was leaving to drive over to your place. I had thirty minutes between ending the call and arriving to see you. My head was a whir. I had no idea what to think. When I think back now, I realize she's as good as her daughter when it comes to manipulation."

"What do you mean?"

"She said something along the lines of how I had a chance to make it up to Eve after letting her down so badly."

"Not exactly subtle."

"She can be very manipulative," Buster said. "I know she has Eve's interests at heart, but she just has no idea what it was like being married to her daughter." He went on to tell her that he'd visited Eve the previous day, and a similar discussion had taken place. "It took me right back to every reason our marriage would never have worked. I appreciate now that the extreme behavior Eve displayed after Holly was born was affected by postpartum depression, but it wasn't brand new behavior. I'd seen it before and hadn't liked it. I'm guessing it would have escalated over time, and our marriage might not have survived anyway."

"What does this all mean, Buster? I'm glad you're telling me now what's going on, but I'm not sure exactly what it means. What are your plans with Eve?"

"I've said I'll support her application for the appeal and stand by her through that. But that's all. I haven't elaborated on what will happen after that, partly because I don't know."

"Does she have any reason to believe the two of you still have a chance to get back together?"

"I told her I wasn't willing to commit to starting over."

"How did she take that?"

Buster frowned. "I think she deliberately misinterpreted it. She said something about how she agreed, and there was no rush. That we owed ourselves to take it slowly without pressure."

"That doesn't sound like someone accepting that there's no chance of reconciling. Did you clarify it with her?"

He shook his head. "Honestly, I only really worked out what she meant as I was driving home. We do need to take things slowly, even just to rebuild an amicable friendship, but not with anything else in mind. Deep down, I know one hundred percent that she's not the right woman for me."

"But you're letting her sit in prison, thinking that there is a chance of a relationship?"

"At the moment, I guess, yes. I'll be going back again in the next week or two, so I'll ensure she knows for sure that there's no chance. It was hard, Steph. The prison is intimidating in itself, and then we only have an hour to talk. She's good at saying what I want to hear but manipulating the outcome. This might be another example of that. I'm not sure, to be honest. I did tell her about you."

"Me? What did you tell her?"

"Just that I'd met someone who I liked."

"I bet that didn't go down well."

Buster gave a sheepish smile. "No, not really. I'm sorry, Steph, I am. What I feel for you is so unexpected and so good. I didn't anticipate it and haven't known how to handle it. Only a few weeks back, I told Travis I was leaving the business and moving away from the area. That I needed a fresh start."

Steph's mouth dropped open. "Why?" She seemed to struggle to control the growing anger in her voice. "Why would you start something up with me knowing you were planning on leaving? Why didn't you just leave our relationship as friends?"

Pain flooded Buster's eyes. "I couldn't, Steph. The attraction to you is too big. How could I walk away from this feeling? I'm not sure I've ever felt this way before."

"And if things between us went well, were you still planning on moving away?"

"I have no idea. Things have been moving so quickly in all areas of my life, I hadn't made any decisions."

"But it was still a possibility."

"I guess so."

"So not only did you not mention the fact that you left Eve believing you're getting back together, but there's a strong possibility you'll leave the area anyway?"

Buster stared at Steph. Her eyes flashed with anger. He ran a hand through his hair. "I'm not explaining this very well." That was an understatement. All he was trying to convey was that he was confused and hadn't had time to sort through his feelings.

"It makes me angry because even though we hardly know each other, a great part of our discussion at Spicer's Peak was about being honest. You were dishonest as we were having that conversation."

"Not intentionally."

"Leaving out the important parts of a conversation is dishonest. You left me feeling like there was hope for us, that maybe after everything that's happened I did deserve some happiness. That we both did." Steph tore a corner off a piece of bread and dropped it in her soup.

"We both do deserve happiness. I didn't want to mention those things when I had no idea how I felt about either of them. But what I said about the attraction to you being too big to pull away from is still true. I mean it, I just haven't done a good job in showing it."

Steph looked up from her soup as if she hadn't even heard what he'd just said. "I think it's probably best that we press the pause button on us. We've both got so much going on at the moment that trying to make *us* happen is awful timing."

Disappointment settled on Buster's shoulders. Part of him agreed with Steph, but another part of him had hoped she'd be the one to say they should try to be together regardless of anything happening around them. That they should support each other through the challenges they were up against, that it could only make their relationship stronger. Instead, she was telling him that no, he could do it alone and she didn't need his help with her situation.

He scooped a spoonful of soup into his mouth, hoping to disguise his disappointment. Steph had spoken about listening to her gut as far as Matt was concerned and that she should go with it more often. Right now, his head was telling him that he had enough on his plate, and a new relationship was not a good idea. His gut, however, was telling him something completely different.

Steph waited. Was he really going to sit back and eat his soup? Did he really have nothing to say? This was his chance to step up and make it right between them. To acknowledge he'd misled her and to promise it wouldn't happen again, to reassure her that moving would be the furthest thing from his mind if a relationship was to develop between them.

She needed to get away from Buster before he saw how angry she was. She was seething. First, there was Matt and his lies, and now there was Buster. It was one thing to not tell her about the phone call from Cora on their date, but it was another to have sat there talking about honesty and being upfront with their issues. The very first time he had the opportunity to show her what type of person he was, he'd failed miserably.

Steph took a deep breath, pushed her chair back, and stood.

Buster grabbed her wrist. "Don't go. I'm sorry, Steph, really I am."

She extracted her arm. "Sorry for what exactly?" She needed to hear from him that he understood why she was upset.

"For the way this has turned out. As I said, I haven't done a very good job of showing you how I feel."

Or a good job of realizing what you've done wrong. She did her best to ignore the pain in his eyes. "I've got a lot to process regarding Heat Wave and what I'm going to do next."

"Steph…"

She shook her head, refusing to let the anguish in his voice affect her. "I'll see you around."

She turned and left the cafe before any more awkward conversation was exchanged. She crossed over Lake Drive, deciding she'd walk the lake trail and try to clear her head.

Steph glanced at the food truck where Asha waved and beckoned her over. Steph hesitated. She didn't want to talk to anyone right now, not even her sister. Yet, she wasn't given a choice. Asha turned and spoke to someone in the food truck and then walked toward Steph.

"Can I join you for a walk?" Asha asked. "Orla's helping me for the next couple of hours, so she can take over. I could use a break."

It was tempting to say no, that she wanted to be alone, but Steph knew that would end in a barrage of questions from Asha, so it was easier to say yes.

They walked in silence to the lake's edge when Asha stopped and turned to face Steph. "What's wrong?"

Steph sighed. "Is it that obvious?"

Asha gave a small laugh. "I'd normally expect you to ask how I am or what's going on. To be completely silent suggests something's wrong. I saw Buster go into the cafe after you'd already arrived. Did something happen?"

This time Steph couldn't help but smile. "Are you spying on the cafe?"

"Definitely. It's easy enough with the food truck being just across the road from it. I'm keeping track of all of my customers and putting black marks against their names on days I see them go into the cafe but not buy their usual coffee from me. They're all going to pay."

Steph stared at her sister. "You're not serious…"

Asha laughed. "Of course not. You should see your face. Orla mentioned she saw you, and then I happened to see Buster's pickup arrive. I thought he might be coming to chat with me about the pavilion. But then he hurried into the cafe. I assume to see you."

"We had lunch together. It didn't go very well. I told him I wanted to put us on hold. Not that we were really at the stage of an *us* as yet, but it was heading there very quickly. I think it's too hard, Ash. He's got all the baggage with his ex and daughter, and to top it off, she's now pressuring him to get back together."

"Really? Wow, I wasn't expecting that."

"I don't think he'll go back to her, but he knew that she was hoping they might try again when we had our date. He didn't mention it, of course, even though we had a conversation about being open and honest. I can't go there again."

Asha nodded. "No, I can understand that you wouldn't want a repeat performance of Dylan. But Buster's situation is different. He told you about his ex today. Only a week's passed since your date."

"He did tell me, but he hasn't told her there's no chance of them getting back together. She's sitting in prison, probably planning her homecoming. I think that's unfair of him and makes me question whether he's made his decision about her. Also, he gave Travis notice that he was leaving the business and moving away from Drayson's Landing." Steph sighed. "Except for Zane, I think all of the men in this area are worth avoiding. They're all liars."

Asha raised an eyebrow. "That's very un-Steph like. I don't think Ryan or Charlie or most of your male yoga clients would appreciate that either."

"Lucky I only said it to you, then." Steph managed a wry laugh. "I didn't mean it. It's just Buster and Matt. They're on the top of my low-life list today."

"Matt? He's not my favorite person, but I thought you were seeing a different side of him, and that he was being decent about Heat Wave. The computer, phone, and even the temporary contract were pretty generous."

"That was when he wanted something from me," Steph said. "But circumstances have changed." She went on to tell Asha about his decision to use Heat Wave as financial security. "Again, it's not what happened that I have a problem with. It's the way Matt's handling it and the fact that he lied outright to me. Why not just tell me the truth to begin with?"

Asha was shaking her head. "I'd like to kill him. Here we all are being nice, giving him the benefit of the doubt that he's changed, and he goes and does that. He's even got Charlie helping him. He's despicable. As soon as we get back, I'm going to see Charlie. He shouldn't be helping Matt at all."

Steph was about to say no, that Asha shouldn't get Charlie involved, but changed her mind. Who knew what Matt was really up to in terms of using Charlie? There would be some ulterior motive, that was for sure.

"What are you going to do now?"

"I'm not sure. I'll think about it during the week.

Opening a studio is an option, but traveling is too. I might finally do what I always said and take off to India and Southeast Asia. Explore the world and have a break from this place and all that goes with it."

Asha put an arm around her older sister. "I'll miss you if you do decide to go."

"Me too," Steph said. As they continued walking around the lake, she realized that right now, Asha, Zane, and her parents were all she would miss if she did leave Hope's Ridge.

Buster hardly remembered the drive back to Drayson's Landing. He was bitterly disappointed. He knew he wasn't exactly a catch with his baggage, but he thought Steph understood him and liked him. That they had chemistry worth fighting for. He shook his head. He was crazy. Only weeks earlier, he'd vowed never to go near another woman again. He'd made that vow for a reason. Not so much because of what they were like, but because of what he was like.

He pulled into his driveway and, for the first time in a very long time, took in his house and garden through the eyes of a stranger. The garden was an overgrown mess, and the front fascia of the house was still only half-painted from fifteen months earlier, when he and Holly had decided it needed a facelift. He'd barely done anything around the place since her death, which on the one hand was understandable, but on the other it needed to stop. He needed to pull himself out of his funk and get his life back together, and he would start now.

Three hours later, Buster took a beer from the fridge and walked back out to the front garden. It was amazing that he'd been able to transform it so quickly. The lawn was mown, edges done, and he'd cut back the bald cypress trees that had grown out of control. He'd also pulled weeds from the garden beds that bordered the house and tidied up the bed of geraniums Holly had insisted they plant two years earlier. They were flowering beautifully, and Buster realized he should be taking pride in these reminders of his daughter, not letting them grow out of control. The backyard was just as overgrown, but he'd tackle that next weekend. He'd started, and that was what was important.

He walked back into the house just as his phone rang. He picked it up off the kitchen counter.

"Henry Busterling?"

"That's me."

"Henry, my name is Nathan Bromley. I'm your wife's lawyer."

"Ex-wife."

Nathan cleared his throat. "Okay. Do you have time to speak? I appreciate it is the weekend, but I'm in court all day tomorrow. I'm meeting with Eve on Tuesday and would like to speak with you first."

Buster sank onto one of the kitchen stools. "How can I help you?"

"Eve confirmed that you are willing to support her appeal. Is that true?"

"Yes, it is. What do you need me to do?"

Buster assumed he might be called on to back up Eve's diagnosis of postpartum depression. He certainly wasn't expecting what Nathan Bromley asked of him. He listened, his stomach churning. Was he being lured into a trap?

"Let me get this straight. You think if Eve and I reconciled, it would strengthen her appeal?"

"Definitely. If the judge sees that you've accepted that her behavior following Holly's birth was a result of postpartum depression, he's quite likely to be more compassionate. We have the medical diagnosis already, which may be enough, but the extra weight of her ex-husband saying that he believed it to be true and it was why you're willing to try again with Eve will probably push the verdict to a yes without question."

Buster was silent.

"Cora, Eve's mother, led me to believe you'd be okay with this. Is that the case?"

Buster sighed. Cora was trying to control the situation. "Not exactly. I need to speak to Eve, of course, but I'm not interested in reconciling our relationship. Yes, postpartum depression is cruel and played a role in our marriage breakdown, but our relationship had problems well before Holly's birth, and I've had reminders of them since visiting Eve in prison."

"You've only visited her three times."

"Exactly. And I've been reminded in only three visits of why our marriage was never going to work. That confirms we are better leading separate lives. Cora's interference helps confirm it for me too."

"Okay, that puts a different spin on our approach. I'm going to have to tell Eve that that's your decision."

"I would prefer to be the one to do that."

"I'm meeting with her on Tuesday. I'm sorry, but I can't change that appointment. You'll need to see her tomorrow if you want to let her down in person."

Buster ignored the lawyer's blatant dig. "If there's any other way I can help without committing myself to a relationship with Eve, I'd be happy to," Buster said.

Nathan thanked him in a tone of voice that conveyed his annoyance at Buster's stance, then ended the call.

Buster threw his phone onto the kitchen counter, swearing he'd never answer it again.

An hour later, when the caller ID showed Cora calling, he wished he could honor what he'd sworn to himself.

"What do you mean you're not going to stand by your wife," Cora demanded before Buster even had a chance to say hello.

Buster took a deep breath. Eve's lawyer was undoubtedly busy with his phone calls this afternoon. "Cora. Eve is my ex-wife, not my wife, and has been for three years now. And I am going to stand by her, but I'm not interested in giving our relationship a second chance. There's too much pain from the past to cope with."

"You could both seek counseling," Cora said. "Get you through your concerns. You made a promise, Buster. To love and honor Eve. You're breaking your promise."

"We both made promises, Cora. Many of which were broken in the course of our marriage. Fidelity for a start."

Cora fell silent. Buster had never brought up that issue with her, but he knew she was aware of Eve's affairs. From what Eve had told him, she'd taken some of the men to meet Cora. "But Eve was suffering, Buster. If she hadn't had postpartum depression, none of this would have happened."

"I agree, it played a role, but I also acknowledge that there were cracks in the foundation of our relationship very early on. Things that I did my best to overlook or ignore. But they're still there, Cora. Eve,"—*and you*—"can be very controlling, and that's not what I want in my life. Also, as much as we have the shared history of Holly, the constant reminder of her that Eve brings is hard to live with."

"I thought you were a good man, Henry. One who would stand by the woman he openly declared his love for on their wedding day."

"I thought I would too, Cora. I guess neither of us knew me as well as we thought."

"Oh, I think I do. You're selfish. Only thinking about yourself. You let my girls down many times."

"Your girls?"

"Eve and Holly."

The hairs prickled on Buster's arms. "I never let Holly down."

"What about the kinder-concert? The one you were late to? Her little heart broke. You promised you'd be there for her song, and you weren't. I, for one, did not believe the story of you stopping to help someone whose car broke down. It's no different from what you did to Eve. Promised her your love and then walked away. You're doing it again now and are giving her false hope that you'll get back together. Her appeal will most likely be rejected as a result. You let people down and should be ashamed of yourself. I suggest you keep well away from women, Henry. No one deserves to be put through the pain you're capable of inflicting."

Buster ended the call before Cora said anything else. His hand trembled as he put the phone on the kitchen counter, this time turning it off. He knew that her outburst came from a place of love for her daughter, but it didn't change the fact that it was brutal, and it hurt.

12

————

Steph felt reenergized after teaching her morning yoga classes. She'd spent most of the previous evening meditating and trying to center herself. She'd realized that her reactions to Buster and Matt were more extreme than she'd usually be. She rarely felt anger to the degree she had the day before, and it was likely the negative energy surrounding her had put her chakras out of balance. An evening of meditation, relaxing music, and essential oils had helped. She would need to make sure she did that more often and took good care of herself. The difference in how she felt today was incredible.

She was practically bouncing when she reached the food truck for a mid-morning tea break. She wanted to thank Asha for listening to her the previous day. Charlie and Asha were standing in front of the food truck, deep in conversation, when Steph arrived.

Charlie smiled broadly. "Good morning, Steph."

"Morning, Charlie, Ash."

"You're looking happier today," Asha said. "Has something happened?"

"No, just me getting back to the things that make me happiest. Meditation and yoga mainly."

Asha smiled. "Good. Charlie and I were discussing some additional ideas for the pavilion. What do you think about having a bar-style counter running around the three walls of the structure?"

"I thought it was just going to be a floor with a roof and then tables and chairs," Steph said.

Charlie nodded. "It is. But the roof has to be held up with pillars, so we can attach a long counter that connects the back and side pillars. Leave the front open for people to walk in and out easily. It means we can have stools all along the counter areas, and a lot more people can be seated."

"Sounds great," Steph said. "Will the food truck be able to cater for that many at once?"

"That's a good point," Asha said. "The tables and chairs were going to seat sixteen. That's a lot to be serving at any one time."

Charlie tapped his nose. "Ah, but what if there is only one person at a table for four? Suddenly you do not have sixteen people."

"I guess you can always remove some of the stools from the counter if it's getting too busy," Steph said.

"Part of the reason Charlie wants to do this is Zane has some beautiful pieces of old-growth redwood at the Mill. He showed me a counter he made for someone in Tall Oaks. The wood's been thinned, and the edges are exactly as the tree was. They call it a live edge countertop. It's coated with an oil to give it a beautiful finish. He says he can get the right length pieces for here so that the counters are one long piece instead of pieces joined together."

"Enough talk of counters," Charlie said. "Steph came for tea, not to talk business."

Asha laughed. "That's Charlie's signal that his stomach's

rumbling. Come on. I'll get some tea and a muffin for you, Charlie." As she went back into the food truck, she said, "So Charlie called Matt last night."

Steph turned to Charlie. "I hope I haven't caused problems for you."

Charlie tutted. "No. I should have known better. I quit as his foreman. I will never be involved with that man again."

"Don't speak too soon," Asha said, nodding toward the road.

Steph and Charlie turned to find Matt walking toward them. His face was pale, his cheeks drawn. Steph immediately worried his father had relapsed or died.

"Matt, is everything okay? Your dad?"

He stopped, his eyes narrowing. "My dad's fine. But no, everything's not okay. I need to speak to both of you." He turned to Charlie first. "I have no idea why you quit your job. I thought we had come to an understanding and moved on from our old problems."

Charlie turned to Asha, who held a paper bag out to him. He took his muffin and turned back to Matt. "I had hoped that too. But then I learned that you are more underhanded than I would have ever thought. You are a disgrace, Matthew. An absolute disgrace." He didn't let Matt respond, he just walked away from the food truck with his muffin.

Matt laughed, an awkward kind of laugh. "Okay, well, that went well." He turned to Asha. "Any idea where that came from or why I'm back in his bad books?"

Asha shook her head in disbelief. "Are you for real? Just leave, Matt. Go and take care of your dad, and don't come back." She turned her back on him and opened one of the ovens in the food truck.

"Well, Steph, that's two conversations that haven't gone well," Matt said. "Are you able to explain any of this to me?"

"I think you can probably work it out."

"Um, okay. Look, I know I said I didn't need an answer on Heat Wave until Wednesday, but I have a buyer, which means a quick deal can be struck, unless you've decided you'd like to be partners and get the retreat project moving?"

Steph stared at him. Why couldn't he just be honest? She decided to call his bluff. "I was leaning toward a yes, I'd like to join you in a partnership."

"Really?"

The surprise on Matt's face almost made Steph laugh. He was probably now trying to work out how he was going to backtrack out of this. It was tempting to see how far she could take it, but if she did, she'd be as bad as he was.

"That's…"

Steph cut him off before he had a chance to tell her what she already knew, that it wasn't possible. "No, of course not really." She shook her head. "I want nothing to do with you, Matt, or your business. I'll run Heat Wave for the rest of the week, and then you can work out what you're going to do with it."

The color drained from Matt's face. "What? Hold on, what just happened?"

"What happened is I found out the truth," Steph said. "Once again, I fall for a man's lies. After what you did to Asha, and now this, I suggest you stay away from my family. You're not welcome anywhere near us."

"I second that," Asha called from the van. "You're a jerk, Matt." She stepped down from the food truck and picked up a rock the size of her palm. She held it up. "You might recall what a good throwing arm I have?"

Matt flinched.

"I'll use this on you if you don't leave now."

Matt opened his mouth but closed it again when Asha raised her arm with the rock. He shook his head and turned on his heel. "I have no idea why you're acting like this,

Steph. If you want to explain to me or change your mind, give me a call. I will pursue the potential buyer, but contracts won't be exchanged until later in the week at the earliest."

Was he for real? Was he still trying to play the good guy? Steph didn't respond; just watched as he walked back to his pickup.

She turned to Asha. "I think I prefer him when he's yelling at us, telling us how stupid we are. You know where you stand with him when he's like that. That you've called him on whatever awful thing he's done, and he's reacting. Being quiet and leaving with his tail between his legs isn't his style."

"I'm not sure we'll ever work out what Matt's style is," Asha said. "Other than unscrupulous, I don't think there are many words that I'd repeat in public that describe him."

Steph shook her head. "Unfortunately, when it comes to describing Matt, the majority of words are, like his behavior, unacceptable."

The first thing Buster did on Monday morning was call the prison to schedule a visit with Eve. He wanted to see her before her lawyer or Cora did. Regardless of anything that had happened between them, he felt he owed it to her to be the one to tell her that he didn't want to try again. Her mother had gone on so many times about him letting Eve down. While he didn't necessarily agree with everything she had to say, this was one occasion when he could do his best to handle the situation delicately. He would still be letting Eve down on the one hand, but having someone else deliver the blow for him seemed extra cruel.

He called Travis on the drive to Tall Oaks. "I'll be back in tomorrow," he told him. "Can we meet first thing? I'd like to discuss something with you."

He ended the call, glad that if nothing else, he was beginning to make decisions and put things in order.

When he reached the prison and completed the security clearance, Buster dug his fingernails into his palms to stop his hands from shaking. He hated that he'd let her get her hopes up.

Eve adopted a guarded look as they sat down opposite each other. He knew that she was waiting for an answer from him but didn't want to launch straight into disappointing her. Instead, he asked her how she was.

Eve laughed. "We both know why you're here. And I get it, I do."

Buster frowned. It wasn't possible for Cora to have visited with Eve since their phone call the day before. Eve was only allowed one visitor a day, and Buster was the allocated visitor today. "Did you speak with your lawyer or your mom?"

Eve's smile slipped. "No, why?"

"Nothing, I just...I don't understand when you say you get it. What do you get?"

"I get that you don't want to try again. Last time you were here, you were apprehensive and then mentioned you'd met someone. I know I put you on the spot, and I've done a lot of thinking too. Mom's voice was playing in my head when you visited. That we could get back together and be happy, but I don't think it would work."

Buster let out a deep breath, causing Eve's mouth to twitch at the edges. Was she trying not to laugh?

"You don't have to look so relieved," she said. "You could look a little crestfallen just to make me feel better."

Buster pushed a hand through his hair. "Sorry. I'm not

very good at this. You are right, though, in that it wouldn't work. I think we're too different now, Eve."

"I do too. I wasn't sure how I felt when Mom suggested the idea. I'm not even sure she had my wellbeing or her own in mind when she spoke to me. My guess is she's dreading me getting out and needing to move in with her. She enjoys her independence too much. If you and I were back together, that wouldn't be an issue."

Buster shook his head. "I can't believe she'd be so manipulative. Not after everything that's happened and with you in here."

"Manipulation is her specialty." She smiled. "Why do you think I'm such an expert at it?"

Buster decided it would be safer not to comment. "I'm still happy to support your appeal any way I can. Your lawyer called me yesterday, and I told him that too."

"He won't be happy," Eve said. "He thinks Mom's idea of us getting back together is an *excellent* move."

Buster was surprised when Eve rolled her eyes. "You don't?"

"I think if the judge decides I should be released early, then I'm very lucky. If he or she doesn't, then I serve out the rest of my time knowing that I'm paying for what happened. Our child died, Henry, and it doesn't matter how my lawyer presents it, at the end of the day, it was completely avoidable. It doesn't matter what the circumstances were leading to that day; on that day, I did many things I shouldn't have done. I am responsible, and I will live with that for the rest of my life." She held up a hand to stop him from interrupting. "Don't worry, I know that postpartum depression played a role in what happened, but I knew better than to drink and then go and get Holly. That's something someone who doesn't care does." She wiped a tear that rolled down her cheek. "And I did care. She was

209

my little love. The best gift I've ever received, and I had no idea how to accept it and enjoy it."

"Hormones played a big part in that, Eve."

She nodded, wiping away more tears. "They did, but I want you to know that I do take responsibility too. I'm not passing the blame to something else. Not you, not circumstances, not anything. I loved Holly with all of my heart, and I need you to know that."

Tears slipped down Buster's cheeks. "I do know that, Eve. I do." And he did.

"Can we play the memory game?" Eve asked. "Like we did the first time you came to visit?"

"I haven't come up with any for today," Buster said.

"I have. Do you remember that day that we took Holly to the carnival? The day when she insisted on the strawberry milkshake before going on the small roller coaster they had for kids?"

Buster rolled his eyes. "I will never forget that. I had to throw my shoes out after that night. There was so much milk in them and all over my clothes, I couldn't get it all out."

"She was so sick," Eve said. "But once it was all out of her, she insisted on going on the carousel."

"Nothing was going to keep our Holly from enjoying herself."

"She was an amazing little girl, wasn't she? Kind and generous. So much of you was in her."

Buster swallowed as a tightness gripped his throat. He couldn't remember the last time Eve had complimented him. "She had your fierceness and determination, too," Buster said. "Our best attributes were all rolled into one little person."

For the remainder of the visit, they shared more stories of Holly, broken up by moments of silence as thoughts of their beautiful little girl took over. When it was finally time to leave, Buster smiled. "Thank you. I thought today was going to be awful and that you'd be upset. I am here for you, Eve. Once you're out, I'll be happy to help you any way I can. I don't want to be remembered as the guy who let you down."

"You won't be. But make sure you pay close attention to this woman you mentioned you're seeing. Sometimes it's hard to realize when someone needs something from you. We all get so caught up in what we're doing. Look for the signs and step up and help her when she needs it. You don't want to have gone through all of this, feeling that you let Holly and me down, to repeat it with someone else."

Eve's words played over in Buster's head as he made his way back to Drayson's Landing. She was right, letting people down wasn't something he ever wanted to repeat with someone else.

Steph sat bolt upright, stifling a scream. She put her hand to her chest, willing her heart rate to calm. Her face was wet with tears. She took a deep breath. It was just a dream. But it had felt so real.

After the stress of the last few days, she'd repeated her meditation routine before going to bed early. She knew a big part of getting her chakras back in alignment was taking care of herself. The irony, of course, was that sleep never came quickly, or if it did, she was usually thrown out of it.

She glanced at her alarm clock and groaned. It was only ten p.m. She'd slept for an hour. She could hear the faint sound of music coming from the living room and Asha's gentle laugh. She smiled. At least Asha and Zane's energy left a positive vibe in the house each day. That had to help. But she also didn't want to disturb them. Imagine if she walked out, and Zane was in the middle of proposing.

Although she was sure he was going to leave that until after Jenna's engagement party and would probably think of something more romantic than in their living room. Still, it was their date, and she didn't want to interrupt.

She got up and lit the oil burner she'd placed on her bedside table. Wafts of ylang-ylang quickly filled the room. She closed her eyes and breathed deeply, doing her best to avoid analyzing the dream she'd woken from. As images filled her mind, she knew there was no avoiding it. It was the same dream she'd experienced since the afternoon of the accident. The sheer panic as the car came toward her, the fear she saw in Eve's eyes as they collided, and the car careening off the road, down the embankment, and into the lake. Of Steph's arms and legs being scraped by the undergrowth as she rushed after the car. She lost her footing several times before reaching the lake. She didn't hesitate. She ran straight into the freezing water, trying to reach the car that was sinking fast. The small face in the rear seat pressed against the window. Although tonight it wasn't a small face. It was Buster. And he wasn't calling for help, he was smiling. His eyes were twinkling, his face full of love. Steph's heart raced as she froze, unable to reach the car. Water reached Buster's neck and then covered his chin and face. He continued smiling, and moments before the car slipped out of sight, he raised his hand to his lips and blew her a kiss.

The pain in Steph's chest as Buster disappeared from her life remained with Steph now as she sat in her room. She'd done her best to allow anger to override her true feelings. While she remained angry with him, she could hold the entire situation at arm's length. But now, when she allowed herself to feel, she knew anger was the last emotion she felt toward Buster. She was bitterly disappointed at how things had turned out. They had a connection, one that no one else would ever understand. They'd both been impacted by Holly's death in different ways and been changed by it. And while Steph knew the situation was much harder for Buster, it wasn't the point. It was their connection. They shared an understanding, but it was more than that. There was chemistry between them. For the first time in a very long time, Steph had felt like she could trust Buster implicitly. That he would never hurt her. She realized most people would consider her reaction extreme, considering it was so early in their relationship, but it wasn't. Yet the red flag she had seen was all she needed. She didn't want to spend longer with him, have her feelings deepen, her love for him grow, and then have it all ripped from her.

She stood up and started pacing the room. *Her love for him?* Where did that come from? She didn't love Buster. She shook herself. Of course she didn't. Regardless of all the things she'd just told herself about him, they hardly knew each other. And spending more time together was unlikely to change that. She thought she'd known Dylan and hadn't. She thought she was getting to know Matt and understand him. She didn't. The one thing she did know was that she was a terrible judge of character.

Disappointment settled on her shoulders as she thought about Matt. She honestly thought he'd changed, and part of her wished she could have explored the idea of working with the improved version of him. Now she'd told him she was leaving at the end of the week. Where did that put her?

Laughter filtered down the hallway from the living room. This time, rather than smiling at her sister's happiness, tears welled in her eyes. Asha had found love in both Zane and her business. She was happy and content with an exciting future in front of her. Steph didn't begrudge her this, but she wished she had it too. That she had something. Right now, she was on her own, about to be unemployed with no backup plan. She lay down on her bed, allowing her tears to flow. It wasn't like her to feel so sorry for herself, but right now she felt like she had no control over her emotions, or for that matter, any other part of her life.

Buster operated on autopilot for the twenty-four hours that passed after seeing Eve. He arrived home, walked around each room in the house, and made notes of what work was required to sell. He met with Travis on Tuesday morning and gave him official notice he wanted to leave within the next two weeks.

"Two weeks? But what about the projects you're overseeing?"

"From what I've heard, Matt's selling Heat Wave, so that's not one we need to worry about. The plans for the job at Asha's food truck are with the township for approval. It's a straightforward job once the plans are approved, and I'm sure Charlie will oversee it. The larger project is Matt's apartments. I'm going to have to hand that one over. Charlie's walked off the job, so we need a replacement for him and should get someone capable of overseeing the whole thing. There are plenty of guys in Tall Oaks who'd move out for a few months if needed."

"And then you're just going to go?"

Buster nodded. "I'm going to go skiing in Vail. I might spend the rest of the season there. Possibly even look for some work."

"Skiing?"

Buster nodded. "I need a challenge, and that's something I've always wanted to do." It was something Holly had said she wanted to do actually. Buster had been on a couple of ski weekends before but hadn't done much skiing. He'd promised Holly they'd go when she was seven. She would have been seven now, so he would go for her.

"Okay. Well, once you're settled, let us know where you are. Jodi and I might come and visit for a weekend."

Buster nodded, knowing he had no intention of inviting them. He needed a complete break from his regular life, and somewhere like Vail was where he hoped to find it.

The same thought went through his mind when later that evening, he started boxing up belongings around the house. He wanted to get it decluttered and suitable for selling. He moved from room to room, leaving Holly's until last. Eventually, he got up the nerve and pushed open the door. This was going to be the hardest task of all.

He put the empty boxes on the floor and sat down on Holly's bed. Where did he even start? He didn't want to get rid of anything but knew that he should. He picked up her soft toy dog, closed his eyes, and hugged it to his chest, a flood of emotion engulfing him.

The ache he knew so well crushed his chest, and for a moment, he felt like he couldn't breathe. This was when images of Holly would usually flood his mind. Her gorgeous little face, her smile and bright eyes. But tonight, that's not what filled his mind. It was another magnificent smile, another kind heart. Another woman who he'd lost, but this time he'd lost her before he'd even had the chance to know her. He wasn't sure what was worse, to break up after a long relationship or never have the opportunity to explore something he knew deep in his heart was a gift. He opened his eyes. But he was not a gift. As much as he appreciated Eve's words that he was kind and generous, he'd still let her down. And he'd let Holly down in the worst possible way. He realized at that moment that Steph reminded him of Holly. Not in her looks, although they were both gorgeous, but in her smile, her kind heart, and her humor. She was a lovely person, just like his daughter had been.

He buried his face in the soft toy, the realization hitting him. It didn't matter what he had or hadn't done with Steph. She deserved better. Someone who would love her with all of their heart. Would be there for her at every moment. Would never let her down. And that was the kicker. The one thing he couldn't guarantee—that no matter how hard he tried, there was always the possibility he would let her down. And he would never forgive himself if that happened, so he could never take that risk.

The tears that flowed from Buster were for what he'd lost and for what he would never have. As he pulled himself together and looked around his little girl's room, he reminded himself that he had been lucky. He had had what some people never had the opportunity to experience: the unconditional love of a child. He would be eternally grateful, even if in his heart, he knew he would also be eternally sad. He hoped that wherever she was, love and kindness surrounded Holly. She would attract it, *that* he was sure of, and it gave him some comfort.

When Buster eventually dragged himself from Holly's bedroom, having unpacked his grief, rather than packing her belongings, an additional sadness settled over him. He knew a change would be good for him, but he also knew he'd be taking every bit of sadness and emotion with him. Steph had given him a brief taste of what happiness could be like, and just as quickly, it was shut down again. It was what he deserved, and he needed to accept that this was how it would be moving forward. Next time, if an opportunity arose, he needed to walk away immediately. Not give himself a chance to let someone else down or crush even more of his heart.

13

*B*uster was surprised when Matt pushed open the front door of J.R. Construction and stepped inside. They didn't have a meeting scheduled as far as Buster knew.

"Matt, everything alright?"

"It is if you've found me a new foreman. Charlie was doing such a great job; it's frustrating."

"Travis mentioned he'd quit."

"Yep, completely out of the blue. I had him quit one minute, and then the next minute, Steph got angry and told me she wanted nothing more to do with me or Heat Wave."

"That was understandable under the circumstances. I should warn you, she thinks you're a despicable human."

Matt gave a wry smile. "Unfortunately, she might be right." He narrowed his eyes. "You're going to have to fill me in on what despicable things I'm supposed to have done. But first, you care about Steph, don't you?"

Buster nodded. "I do—or did. But I'm no good for her. I'll just let her down like I did Eve and Holly."

Matt's mouth dropped open. "Let them down? Are you for real? When it comes to Eve, you were a saint."

Buster laughed. "You hardly knew her. How did you come up with that?"

"I knew Eve. We were at school together, remember? She and I had drama class with Mr. Herbert. Herbie, as she insisted on calling him—to his face! I ended up dropping out because she controlled the whole thing."

"Two control freaks never work," Buster said.

"Touché! No, she made me feel uncomfortable. She was so sweet one minute and would turn on me the next. I had no idea whether I was coming or going when it came to Eve. She seemed to have a lot of different personalities. She also made me feel bad about myself."

"Really?" Buster couldn't imagine Matt ever feeling that way.

"Yeah, she said things to belittle me. It made me question my intelligence, my appearance, all sorts of things. She had the kind of personality that got under your skin. I wanted her to like me, yet I couldn't work her out. I found it easier to stay away from her, even though part of me would have liked to have been close to her. Those thoughts were before you two got together, of course."

Buster nodded. He understood what Matt was saying. It was part of his dilemma with Eve. The most beautiful person one minute, and a manipulative and nasty one the next.

"I was shocked when you two got together."

"Why's that?"

"You're too nice. Way too nice for someone like that. When you announced your engagement, my first thought was she would trample your heart."

"You were right there. Although I think I did a pretty good number on her too."

"See?" Matt said. "Even after everything, you still defend her. You are an amazing guy with a heart of gold. Steph would be lucky to have you."

"Steph doesn't want me, and I can't go there anyway. I have good intentions but seem to mess things up with women and let them down. It would be heartbreaking if it ended like that with Steph."

The look on Matt's face was incredulous. "So...what? You give up now before you even make an effort? That's letting her down, Buster. If you love someone, you do everything possible to make sure they know it. Yes, your heart might get broken, but it means you feel things. That you love and want to receive that back. You can't just walk away. You'll forever wonder if she was the one."

"She is the one." The words came out of Buster's mouth before he had a chance to think about them. He shook his head, his cheeks heating. "I don't know where that came from."

Matt tapped his chest. "It came from here. From your heart. From the part of you that's wishing right now you'd let it take the lead rather than relying on that ridiculous brain of yours."

Buster couldn't help but smile. He would never have expected such a passionate speech from a guy like Matt.

"I'm saying this," Matt said as if he could read Buster's mind, "because I admire Steph. I would love to take her out, but I'm smart enough to know that first of all, we're better being friends, and second of all, she would never agree to date me. And even more importantly, I think she hates me anyway."

"After your recent stunt," Buster said, "you'd be nuts to even go near her."

Matt frowned. "Okay, you might need to enlighten me here. What stunt? Things went weird with Steph over Heat Wave. I thought she was going to go into partnership with me." He shifted awkwardly. "I know I'm not an expert, but

I've drawn up some sketches of what I imagine the retreat looking like."

Buster stared at Matt. He sounded genuine. But he couldn't be, could he? "Hold on, aren't you in the process of selling Heat Wave so you can invest in some project in Tall Oaks?"

"News travels quickly."

"Steph mentioned it to me. On the same afternoon, she told me there was no point in us pursuing a relationship."

"When was that?"

"Last Sunday. She was pretty upset."

"Sunday? But I didn't talk to her until Monday when she pretty much suggested I was the lowest of low and there was no way she'd work with me. I hadn't told her about the investor. The investor that's fallen through, by the way."

"Seriously?"

Matt nodded. "I'm going to have to find someone pretty quickly now that Steph's leaving this week. I doubt I can talk her into staying at the studio. She's furious with me, and I still have no idea why."

Buster wished he could trust Matt, that the man in front of him had a better reputation. His gut told him Matt was genuine. He thought back to Steph's comment about trusting her gut. Maybe he should follow her advice and assume Matt was telling the truth.

"Steph was under the impression that you'd decided to use Heat Wave to guarantee your investment in Tall Oaks. That you were going to do your best to sell it as quickly as possible to convert the property to cash so you could move forward with the Tall Oaks deal."

"Only if Steph said no to going into business together."

"Really?"

"My decision came down to Steph's involvement. I've wanted to do a retreat for years, but the timing isn't ideal with the other projects I have going. Steph's the perfect person to partner with on a project like this. She's passionate and has an amazing eye for detail. Without her it just isn't the right time for me to embark on this project. I will do it one day though. Ever since Mom died, I promised myself that I'd set up something that could help people like her."

Buster fell silent. He'd forgotten about Matt's mom. They'd been quite young when she died. She'd had multiple sclerosis, which hadn't killed her, but a minor operation had led to an infection and pneumonia, and that did.

"I wanted the retreat to be for wellness. So rehabilitation and all sorts of things. Even respite, if needed, but for people who are still well enough to enjoy it. I would put in a pool, for instance. Mom was losing the use of her legs before she died, and the one place she still loved to be was in the pool. The weightlessness made her forget, even just for the hour she was in there, that she had any limitations. That was just one thing I wanted to do. I haven't worked it all out, but I do have a lot of other ideas. We'd still offer the upscale experience, of course, but the whole point of calling it a wellness retreat was to help people heal both physically and mentally."

"Did you tell Steph all of this?"

Matt shook his head. "No, we never got down to details. It all happened too quickly, and then Dad had his heart attack, and there hasn't been time to go through everything. The main thing I wanted was an idea of whether Steph was interested in being involved at all. We would have discussed it in more detail before signing a partnership agreement."

"You could have done it all without Steph," Buster said.

"I could, but I wanted her in on the project." Matt blushed. "Her energy reminds me of my mom. Mom was always doing yoga and was very spiritual. She and Dad were opposites. They probably would have split up, I'm guessing, if she hadn't died. Steph brings something to it that I can't explain, but I feel like it's needed. She makes me want to be a better person."

Buster's mouth dropped open. "Are you in love with Steph?"

Matt's blush deepened. "No, but I admire her and believe Heat Wave is her. Bodhi ran it, but it was Steph everyone talked about. She has a magnetic energy, and anything she touches will turn to gold."

Buster nodded. He agreed with Matt.

Matt frowned. "I wonder why Steph thought I was going to sell the property before I had her answer?"

"Ryan. He mentioned that you and he had had a few drinks, and that was your plan. It was a couple of days after you'd come to see Steph to tell her how much you hoped she would go into partnership with you. She assumed everything you'd fed her were lies to try to make yourself look better before pulling out of the deal."

Matt threw his hands up in the air. "Where did he come up with that? I told Ryan that was my plan *if* Steph said no. It was probably the beer. He was singing by the end of our catch-up. I should fire him."

Buster was about to object when he realized Matt was joking. "You should probably go and see Steph. She might change her mind."

Matt shook his head. "You know, I think there's so much bad blood between Asha and me and Charlie too. I can't see them ever coming around. At this stage, it's probably more important that you tell Steph how you feel. She's a gift, Buster. One you can't ignore. Imagine how you'd feel waking up with her in your arms every morning. Telling her you love her, protecting her. You can't let that go."

Butterflies flitted in Buster's stomach. It's what he

wanted to believe and wanted to do. He just wasn't sure if he dared to do it.

"You've got nothing to lose," Matt said. "You've lost so much already. In fact, if she says no to you, which I think is highly unlikely if you lay your heart on the line, I'll make everything on the Sandstone Cafe's menu free for a week."

"What?"

"I mean it. I'm that confident. You're an amazing guy, and she'll say yes."

Buster stared at Matt. Could he be right?

"You know what?" Matt said. "I have an idea. If you want Steph back, you need to do a few things. You need to sweep her off her feet, and you need to give her a reason to give you another chance. And I think I have the solution to both of those."

Steph wiped down the studio's reception area before doing the final count of the till and locking the day's earnings in the small safe Bodhi had installed. Most of the payments were by card or monthly membership, but there were always some cash payments for each class. She looked around the studio. She was going to miss Heat Wave. She and Bodhi had built it up over several years, and the energy the studio housed was magical. She hoped she'd be able to recreate this if she was ever to set up her own place.

"Knock, knock."

Steph's heart lurched as Buster's familiar deep voice called to her from the front door.

His smile was cautious, his eyes searching hers as he stepped into the foyer area. "Is it okay to come in?"

"Sure. I was just cleaning up for the night. Tomorrow's my last day. Although," she turned away from him, "I haven't told anyone, so I'm not sure how that's going to work."

"What about future classes?"

"I guess I'll put a sign on the door after I leave tomorrow night." Steph raised an eyebrow. "I'll add Matt's phone number if anyone has inquiries."

Buster nodded. "Fair enough. Steph, I need to talk to you. I've been so stupid, and I want you to know how I feel."

Steph swallowed. She couldn't imagine what he was about to say, but she wasn't sure if she was ready to hear it either. She was planning to book her flight to Thailand over the weekend, and nothing was going to stop her.

"Can we sit down?"

Steph nodded and gestured to the small sitting area. Buster sat down, and she chose the chair furthest from him.

Buster took a deep breath. "I've done so much thinking the last few weeks. Way too much, in fact. From the day we climbed at the Bluff, to my visits with Eve, to my abysmal communication with you over what was happening and what I wanted, and now over what my heart is telling me."

Steph's heart raced.

"I realize I have a reputation for letting people down," he continued, even though Steph attempted to interject. "But I've made a promise to myself that I'm not going to be that person anymore. I'm going to believe in myself. That I'm a good man, a man who would do anything to make you realize that."

"I do realize," Steph's voice was a whisper.

"Do you know that I love you, Steph? I'm falling completely in love with you. You're the person I would do anything for. I want to be part of your life. I want to show you my love and be wrapped in yours. I want to do this life thing together. The fun parts and the hard parts."

Steph stared at him, hardly believing what she was hearing. "I thought you were leaving the area."

"Not if you'll let me be part of your life. I'd only leave now if you said no. I don't think I could bear staying and seeing you when I know that we could be so good together."

"But I'm planning on traveling to India and Thailand."

"You are?"

"Possibly. I've convinced myself I need to explore beyond Hope's Ridge to have any chance of happiness."

"I'll come with you if you want to go. I don't care where I am, Steph I just want to be with you. I love you. I do." He reached for her hands, which she let him take. Then he stood and came around in front of her. "I want us to move forward together. We'll always have our baggage and things from our pasts, but they're things we can help each other with. Talk about them, reminisce, or just sit together and remember. But just as importantly, I want us to create new memories. Times to cherish together. I don't think happiness for us is only beyond Hope's Ridge; I think it's right here. It's wherever we are together."

Tears filled Steph's eyes. Her gut was screaming at her to embrace Buster, to reflect everything he'd just said back at him. Her feelings for him were so strong. It was hard to believe she'd pushed them aside and done her best to dismiss them.

"But what if you decide you can't handle it?" Steph said.

"I won't. And on the unlikely chance I felt like that, I'd talk to you. I will be an open book from now on." He grinned. "You'll be so sick of me telling you everything you'll ask me to stop. What do you say?"

Steph didn't need to think. Her heart told her precisely what she needed to know. She leaned forward and brushed her lips against Buster's. "I say definitely."

14

─────────

*I*f cloud nine existed, Buster could honestly say it was where he was right now. Steph had said yes! He couldn't believe Matt had been right. He'd laid his heart on the line, and rather than trampling it, she'd accepted it lovingly and handed hers to him. It was a magical feeling, one that he hoped would stay with him for the remainder of his life. He was confident that with Steph by his side, it would.

They'd closed up the yoga studio and were now walking hand in hand along the lake trail. The moon was dancing on the water, the trees rustling in the light breeze. It was dark and cold, yet warmth and happiness wrapped around Buster.

"What made you do this tonight?" Steph asked. "I'm curious."

"Someone gave me a kick up the backside. It made me realize that my feelings for you were so pure that I couldn't walk away without trying one last time."

"Who? Asha?"

"No, Matt."

Steph stopped walking, dropped his hand, and turned to

face him. "Matt Law made you realize you're in love with me?"

Buster saw the fury in her eyes. "No, I knew I was in love with you. It was Matt who made me realize I had to tell you."

"What's in it for him?"

"Steph! That's a horrible thing to suggest."

"Why? He doesn't do anything that doesn't benefit him. Look at what he did with Heat Wave."

"He didn't do anything. Now, let me retake your hand so we can keep walking, and I'll explain what happened with Heat Wave and why you need to be angry with Ryan, not Matt."

Ten minutes later, nausea replaced Steph's fury. "I feel awful," Steph said. "I can't believe I didn't let him explain."

"It's okay. He understands. After the situation with Asha and Charlie, he knows you'd suspect the worst from him. He did tell me that the situation with his dad has helped him get a better perspective on what's important in life. He doesn't want to end up like his old man. Unwell with only a few acquaintances checking up on him. He doesn't appear to have any friends, and Matt says that's because he's burned them all with his unfavorable business dealings and developments. Matt doesn't want to be that person."

"And he still wants to develop Heat Wave?"

"There's a bit of a catch with that. He sold the property yesterday."

"Oh."

Buster could see the disappointment on Steph's face.

"You wanted it didn't you?"

"I did, but I kept flip-flopping on whether working with Matt would be a good idea or not. My gut told me not to trust him. I'm beginning to think my gut's not that good at giving advice."

Buster tightened his grip around Steph's shoulder. "It told you to say yes to me, didn't it?"

Steph nodded.

"Then it is reliable."

Hours later, after Buster walked Steph home, and he drove back to Drayson's Landing, he lay in bed, a feeling of euphoria settling over him. Steph had said yes! He wouldn't rush things with her but would make sure that every minute they spent together built trust and more love between them. He couldn't wait until the next morning.

The build was starting on Asha's pavilion, and he'd asked Steph to meet him at the food truck to celebrate breaking ground on-site. What she didn't know was he had an ulterior motive. One that he hoped she was going to love.

———

Steph hurried along the lake trail after her seven a.m. class ended, hoping she'd make it in time for the ceremony. It sounded a bit strange to her, celebrating breaking ground, but she couldn't wait to see Buster again, so she would have been happy to attend for any reason. He'd said they would wait for her to arrive, but she couldn't imagine them holding up a construction crew. It would be expensive, that she was sure of.

She was breathing hard when she arrived at the food truck. Asha was handing out coffee to a group of construction workers and Buster was standing with Charlie, his hands gesticulating wildly. Steph's heart lurched when Buster's face suddenly broke into a broad smile, and he said something to Charlie before striding over to her. He swept her into a giant hug, causing her to laugh.

"Now that's the kind of greeting I like."

Buster grinned. "Good, expect plenty more. Now, these

guys are going to be an hour or so before they break ground. They need to take measurements and lay out some markers and other bits and pieces. While we wait, let's get coffee, or tea in your case, and I'd like to go through the plans with you."

"With me? Shouldn't you be doing that with Asha and Charlie?"

"They've already been through the plans. I would like your input on a few things, if you're okay with looking them over?"

Steph nodded. "Sure, although I can't see myself being much very helpful."

Buster winked. "I think you'll be surprised. Let's get the drinks and grab a seat."

Steph followed Buster to the serving window, raising her eyebrows when she saw the grin on Asha's face. "Is something weird going on?"

"What do you mean? It's groundbreaking day, and we're all excited."

Steph nodded. That made sense, but she had a feeling there was something else at play.

Asha handed her a cup of tea without asking what she wanted and a plate with a heart-shaped muffin on it. "For you and Buster to share."

Steph blushed. "News travels quickly."

"Sure does," Asha said. "And I just happened to bake a tray full of lovins, as I like to call these muffins, so it all worked out perfectly."

Steph stared at her sister as she followed Buster to a table. "Ash is acting strangely." Buster laughed, and Steph couldn't help but notice it was a nervous laugh. "Why am I suddenly getting worried?"

"I have no idea. Now, let me show you these plans.

They're just a starting place, so you can add anything you want to them."

"A starting place? But they're about to break ground. The township had to approve these plans before construction started. We can't change anything now."

Buster smiled. "Just take a look and see what you think." He typed something into his computer, took a deep breath, and moved his screen in front of her.

Steph's mouth dropped open. She was not looking at the design of the pavilion, she was looking at a 3D design of a retreat.

She turned to Buster. "Steph's Place?"

He nodded. "What do you think?"

"But it's Heat Wave. Heat Wave that Matt sold. Is the new owner thinking of going with the retreat idea?"

Buster nodded. "I think so. Take a look at these concepts he asked me to show you. See what you think."

Buster used the mouse to drive the presentation for Steph. The drawings were very detailed, going into the existing studio and showing the cottages after the renovation.

"He wants wheelchair access?" Steph noticed the inclusion of many facilities for those with disabilities.

"He'd like the retreat to be a wellness center as well as for yoga and spiritual journeys."

Steph nodded. "Matt would be happy with that. He's always referred to it as a wellness center, not that he was necessarily going to include these types of facilities."

"You like it?"

"I do, but why would the owner call it Steph's Place? He hasn't even met me."

Buster took her hand. "I bought fifty-five percent of the business from Matt. I have a contract with the option to purchase the other forty-five percent, but I wanted to talk to you before I do that."

"You bought it?"

Buster nodded. "Matt has excellent reasons for wanting the retreat to provide relief for people with disabilities, and he wants it to go ahead."

"But what about the Tall Oaks investment?"

"He's looking at other ways to finance it that don't involve Heat Wave. I was hoping that this is a project we could work on together. My skills are obviously useful for getting the plans drawn up and construction underway, and I know you'll be amazing in helping design it, to begin with, and then fitting it out and making the decisions on the landscaping and other touches."

"I…" Steph wasn't sure what to say. "I don't have money to invest in this."

"You don't need to. This is for us, Steph. *Us* is long term. We can create an arrangement so it's all fair, if it makes you feel more comfortable, but this isn't about money. It's about creating a lifestyle and something that we can be passionate about."

"And you're going to buy the other forty-five percent from Matt?"

"I wanted to talk to you about that first." Buster went on to explain Matt's reasoning for wanting to do the retreat to begin with.

"I'd forgotten about his mom," Steph admitted. "He was so young when she died."

"And he promised himself that he'd do this one day in her memory."

"And he'd like to be involved?"

"Ideally, yes. His forty-five percent ownership means we have the final say on everything. He suggested that. It was his plan all along. He wanted you to design the retreat and pour your energy into it. He's very complimentary about you, Steph, says you remind him in many ways of his mom, which is one reason he wanted to do this with you. I believe he's been completely honest with you since day one when it comes to this project."

Steph smiled. "You know, I'm so happy to hear that. I was so disappointed when I thought he'd lied to me. I thought we had a connection and would work well together."

"So you'd be okay working with him?"

"Of course. It's a shame he's not here, we should be celebrating."

Buster grinned. "He's over at the cafe. I said I'd give him a thumbs up if it was safe to come over." Buster turned and waved in the direction of the cafe and gave a thumbs-up signal.

Within seconds Matt came racing out the door and jogged over to them. He had a tentative smile on his face. "Good news or bad news?"

"Good, Matt," Steph said. "And I'm sorry I doubted you. I would love to work on this with you and Buster. I think we'd make an amazing team."

"You had every right to doubt me, Steph, as does everyone else around here. Hopefully, over time, I'll have you all believing my new image is genuine." He nodded toward Charlie. "Even Mr. Li, I hope."

Charlie scowled and walked over to them. "I will keep an eye on you, Matthew. You keep messing with my emotions."

"Your emotions?"

"Yes, one day you are bad, then you are good, then bad, and then I just don't know. I like to live in a peaceful town, not one with a roller coaster called Matt Law."

Steph laughed at Charlie's description. "I think that the roller coaster's just a part of life, Charlie. And we all owe

Matt an apology. I got it wrong about Heat Wave. We're just looking over plans for the new wellness retreat that the three of us are going to work on together."

Charlie smiled. "That is excellent news. Will you offer silent meditation retreats?"

"I imagine we'll offer all sorts of services, Charlie."

"Will you still call it Heat Wave?" Asha asked, joining the group.

"Steph's Place has a nice ring to it," Matt said.

Steph shook her head. She looked from Buster to Matt. "I have the perfect name. It's one that means a lot to both of you. How would you feel about simply calling the retreat Holly's?"

Buster's eyes filled with tears. "Really? I'd love that. But why would that mean anything to Matt?"

All eyes turned to Matt, whose eyes had also filled. He wiped his eyes on his sleeve. "Because Holly was my mom's name, too."

15

*S*teph stopped in the entrance to the function hall, awed by the extravagant display in front of her. A smile played on her lips as Bruno Mars' "Marry You" burst from the speakers. There would be no doubt in anyone's mind of what they were celebrating tonight. Jenna's engagement party appeared to be every bit as extravagant as she'd promised. Her eyes flitted to the enormous floral centerpieces on the exquisitely dressed tables. The white tablecloths and silver ribbons adorning the backs of the chairs with their giant bows screamed *wedding*. Steph's eyes traveled to the ceiling, which was a sea of silver balloons. She had to hand it to Jenna, it was extravagant but tasteful.

It was amazing for Steph to realize how different she felt compared to only a few weeks ago. She had energy she hadn't experienced since before the accident. Energy brought back to her through love and plenty of sleep. In the last month, she'd only woken a handful of times in the middle of the night. Holly still appeared in her dreams, but she was smiling and happy, not scared and asking for help. It seemed Steph's subconscious was rewriting the dream, while Buster was rewriting her fear of being in a car. Each weekend they'd driven somewhere, a little farther each time. She found her fear lessening with each trip and hadn't dreaded the long drive to the city for the party, as she would have only a month earlier. According to Buster, she'd be driving herself by the time Holly's officially opened.

"Steph, Buster!" Jenna appeared in front of them dressed in a white lace maxi dress with a plummeting neckline and a split up one leg. Her usually straight honey-gold hair had been styled with loose waves, which gave it more volume and a beautiful soft look.

Steph immediately leaned forward to hug the bride to be. "You look amazing."

"You do too!" Jenna pulled out of the hug and looked Steph's midnight-blue cocktail dress up and down. Her eyes returned to Steph's face and she grinned. "You're also glowing. I assume this gorgeous man has something to do with that?"

Buster wrapped an arm around Steph. "She was glowing long before I met her; radiating health and beauty. I'm just hoping it's going to rub off on me. Congratulations, by the way." He leaned forward to kiss her cheek. "And where's this fiancé of yours?"

Jenna grinned and pointed across the room to where Brad was talking to a group of people. Steph had met him briefly twice before. All she knew about him was what she'd heard from Asha and Zane, and none of it was particularly complimentary. She hoped for Jenna's sake their summing up of him was wrong.

Asha appeared by Jenna's side with two glasses of champagne. She handed one to Jenna.

"Where's Zane?" Steph asked.

"Mingling." Asha rolled her eyes. "Jenna invited every person the family's ever associated with, and Zane's dad's insisting he does the rounds and chat with all of them."

Jenna laughed. "The wedding will be worse. I'm planning on inviting at least four hundred to that."

Buster gave a low whistle. "Four hundred! If I invited every person I'd ever met, I doubt I'd reach that number."

"Jenna's inviting all of them plus strangers she's hoping she'll see one day," Asha joked.

Jenna slapped her arm playfully. "Enough out of you. When's that brother of mine going to make things official with you, that's more what we should be focusing on tonight."

"No," Asha said. "This is your night, so let's concentrate on you. Look, there's Matt." She waved as Matt appeared in the doorway of the function room, his broad, athletic body filling the doorframe.

"He looks pretty good when he scrubs up," Jenna said.

"Should you be noticing other men tonight?" A smile played on Steph's lips as she asked the question.

Jenna laughed. "I can notice, I just can't touch. And anyway, it's Matt. I'm glad to hear he's turned over a new leaf, but I can't imagine any woman in her right mind going near him. She'd be crazy."

"Oh?" Steph asked. "What have you heard?"

Jenna raised her eyebrows. "A lot. He's a friend of Brad's, and Brad has plenty of stories about him."

"Time to change the subject," Asha murmured, as Matt made a beeline for them.

"Congratulations." Matt leaned in to kiss Jenna. "You're stunning. Brad's a lucky guy."

Jenna looked surprised at Matt's kind words. "Thanks, Matt, that's very kind of you."

"Not kind, it's the truth. I'm amazed Zane's letting you anywhere near Brad, to be honest."

"Zane hardly knows him."

"Ah, that explains it then." He winked. "I'm only fooling around. As I said, Brad's a lucky man."

"He is, and he looks like he might need rescuing," Jenna said. "My nosy aunt is giving him the third degree by the looks of it. Excuse me." She smiled and made her way over to where a group of women in their fifties and sixties surrounded Brad. The relief on his face when she arrived confirmed he needed rescuing.

"I wasn't joking," Matt said quietly. "I can't believe she's marrying that guy. Jenna's a smart girl. How can she not see what he's like?"

"What do you mean?" Asha asked. Steph could see the concern in her sister's eyes. "That's my best friend you're talking about."

"I know," Matt said. "I spoke to Zane about him a while ago, but Zane said Jenna won't listen. She's infatuated with him and no one's going to convince her otherwise."

"Everyone sees people through different lenses, Matt. It might be that Jenna sees the good in him and chooses to overlook things that we might consider less than desirable," Steph said.

A flush crept across Matt's cheeks, and Steph realized he thought she was comparing him to Brad. She wasn't. "I'm not suggesting anything by that. I just like to think most people are good at heart and sometimes it takes someone special to see that."

Matt nodded. "You're right. Let's hope that's the case with Jenna and Brad."

"He certainly looks like he's in love with her," Buster said. "He couldn't look prouder."

They all turned their gazes to the engaged couple. Steph had to agree with Buster. Brad looked as enamored with Jenna as she did with him.

"I stopped in at the food truck this morning," Matt said.

"The pavillion area is amazing. I love those counters you've used on the sides, Asha. I'd love to talk to Zane about doing something similar to the rooftop bar at the Sandstone Cafe. It's an amazing touch."

Matt was right. Steph had been blown away when the finishing touch, the counters, had been installed. The wooden structure had been done tastefully and blended in well with the surrounding trees and area, but it was the counters and other carvings that made it special. Zane had presented Asha with two beautifully carved doves to add to the structure.

"They represent peace and love," he'd told her when she unwrapped the gift. "My love for you and the hope that your business continues to operate in a peaceful way moving forward."

There had been plenty of laughter when Matt had called out, "That means no throwing rocks, Asha!" The carvings were beautiful, and Steph knew her sister was incredibly touched that Zane had gone to the effort of creating them. He also gave her a carved four-leaf clover to hang in the doorway for eternal luck.

Steph smiled as Ryan and Margie entered the function room with Travis and Jodi close behind. Steph thought it was lovely of Jenna to have invited all of them. She'd wanted to include most of the town, but her father had eventually drawn a line and said no more, pointing out that if Jenna wanted him to pay for a wedding, there would be no money left at this rate.

"How's Holly's coming along?" Margie asked after they'd all greeted one another.

"Fabulously," Buster said. "We've finished the design and the plans are with the township. They'll take a few weeks to go through the approval process, but we're hoping to get started on the buildings in a couple of months."

"We're going to start on some of the landscaping now," Steph added. It had been fantastic working with Buster and Matt to turn a vision into real plans. Steph had been brought to tears several times listening to Matt's stories of why he wanted certain features included. It went beyond the facilities such as ramps for wheelchairs and the practical elements a person with a disability might require. It included a variety of pastel-colored water lilies for the lake. "Mom loved them," Matt had said. "She made me help her dig out a small pond in our yard when I was about six so that she could fill it with them. She'd sit beside it and sing to me. They were her absolute favorite." He'd also insisted on planting a hedge to surround the entire retreat and had chosen Dragon Lady Holly for this. Steph was moved by the number of touches he added that held such meaning.

She was so glad she'd gone on this journey with him and Buster. She knew deep in her gut that what they were building was more than a business. It was going to provide a lifeline to many people and be incredibly rewarding for all who worked there. Steph had also realized that it was going to create quite a lot of employment. They were looking at a range of specialty offerings that they would need experts to run. They were still months away from being operational, if not longer, but she would need to start contacting people to see what might be possible.

"What about you?" Steph asked Ryan. "Any news about getting some classes up and running at the cafe?"

Ryan shook his head. "To be honest, Margie and I have only just pushed our heads above water since we started running the cafe." He laughed. "It's a lot more work than I imagined. Mind you, Margie's doing most of it."

"And loving it," Margie said. "Which we should be thanking you for, Matt."

"Don't thank me. You bringing your skills to Hope's

Ridge is something we're all incredibly grateful for." He looked across at Asha. "I'm pretty sure I saw you there the other day, Ash, buying a slice of cake, if my spies have the correct information."

Asha laughed. "I would like to say it was to check out the competition, but I just love Margie's butterscotch pie. It's to die for."

Matt chuckled. "I agree. And my spies have told me that both Margie and Ryan sit at Irresistables enjoying coffee pretty often. It appears we are all supporting our respective enemies."

"You're hardly in town at the moment, Matt, so how do you know all of this?" Steph asked.

"Like I said. My spies."

"That wouldn't be a spy in the form of a ninety-six-year-old man of Chinese ancestry by any chance?" Buster asked.

Matt raised an eyebrow. "I'd have to kill you if I told you."

They all laughed.

"You've given Charlie a new lease on life with that development, Matt," Buster said.

"You sure have," Zane said, joining the group. "He's incredible. The construction guys are complaining about the pace he's pushing them to work at. Those apartments will be finished ahead of schedule, the way he's going."

Matt nodded. "They are ahead of schedule. I gave him a raise yesterday."

"What, he accepts money from you?" Asha said. "My rent is paid in coffee and muffins."

Matt laughed. "No, he won't take any money. He brings his neighbors into the cafe twice a week for lunch, and the raise he wanted was two massage vouchers a week. He's going to accumulate them and come for a daily massage once we get that up and running at Holly's. I said I was happy to make his raise a daily massage for the rest of his life, that he didn't need to accumulate vouchers, but he refused. He said, 'If you offer me the world now, Matthew, what reason will I have to do better?'"

The group laughed.

"He'll be the most chilled out resident in Hope's Ridge with a daily massage," Zane said.

"I think he already is," Steph said. "And I think it's the secret to a long and happy life. He keeps fit, healthy, and uses his brain daily. There's no getting old for Charlie."

Jenna's dad tapped his wine glass, silencing the room, and invited everyone to find their places for the sit-down dinner. Steph and Buster found themselves at a table with their group of friends from Hope's Ridge. The only one without a partner, she realized, was Matt. Zane noticed too and commented, "We need to find you a girlfriend, Matt."

Matt blushed. "You wouldn't want to inflict that pain on anyone."

They all laughed, but Steph saw sadness flicker in Matt's eyes. She did a mental check on the women she knew in Hope's Ridge. There were a few single ones, but she didn't see any of them as a match for Matt. He needed someone strong, ready to stand up for herself, and not afraid to speak her mind. Holly's, once it was open and they had employees, would bring new people into the area. Maybe Matt would find his perfect match then.

The evening passed quickly with a wonderful dinner, speeches, and finally dancing. Steph had been looking forward to this part all evening. To being wrapped in Buster's arms, just the two of them together in a sea of people. She melted into him as the band started playing Ed Sheeran's "Thinking Out Loud".

"This is one of my favorites," Buster said.

"Me too." Steph moved with Buster in time to the music.

"I can't believe we're here, Steph. I feel like the luckiest man alive."

"At the party?"

"No, here." He touched his hand to his heart and then to hers. "I absolutely adore you. You've brought a light into my life I was sure had been extinguished. With everything that happened with Eve, I never expected to have an opportunity like this."

Tears pricked the back of Steph's eyes. She knew precisely what Buster meant because she felt it too. "Let's pray things will work out for Eve too," she said. "That she'll find her own opportunity." Eve's appeal was scheduled to take place the following month. Hopefully, she would be released and given the opportunity to start again.

"I hope so," Buster said. "I'm sure she wishes the process would speed up. She's missed out on a lot."

"She's gained a lot too, though. She's had help to understand what happened to her and to cope with her alcoholism. There's no rushing those things. If you're patient, life will unfold as it's meant to."

Buster gave a little laugh. "Yet neither of us took that advice following our first date. If anything, we rushed as quickly as we could into ending this before it started."

"We did, but that's because we were scared. I was scared. I know that. And do you know what's good about being scared?"

Buster brushed his hand against her cheek. "No, tell me."

"It's a sure sign that something is so important to you, you can't even face it because the thought of losing it is too painful. Sometimes you'll push it away before giving it a chance to hurt you. For me, my fear was because I had feelings for you I couldn't handle. They were so strong and full of love, and to be honest, they hit me with an intensity

I've never felt before. Rather than feel that and be excited by it, I did exactly the opposite and pushed you away."

"But that also made us stronger," Buster said. "In a short space of time, we've learned so much about each other, Steph, and we continue to learn."

Steph nodded and smiled.

"What's that look for?"

"I'm just thinking about one important thing I've learned about you, that's all."

Buster raised an eyebrow.

"That I love you with all of my heart, and nothing else, other than you feeling the same, matters."

Tears welled in Buster's eyes as he pulled Steph against his chest. He lowered his mouth to her ear, his words a whisper.

"And I do, Steph. I absolutely do."

The End

FREE BONUS SCENES

Would you like to read more about our friends in Hope's Ridge? Sign up to my mailing list at www.silvermckenzie.com.au for exclusive access to bonus scenes featuring our Hope's Ridge family.

These aren't deleted scenes, they are bonus scenes written exclusively for my mailing list subscribers and new scenes are added each month. You'll also have opportunities to win free books and Amazon gift cards.

He broke your heart and destroyed your business. Would you give him a second chance?

Asha Jones has lived and breathed the small town of Hope's Ridge her entire life. She's built a successful business on the shores of Lake Hopeful, and now, with the iconic Sandstone Cafe up for lease, she has an opportunity to expand her business and fulfill a dream.

But one mistake is all it takes for Asha's dream to crumble overnight. She's made an enemy of an influential property developer, and just when she thinks things can't get any worse, the man who crushed her heart ten years earlier returns to town.

Suffering from PTSD and dealing with the trauma of recurring nightmares, Zane Larsen returns to Hope's Ridge, resolved to recover his self-confidence and find a new direction for his life. Teaming up with a local property developer provides a new career path and gives him a much-needed reason to get up each day.

As Zane slips back into small-town life, he doesn't anticipate feelings resurfacing for Asha, the one woman in Hope's Ridge who's hated him since high school. And, while Asha does her best to ignore Zane's existence, she can't ignore the feelings for him that reappear. She can't go there again—can she?

Zane needs to redeem himself and fight for a second chance at love. But is working with the man who wants to destroy Asha's business a guaranteed way to reignite her hatred - or could it be an opportunity to change her opinion of him?

Available now from Amazon or
www.silvermckenzie.com.au

Dream wedding—or nightmare?

When Jenna Larsen dreamed of her wedding day, she never visualized it being the most humiliating day of her life. But it was.

Devastated and mortified by the turn of events, Jenna returns to Hope's Ridge single and seeking solace in the comfort of her parents' home.

Matt Law has spent the last six months proving to the residents of Hope's Ridge that he's changed. He wants to be part of the town and part of the community, but one act undoes all of his hard work and makes him an enemy—Roy Larsen: the influential owner of the town's mill; a major supplier to Matt's businesses; and furious father of the bride.

While Matt does his best to tame Jenna and her father's

fury, there are bigger issues brewing. His father, the majority owner of his businesses, is persuaded by an outsider to move his investments from Hope's Ridge. But who exactly is venture capitalist Susan Lewis, and why does she have so much influence and power over his father?

As Jenna does her best to move on from the wreckage of her wedding day, an opportunity arises for her to work with Susan. Their business collaboration could ultimately destroy Matt's businesses. Matt ruined Jenna's life—she's single, unemployed, and without a home because of him—and now she has the opportunity to ruin his. But will she?

Available now from Amazon or
www.silvermckenzie.com.au

ABOUT THE AUTHOR

SILVER MCKENZIE is a pen name of women's fiction and domestic thriller author, Louise Guy.

Louise decided to write the Hope's Ridge series under a pen name as while the series sits nicely in the women's fiction category, the books have a stronger romantic story line than her other women's fiction titles which tend to have more intrigue and suspense. The Hope's Ridge series is also set in a fictional US town so the books are written in US English compared to Louise's other books that are set in Australia and use Australian English. She also decided Silver was a pretty cool name and it might be the only chance she has to name herself!

Silver has lived in the UK, New Zealand and Australia as well as having traveled to over thirty countries. Today, Silver and her husband are permitted to share a home in Queensland, Australia, with their two sons and a rather bossy, but beautiful cat named Pud.

If you are interested in checking out books written by Louise Guy, go to: www.louiseguy.com

And, both Silver and Louise are easy to find on Facebook.